*A Woman Undefeated*
*Dreams Can Come True*
*Ping Pong Poms*
*Innocence Lost*
*Shattered Dreams*
*Her Heart's Desire*

A
# Distant
# Dream

## Vivienne Dockerty

DISCLAIMER.
Although places and events exist in my story, this is a work of fiction.
All the characters, names, incidents and dialogue is from my imagination
or have been used fictitiously.

Matador
9 Priory Business Park
Kibworth Beauchamp
Leicester LE8 0RX, UK
Tel: (+44) 116 279 2299
Fax: (+44) 116 279 2277
Email: books@troubador.co.uk
Web: www.troubador.co.uk/matador

ISBN 978 1783064 472

British Library Cataloguing in Publication Data.
A catalogue record for this book is available from the British Library.

Typeset in 11pt Aldine401 BT Roman by Troubador Publishing Ltd, Leicester, UK
Printed and bound in the UK by TJ International, Padstow, Cornwall

# Acknowledgements

I'd like to thank the volunteers who do such a good job at the Courthouse and Slate Museum in Willunga, South Australia, particularly a lady there who told me that an ancestor of hers was one of the early settlers in the township.

I would also like to mention two books that I found invaluable during my research: *Willunga: Town and District,' 1837-1900* by Martin Dunstan and *Cradle of Adversity: A History of the Willunga District* by Rob Linn.

I'd also like to thank everyone who has bought my books either online or from the bookstores and those that I have met at the many events that I like to go to.

One of the readers of *A Woman Undefeated* wondered if Molly had been left behind in the hamlet to starve. I decided to give her an answer.

I would like to dedicate this book to Denis Gavaghan, who was a source of inspiration when I was trying to finish this book. A kindred spirit, an Irishman, from the very region that gave birth and shelter to my ancestors, I was fortunate to meet him and his wife Maureen, whilst on a trip to Loch Awe in Scotland, a beautiful place.

Denis has given me permission to publish a poem that he wrote recently, *The Moment at Hand*, which is all we really own, as we travel along life's way.

Last night I had a dream about dying
And although it caused sorrow and fear
I knew that my dream held a message
A reminder of things I hold dear.

So I lay in my bed and I wondered
How the years could so quickly have flown
Why the moment at hand we should cherish
It's the only thing we really own.

Our past, just a gathering of memories
Our future is yet to unfold
But this moment is ours for the living
It's the most precious present we hold.

So live each victorious moment
Don't let worries and cares hold their sway
Count your blessings instead of your troubles
And thank God for the gift of today.

Denis Gavaghan.

♣

# Chapter One

The sun had appeared from behind the rain clouds, much to the relief of the middle-aged man and woman who hurried into their farmhouse, situated as it was above a small hamlet a few miles away from the village of Killala.

"I'll boil a kettle, Filbey," the woman said once they were in the kitchen. "You go and get the tin bath and we'll put her in it. I'm not takin' her stinking to high heaven to Sara's house. It'll be bad enough expectin' your cousin to feed another mouth until we get on the boat."

"She's only weeny, Bessie. To be sure Sara won't even notice the little dote. Go to your Aunt Bessie, Alanna, and she'll make you nice and clean."

"Want Maggie." The little girl stood with her thumb in her mouth, staring at the farmer with wide eyes, as she watched him place the tin bath in front of the kitchen fire, where there were still enough glowing embers to boil a kettle.

"Yer'll see her later. She said we could take yer on a little 'oliday. We'll go to the seaside. You'd like that, wouldn't yer?"

"Want Maggie."

"Oh for heaven's sake, Filbey. I hope she isn't going to be whinin' for her sister all the way to Sligo. She should think herself lucky we've decided to take her away from all that misery and look at the state of her. You'd think somebody would have given her a wash now and again."

"Bessie, have some pity, they're buryin' her mother today. The

*1*

last thing on any folk's mind would be the cleanliness of the poor child's body. Now, that water should be warm enough. Strip 'er out of that terrible bed gown and I'll pour a bit of the kettle in the bath."

The child started to scream, as the woman gripped the hem of the nightdress and yanked it roughly over her head. She ran for the door, flapping her arms wildly, her skin the colour of alabaster against the darkness of her long matted hair.

"Grab 'er," shouted Bessie, over the child's cries, after turning back to test the temperature of the bath water, before picking up a piece of towelling in readiness. "I bet she's never had a bath in all 'er three years."

"Come 'ere, Molly, we won't hurt yer." Farmer Filbey's voice was gentle and his plump face full of sympathy, as he ambled across the short distance to where the girl was trying to jump up and pull at the door latch. "Let's make yer nice and clean and then we'll go on that little 'oliday."

Defeated, but still sobbing, Molly allowed herself to be carried, but began to scream and thrash around wildly once she began to feel the tepid water being sloshed onto her skin.

"Give me that soap," Bessie shouted above the bedlam, pointing to a jar on the well scrubbed, pine table that held a thick, green, carbolic solution. "Needs must," she muttered grimly as she placed a dollop in her hand, then rubbed the glutinous fluid over the child's head and body.

"Now the jug. Filbey will you ever take a look at this, just look at the colour of this water."

"Ah Bessie, take a minute to be gentle. She's been ill. Didn't Maggie say she's had a fever? It's not the child's fault she's in the state she's in. Here, give me the cloth and I'll dry her in it, while you find her a biscuit."

It took the soothing voice of the man, the comfort of his arms around her and the tempting look of one of Bessie's homemade biscuits, before Molly's sobs changed to an occasional hiccup. She stared across from the safety of Filbey's arms at the old, wooden chiming clock that ticked from where it sat above the kitchen dresser, then watched as the woman carried the bath to the scullery, where she heard the sound of water swishing away.

"We'll have to get on."

The woman had come back, wiping down the table and moving the jar back to its original position on a nearby window sill.

"Yer said Colooney would be here as soon as he'd fed his animals. I hope to 'eaven yer'll manage to get them boxes on. There's not a thing in there that I'd leave behind for the next one's to make use of."

The farmer nodded, his manner one of resignation, as if this kind of conversation had gone on before and he didn't want to hear it again.

"We're ready aren't we, just a case of tampin' down the fire? What are we going to put the child in, Bessie? She can't travel all the way to Sligo in this old towel, she'll catch 'er death of cold and what'll we do if it rains on the way I don't know. Look, already the poor dote's shiverin'. Is there anything we could use in your travellin' bag?"

"Me change of clothin', that's all, I've thrown 'er dirty bed gown on the muck heap. Not that it would have been fit for wearin' anyway."

Bessie's face wore a long suffering look. She was dressed in her best blue, linen gown with a white, lace collar, when normally she would wear a dark, homespun skirt, a white blouse and an all enveloping pinafore for the farm work. "I'll have to wrap her up in one of me clean petticoats and me second best shawl."

The sound of a horse's hooves clattered into the cobbled farmyard and Filbey, dressed in brown, moleskin trousers, a white and brown, striped collarless shirt and black, shiny shoes, with the few hairs on top of his head smoothed down with a type of pomade, went to the door after placing the little girl, who was still wrapped in the towel, into Bessie's arms. The child began to cry again, her damp hair clinging to the woman's face and her small body shuddering.

"There, there, Molly," Bessie crooned, trying to fight off the frustration she was feeling, as she carried her burden to one of the large trunks placed near the doorway. Here she was, being given the gift of a lovely little girl to love, but in circumstances that were going to take every ounce of her willpower to get through. This wasn't a little holiday that her husband, Filbey, had tried to soothe the child with the promise of, they were to sail across the ocean to the other side of the world.

"*Dia dhuit,*" said the tall, thin man who tenanted the neighbouring farm. "Didn't I tell yer, I'd be over at this time of the mornin?" Not that Filbey had uttered a word other than "*Failte,*" but Colooney took his worried expression for reproach. "Got yer boxes ready? I'm hopin' to make it there and back agin ter Sligo by the end of the day."

"Piper won't let yer down," Filbey said in reply. "He's been a good horse since I bought him as a youngster and I give the axles a good greasin' on the cart. Shall we load up then?"

He turned away quickly, lest the man saw the ready tears that had come into his eyes when he looked upon his faithful horse. Piper had been part of his family for the past ten years.

"Is she ready?" Filbey's eyes were drawn to the pretty little girl, standing in the doorway, now ensconced in a white petticoat, the drawstrings of the waist pulled up around her neck and a dark brown woollen shawl tied in a knot over it. Her dark hair, now that it had dried, sat squeakily clean just touching her shoulders and he noticed that her large eyes were blue, though filled with tears again.

"Come to Filbey," he said kindly and picking her up he carried her to the cart.

"What are yer doin' with the Mayo child?" asked Colooney, looking puzzled. "Isn't it today that they're buryin' her mother up at Ballina?"

"She's ours now," Filbey said stoutly. "The sister's gone off to England with the young Haines lad and seeing as 'ow their Aunt Tess 'as her 'ands full, we were allowed to take 'er. All above board, Father Daley knows about it."

4

"Fine, fine, none of me business really, I just wondered" Colooney said, pulling back a tarpaulin in the cart in readiness for covering his load. "Do yer want 'er to sit up here with you or back there with yer missis and the boxes?"

"She can come with me. The little dote keeps cryin' for their Maggie. Not that it matters now, but you'd think that she'd have been taken over the water too."

*Which wasn't true, Maggie hadn't had a say in the matter. They'd snatched the child from her cot whilst her Aunt Tess had attended Mairi Mayo's funeral.*

"Anyway, me and Bessie can give her a better life than her sister could."

"A matter of opinion, Filbey. Sure, I'd rather sit out the famine here, face the *drochshaol,* (the bad times) which my family has done for generations, than go off to God knows where, across miles and miles of sea. *Bionn adharca fada ar na ba thar lear.*

"So they say, Colooney, the grass is always greener on the other side and let's hope it will be." Filbey shrugged and left the child on the bench, where she stared ahead at the rear end of the patient horse, watching its twitching tail in fascination. A few minutes later the two men loaded the first of the heavy trunks behind her.

"Come on Bessie," Filbey said, as he went in to drag the second trunk to the door and noticed his wife was still wiping down the kitchen range with a bit of old rag. The stone flagged floor shone from a recent mop up of where the tin bath had been. "This is the first day of our great adventure. Pick up yer bags and off we'll go."

It was hard for Bessie to stand in the yard and not look back at the place that had been her home for almost twenty years. Brought here all that time ago as Farmer Filbey's bride, she had been a pretty young thing, full of hope for a happy future, blessed as she would be with a quiver-full of children to help on the farm. Now her sharp, pointed face was etched with lines and her down turned mouth showed unhappiness. There had been no pitter pattering of tiny feet after all.

Bessie, not usually a sentimental woman, couldn't help but

shed a tear as she looked at the four square, stone built house, with its now empty cow byre and one of its doors having been left hanging by one of its hinges, and at the deserted barn which usually stored a glut of hay or barrels of healthy potatoes. She thought of the hens that had clucked and the geese that had waddled around the now deserted yard. If it hadn't been for the blasted famine and the increasing amount of rent they'd had to pay, they would have tenanted the farm for the rest of their lives.

Yes, the past twenty years had been hard going. The youngest daughter of a slater, she had been unused to supervising the staff needed to run a small dairy and arable farm. It had taken determination and fortitude to help the farm make a small profit, along with her husband Clarence, and she had quickly learnt how to handle a lazy kitchen girl or dairymaid, though recently there hadn't been much work for Maggie, her latest servant. Maggie had left the hamlet the day before, bound for England in the company of Michael Haines and his family, who had worked as a *gillie* on the estate of the local Big House. Now her house and dairy would be empty except of course for the furniture that would sit there gathering dust whilst waiting for the blighted land to revive. Then someone else would cook in Bessie's kitchen, sleep in her bed and take advantage of all of those bottles of preserves that she'd had to leave behind in her larder. All that hard work had been for nothing. It was a crying shame.

"Give me the child," she said to Filbey, after seeing that Molly had been placed upon the bench seat of the cart and looked a bit wobbly. "I'd sooner have her down here with me, where she can 'ave a sleep under this blanket I've brought."

Molly looked wild-eyed as she was handed over, having settled in her place with a rear view of the patient Piper, but she became resigned as Bessie took charge, especially as the woman had now placed the yard cat in the cart beside her.

"Sara might want it" Bessie said in explanation, after Filbey had raised a quizzical eyebrow. "Can't leave the poor thing to fend for itself and I wouldn't want it to."

Piper set off along the rutted lane at his new master's command with his harness jingling and the cartwheels creaking under the weight of its cargo. Filbey glanced back to the row of grey roofed, stone built cottages that had been built forty years earlier to house his father's farmhands. They were all empty now except for one, as most of the workers had gone off to live in pastures new. Only Widow Dockerty lived there now, visited by her sea captain son, Johnny, when his ship docked across in Sligo, a small town on the Atlantic coast. Filbey hoped to God that the widow didn't perish in the winter storms that would soon be on their way.

*Is this a foolish dream?* He asked himself again, as the vehicle rounded a corner and the place of his toil for twenty years disappeared from view. He had sold everything he could to the man who sat beside him, in order to pay for his passage to a distant land. It was very distant, on the other side of the world to be precise, a place they called Australia. Why he'd got the notion was beyond him, as he had always felt homesick after a couple of days when they had gone to stay in Sligo with relatives. Perhaps it was a feeling of growing old and never achieving more than his forebears, or maybe it was the thought of struggling to make a living now that the landlord had raised the rent and was insisting that the land be given over to rearing sheep. When he had seen the poster, placed in the window of a government building in Sligo town by Her Majesty's Colonization Commissioners, exhorting all skilled workers to travel across the ocean to a new life in Australia, it hadn't taken him long before he was sitting at the recruitment table. After listening to the official in command, he had watched as the man filled out the application form.

Outwardly, and mostly to his wife in an effort to keep the poor woman's spirits up, he boasted of the nice, long sea voyage they'd be having, with plenty of rest, enabling him to take up the tools of his trade again when they got to the other end. Inwardly, he quaked at the notion that the ship might go down or there'd be nothing for them when they got there, though now he had another reason to leave this life behind and find a new one – his little girl. She'd be Molly Filbey when they boarded that ship to Adelaide and Molly Filbey was going to have the best of everything when he and his wife reached the New World.

*Beidh la eile ag an bPaorach.* We will live to fight another day.

# Chapter Two

Sara's house overlooked a river which flowed past their house and out into the Atlantic. It wasn't far from the docks, where a vessel bound for the south of England would take the Filbeys to join the migration ship in Plymouth. They were to stay in Sligo for a couple of nights, time enough to say their goodbyes to Sara, Filbey's cousin, one of Bessie's sisters and any other members of the extended family who lived around the town.

Clarence Filbey, no longer a farmer and only called "Filbey" as a term of respect by his wife, had spent the last few miles of their journey from Killala with a worry on his mind. Coolooney was known to be a bit of a hard bastard when it came to negotiating the price of a deal, which he could be when he was in the driving seat and you were the poor sod who was waiting for his money. What if he began to haggle over the price of the horse and cart? Coolooney hadn't been particularly generous when taking the small herd of shorthorns, which had been good milkers and had prolific births. He had given them a trivial amount for the geese and hens and had only offered Bessie a paltry couple of guineas when she had shown him some good pieces of furniture from the contents of the sitting room. Luckily, he had a little tucked away, but the extra money for the horse and cart would have made life a whole lot easier. Still, he was better off than the poor buggers they'd passed along the way, struggling to keep to the muddy track with their possessions on their backs or on a wobbly handcart, their kids crying with tiredness and their thin and starving parents looking as if they were at their wits' end. Colooney had told him in a lowered voice that the soldiers had been sent from Dublin Barracks in order to clear up the sick and the dying and had made the ditches wider to pitch the poor sods in.

The cost of emigration wasn't cheap. It might have been, if Clarence had been under thirty five and had one or two children. Then their voyage would have been completely free, underwritten by the government of Her Majesty, but he was fifty two and childless when he'd applied, though he was able to qualify on two counts – he was married and a skilled agricultural labourer. "Agricultural labourer" was not a term he liked to use, as in his opinion running his own farm, though tenanted, made him a farmer. Though if lying got him to where he wanted to go, he was happy to stretch the truth. He did have the option of borrowing money from Sara's husband, who was a moneylender. It was something that Bessie had urged him to do, when he had told her that they couldn't afford to travel in a second class cabin. At £25 per person, they could save that money, travel in steerage and buy more land when they got to their destination. At his age and not being used to taking orders, he didn't want to have to work for the benefit of another. Why should he now be beholden, like he had been to the absentee English landlord who owned all the land around?

The child awoke as the horse and cart pulled up outside a row of sturdy, brick-built villas. She lay quietly for a moment, her eyes focusing on the cloudy sky, watching as a flock of seagulls wheeled around in the air above. She felt warm in the little nest that Bessie had created, especially as the cat had joined her and was purring quietly at her side. Though she felt sad that Maggie hadn't come along with her, perhaps she would enjoy a little holiday.

The sound of angry voices, the squeal from the cat as it was wrested from its perching place, the shrill tones from the woman and shouts of the man, all brought Molly from contentment to alarm. She was whisked into the air, scratching her shin on the side of the wooden cart and then deposited with someone who was wearing a long, black dress covered with a long, white pinafore and had a frilled, starched hat upon her head.

"Take her somewhere, Bridie, just while we sort this one out," she heard the woman say. "We'll be indoors in a minute or so. Perhaps you can give her a drop of milk."

Molly sat on the nice girl's comfortable knee in a place that looked like a kitchen. At least it had a warm fire glowing in front of the chair where they were sitting and the girl called Bridie was dabbing something soothing onto her bleeding shin.

"Wheesht, Alanna, would yer ever look at this, what have they done to yer? Where have yer come from and dressed like some sort of a marionette from a puppet show? Sure, all ye'd need is a bit of rouge on that poor little face of yours and yer'd be the spit image."

Molly stared up at the kind looking girl who looked to be as old as her sister, and gave her a tearful smile.

"There now, isn't it good to see that cheerful face, instead of the sad one that yer had on yer before. Yer shin will be as good as new soon and I'm sure I can find yer a cup of milk and one of Cook's tasty biscuits. Sit there, Alanna and I'll be with yer in a second."

Bridie disappeared into the scullery and was soon back with the promised treats, which Molly ate and drank hurriedly, not having had anything to eat since the biscuit at the Filbey farm.

A woman with light brown, curly hair that was pulled back in a colourful, woollen bandeau, put her head around the kitchen door. Bridie bobbed a curtsey and asked what she could do for her?

"Just checking on the little girl, Bridie. There's a bit of an altercation between the carrier and my visitors, so shall we say dinner at half past the hour? Will the child be a nuisance? I can take her from you if you want me to, though Mrs. Filbey has asked me to look out some of Kathleen's old things, so I'll be doing that for a while."

"No, she's fine, Madam, she can watch me while I'm dishing up. Cook left everything prepared. Looks as if the orphanage was a little short of clothing."

Her employer nodded and it wasn't until Bessie came to take the child to a bedroom that Molly saw the woman again.

"They're probably a little on the big side," she was saying when Bessie walked into the room, holding Molly by the hand. "I kept them for sentimental reasons, hoping that Kathleen's children could make use of them, but she turned them down flat, said that her husband was quite capable of providing the clothes for their children."

"That's young women for you Sara, but I'll be very glad to take them off your hands as they are really quite beautiful. Come Molly, let's try on this little dress and make you look like a princess."

Molly, not sure what a princess was anyway, found herself in front of a cheval mirror, being pushed from side to side, whilst Bessie put a few pins into the hem of the white, muslin dress. Then there was a brown one with white lace on the bodice and a pink, stripy one with a white frill around the neck. Two pretty bonnets, three pairs of pantaloons, white gloves and a pair of shiny, black shoes later, Molly found that she quite liked the idea of being on a holiday.

"I threw away the rags that the orphanage had dressed her in, that was why she was dressed in my shawl and petticoat. I just need to get her a couple of liberty bodices." Bessie and Clarence had decided on a simple tale regarding the young child's origins.

"There's a small shop in town that sells just about everything. We can go tomorrow. Would you like me to get Bridie to do the hems later? She's a very willing girl."

Molly had eaten her dinner in the kitchen, with Bessie and Clarence not being sure of how she would behave at a grownup table, so she missed the heated discussion in the dining room. She had been happy in the kitchen with Bridie and was full to bursting with the mashed potato and gravy, a little piece of meat and a few boiled carrots that she had been fed with. She had been taken to use the lavatory in the yard outside and had made no protest when she was dressed in a long cream nightgown and put into a comfortable bed.

The day had been a tiring one for all concerned and the couple's nerves were taut when they sat down for a meal with Sara and Finbar, her husband, a genial man. Bessie, not used to more than a glass of red wine occasionally, something their host had imported from Burgundy, felt empowered to speak her mind.

"I think Coloney's a miserable sod, fleecin' them that has no option than to take what he offers and be pleased about it. I heard say that he is nearly as rich as him that lives in the Big House."

"Needs must, dear Bessie," said Finbar, who was large, with mutton chop sideburns. "You could say that of me. Perhaps people are saying that I fleece the poor by adding interest to the loans I give them, but that is what I do for a living: I'm a money lender."

"A bit of a difference, I would say," said Clarence. " Yer've been in business, father and son, for fifty years. People in Sligo know that yer 'onest as the day."

"Well, you could say that I suppose, though I like to think I'm philanthropic. Anyway, let us make a toast to you both, to a pleasant journey and health and happiness in a new country."

He raised his glass, but Bessie's face was mutinous.

"A pleasant journey? Six months breathin' in the smell of someone else's sweat, livin' cheek by jowel with a hundred others, listenin' to other people's carnal and dare I say it, *lavatorial* habits and yer want to wish us a pleasant journey? We will probably catch all sorts of diseases and end up in a watery grave."

"Nonsense," Clarence said. "I expect we'll have to share with around about fifty and I'm sure there will be rules regardin' such delicate things or the captain wouldn't allow it. Besides, our fellow passengers will be artisans, people with a useful trade, not just any kind of riffraff. We'll probably make lots of good friendships on our way."

"Did you see those people when we were on our journey over 'ere?" Bessie was not going to be silenced by her husband's attempt at diplomacy. "They were raggedy lookin' people, with their scant possessions tied up in pieces of tarpaulin. They looked hollow-eyed and sickly and we'll probably be expected to travel across the ocean with them."

By this time Bessie was beginning to work herself up into frenzy and started to point a jabbing finger towards Filbey.

"I have been married to you for nigh on twenty year, yer've had the sweat off me brow and total obedience and I have never frittered away a penny of my housekeepin' on *gewgaws* or frivolity, but what I do know Filbey, you can be a meanie of a man."

Filbey looked annoyed. He wasn't going to have his wife show him up in front of his cousin and her husband.

"I repeat Bessie, they will not be the kind of people who will be boardin' the ship at Plymouth and while I'm on about it I'll say it again. I am not payin' out for a cabin: we'll be needin' every shillin' when we get to Australia. Anyway, I think yer've said enough. Yer tired and yer've been gulpin' that wine inside yer for the past couple of hours. When we've finished 'ere, I suggest yer go to the room and get some shut eye, we'll talk about this problem that yer seem to be 'aving with our travel arrangements at another time."

Finbar, who had been listening to Bessie's berating with surprise as his own wife had never raised her voice in anger since they had married twenty seven years before, felt he must interject on Bessie's behalf, especially if it would help the situation.

"I have to say that Bessie may have a point, Clarence. Some of these people are desperate and might have found their fare in a heinous fashion. Only the other day one of the grain stores was attacked, not that the mob got away with it as the British soldiers used their muskets, but even I have to carry a pistol and employ a guard to watch over my office in Ashbourne Street. Perhaps you and I could adjourn to my study later, smoke a pipe and think on the money that might be needed. Do you know how much it will cost you for a piece of land?"

Clarence was appeased and Bessie, feeling a little ashamed at her outburst, finished their main course, which was a simple meal of roast lamb and vegetables as it was Cook's day off, and the matter for that moment was forgotten. The subject turned to Molly, as they ate an apple dumpling for dessert.

"We got 'er from a destitute children's home in Ballina" Bessie lied, the couple having decided that this story was a better one, rather than saying they had taken the child from her cot whilst Aunt Tess, the only family Molly had left, was away at the funeral. "Her mother had left her on the doorstep, according to their records, so we don't have any papers belonging to 'er. Of course we made a donation, these places can't exist on fresh air, but as yer saw, I had to dress her in me change of petticoat as the clothes she wore were rags, only fit for the *midden* as far as I was concerned. I'm really grateful for the clothes yer gave me, Sara. She looks such a little princess."

"I was pleased to be of help, Bessie. Like Finbar, I like to be philanthropic too."

The bitter wind that could cut a body to the bone, didn't deter the family from sallying forth along the riverside to the bustling town the next morning. Two liberty bodices and a brown, lightweight coat were purchased in the High Street for Molly along with a couple of personal items for Bessie. Filbey bought a large wad of shag, a coarse type of tobacco that he hoped would keep his pipe filled until they reached their destination.

They averted their eyes as they hurried along the heaving pavements of O'Connell Street, passing the beggars who were quite vocal if you didn't put a coin into their outstretched hand. They skirted around a family group who were blocking their way menacingly and kept their reticules, wallets and purses out of any roving pickpocket's reach. Clarence, not used to shopping, finding it boring unless he was the purchaser, kept a firm grip on Molly, who shivered with fright at the throng of people, carriages and dray carts that were trundling along the busy streets. It was good to arrive at the quiet cul-de-sac, where Sara's daughter Kathleen lived with her husband, who was a Marine solicitor.

Molly was taken to the nursery, a noisy place on the second floor of the large, semi-detached dwelling, where three children, two girls and a boy, were playing with their many toys. She sat on a cushion in a corner, her thumb in her mouth, staring at the active trio, who after giving her a moment's glance, carried on.

The boy swung on a wooden rocking horse, whooping loudly as if he was a Red Indian; the girls giggled as they walked their pot-faced dolls into the various rooms of a dolls house, one shouting orders at an unseen maid to pick the clothes up from the floor. The nursery maid, who had smiled at Molly when she had first arrived and had been placed on the cushion by Bessie, returned to her chair where she continued her mending, blocking out the noise from her rowdy charges.

"Lunch time" sang a young woman dressed in a maid's uniform, coming into the nursery carrying a tray with the smell of something delicious wafting from it. "I've brought enough for our little visitor."

The children ran across the room to where a couple of small tables and chairs stood, which had been set with a variety of utensils.

"What have yer done with 'er, ye wee rascals?" She asked, as she put the tray down on a sideboard.

"She's behind you," the boy shouted, jumping up and down in excitement. Molly got up, ready to run.

"So she is," said the maid. "Didn't she want to join in with your games?"

"She's from an orphanage." The elder of the two girls spoke for the trio, disdainfully. "Aunt Bessie said so when she brought her in."

The two maids exchanged glances. It wasn't their place to chastise their employer's daughter, but something should be said all the same.

"She's still a visitor and we should be her gracious hosts, young lady. Now, Molly would yer ever sit up at the table and have a little soup."

After a nursery lunch of mashed potatoes and carrots, some sort of mushy pie and gravy, with slices of apple for dessert, the children were taken to the lavatory, then settled down for a nap.

Molly lay on a couple of cushions on the floor of the nursery, the children having been taken to their bedrooms.

"Tis a crying shame," she heard the nice lady say, the one who had brought in their lunches. "They'll use her as a servant when they get her out there. All this show of adopting a child and treating her like a daughter. *Cailin ag Mor agus Mor ag iarraidh deirce.* Anything to keep up appearances. If they'd wanted a child that much, they'd have gone to the orphanage and adopted one many years ago."

"Going to the New World, being a servant or not would be better than living in one of them places," the nursery maid was quick to point out. "She'd only end up being a servant around here, and that would be if she was lucky enough to get a job, like us."

It was early the following morning, just as dawn broke over the rooftops, that Molly was put into a hansom cab, alongside Bessie and Clarence, whilst the driver placed their trunks and bags up above.

Sara and Finbar waved a fond farewell from their doorstep, not wanting to hazard a trip to the quayside, beseeching them to have a pleasant journey – "God Speed, write when you can." Bridie watched from behind the privacy of a net curtain, saying a little prayer for the health of the poor wee three year old. There was a lot of ocean to travel for the unsuspecting girl.

It was as Bessie thought when they arrived at the dockside. It was teeming with what she saw to be life's flotsam and jetsam. It had appeared that a sympathetic captain had offered free passage to England, providing that they didn't mind travelling with the cattle on board. When the gangway dropped he had been inundated and soldiers had been called to stem the brawling amongst the men.

Bessie looked sullen, no doubt still feeling the effects of her husband's chastisement ringing in her ears. He was not about to be thwarted in his plans and had told her so quite strongly, which was quite unusual for the normally placid man. He held Molly's hand firmly, once they had alighted from the cab, the driver placing their luggage in front of a small packet ship, moored between a grain ship and a barge carrying a large herd of sheep. Soldiers stood, dressed in the uniform of Her Majesty, nervously guarding the vessels in case another riot broke out.

"Look, the *Bessie Belle*, Clarence said excitedly, pointing out the name of the ship that they were about to board on their voyage across the water to Plymouth. "How providential; it's a sign, an omen, the *Bessie Belle*. Well would you believe it?"

A sombrely dressed man, standing with his wife and three children nearby, looked over and smiled at Clarence's levity, then relapsed into a certain gloom which could be seen on the faces of many of the waiting people. Seagulls circled overhead, screeching loudly as they swooped to sit on the grain ship's railings, then flying off again as sailors ran along the deck carrying long poled shovels.

"Have you got the tickets?" Bessie asked, on seeing an official looking person, who after walking down the *Bessie Belle* gangplank had stopped to talk to a man nearby, who was fumbling in his jacket pocket.

"Yes, in the carpet bag, all documents, certificates, tickets, all here safely. We'll be away soon, looking at the tide and the way the wind is blowing."

He held out his tickets, which were scrutinised in detail by the official, then he was told to climb up the gangplank and wait for instructions.

"Want Maggie," said a forlorn little voice at the side of Clarence, tears beginning to fall as Molly stared up at the ship, which must have looked like a big brown monster to her.

"And yer will do one day," he lied, picking her up along with his bag, and walking forward, as they followed a crew man who had loaded their trunks on each of his shoulders and was walking ahead. "But today we're going for a sail in the *Bessie Belle*."

The sound of chattering and excited babbling could be heard from the quayside, as the passengers were directed to descend the ladder to the deck below. Clarence looked back as seven young girls and one more mature looking one, rattled up the gangplank noisily.

"Wait at the top, girls", the one who seemed to be in charge shouted. "Best behaviour or you'll be thrown in the brig by the captain."

Clarence grinned at her sauciness, then followed the others into the gloom below. The *Bessie Belle* had been pressed into service as a passenger ship, after its owner, a wealthy shipping agent, had decided it would be more lucrative to carry people than the bales of wool that he normally had carried to the mills of Lancashire. Thus, the hold had been converted by attaching rough planking around its walls. If the voyagers felt dismay as their feet landed at the bottom of the wooden ladder, because of the rancid odour that still lingered, they didn't show it. Soon, when the hold was fit to bursting with humanity, the sound of the anchor being lifted met their ears. They were silent as the ship slipped its harbour moorings and headed out into the choppy waters of the Garavogue River. It was as if the passengers were holding their collective breath. Then one by one a comment was made, a conversation started, a wrap of sandwiches crackled or there was the sound of a bottle stop being opened.

Bessie, having been given a basket of food by Sara, with enough to last the family a couple of days if they didn't make pigs of themselves, brought out some bread, a lump of cheese, a bag of biscuits and a stone bottle filled with a homemade lemon drink. She laid it on a white table square, in the bit of space created on the planking by putting Molly on Clarence's knee. The feast was eyed by one of the girls, who Bessie assumed, from the similar dark grey dresses that all of the seven nearby were wearing, came from an orphanage. She smiled and opening up the paper bag that held the biscuits, she offered one to her.

"No" said a sharp voice nearby, making Bessie jump, as if the person thought she was about to poison the young girl.

"She mustn't, I am sure you wouldn't have enough to spare for the others."

"Sorry," Bessie mouthed to the youngster and put the biscuits back in her bag. They could wait for a while until they were out onto the ocean.

"I'll go up on deck now that we've cleared the harbour," Clarence said, staring sympathetically at a woman who had just been sick and was clearing up the mess as best she could. "Somebody has to keep an eye to Molly, so I'll smoke my pipe then come back down again."

Others followed his example, no doubt waiting for the smell of sick to disappear.

"Are yer bound for Adelaide?" He asked a man who appeared to be in his mid-thirties and was staring out across the ocean, seemingly weighted down with the troubles of the world on his narrow shoulders.

"That I am," he replied. "And you?" Clarence nodded, about to light his pipe, but a playful wind kept blowing his matches out so the man cupped his hands around the next match and Clarence was able to start his pipe.

"George Comayne," the man took Clarence's free hand in his and shook it. "Recently from Westport, but my wife and I have decided to seek a better life for us and our children."

"Clarence Filbey. Me wife and I have a little girl called Molly. We had a farm, been in our family for generations, but what with the landlord wanting us to start rearing the sheep and increasing our rents for the privilege of it, we decided to leave these shores for a new life."

George nodded in agreement.

"Aye, that was what caused me and the wife to look for pastures new. I had a little school not far away from St. Mary's, in one of the rows of cottages. Just a single classroom where I taught the sons of a few farmers and one or two of the better off from the village, but last year as you know, times were hard especially after that terrible winter. It wasn't worth opening my door to the few who attended in the end."

"They'll be plenty of work fer yer in the new country then," said Clarence, wishing that his farming parents had, had the foresight to give him a little education too. "I can just about sign me name meself, it's my Bessie who's got the brains."

"We've a lot of water to travel to Australia, Clarence. I am sure I could help you with a bit of learning if you'd like me to." George looked pleased. Perhaps he could charge a few shillings for his tutoring; there must be plenty of people that were emigrating who couldn't read or write.

"Aye, mebbe yer could, though I warn yer I'm a slow learner, but it'll give us both something to do when there's nothing but the ocean to feast our eyes upon."

♣

# Chapter Three

The two men stayed talking, until Clarence suddenly remembered that he had left Bessie with the promise that he would be back as soon as he had smoked his pipe. He didn't want to antagonize her further as she was still annoyed about the fact that they were to travel in steerage with the "hoi polloi."

It wasn't as if she had come from a grandiose family. She was only the daughter of a village slater after all, although her father had scraped the money together to send her to a hedgerow school. She enjoyed rubbing shoulders with Sara, who had a good living with her money lending husband and one of Sara's daughters had married a solicitor, which in Bessie's opinion had brought the family up a notch or two. She appeared content when he arrived to take his place on the planking beside her, though the noise below was deafening, people having relaxed now that the journey was underway. Molly seemed to have been taken under the wing of the young girl whom Bessie had offered the biscuit to. They were playing some kind of game on the floor with a cotton reel and Bessie had been chatting with the older girl in charge, telling her a little of her life on the farm.

"A bit happier?" he asked, squeezing her arm in a friendly fashion, hoping that her frown would turn into a smile. "Would yer like to go up top whilst I keep an eye to Molly, though she looks as if she's enjoyin' herself with the young one there?"

"I could do with the air," she replied, not letting him off the hook just yet, as he still had a bit more suffering to do, considering he had been most unsympathetic towards her, especially as she knew he could afford to pay for cabin class on the ship that would take them to Adelaide. "Come with me, Filbey. Hannah can keep an eye to Molly and I'll reward her later with a biscuit."

She leant over to ask permission from the young woman whom she had begun to call Maura and who it seemed had the spurious title of Matron to the youngsters in her charge. It appeared that Maura and another girl were guardians of the orphans until they got to Adelaide, where they would be handed over to the authorities and set to work.

"It's the best decision," Clarence said, as the couple stood on deck looking over to the tiny fishing village, then across to the islands in Killala Bay. He had played on those islands with his now dead brothers and his cousins from Sligo, when they had come to stay at the farm in their holidays. "It would have been the divil of a future, livin' hand to mouth, tryin' to find the extra rent for his mightiness. They'll turn the land over to grazin',now they've got rid of me."

"Aye Sara was sayin'." Sara had given her ten pounds, one pound for every Christmas present for the next ten years, but Bessie wasn't going to tell him so!

"Those young girls, they're from an orphanage in Crossmolina. Maura, who's their guardian, was tellin' me. She and another woman with a group from Foxford are to take them all to an office in Adelaide, where they'll be given jobs as servant girls. Poor girls are only eleven or twelve, tis a long way for them to travel."

"Better than no jobs at all, Bessie. Will Maura be looking for a job when she gets there too?"

"I think so. She didn't say, though she did say she liked working with children in the orphanage. I didn't tell her we got Molly from an orphanage; she can think I had a late baby."

Clarence nodded in agreement.

"I was talkin' to a man from Westport. See, he's over there, with his wife and youngsters. He was sayin' he's a teacher, but the ten pupils attending his school two year ago dropped down to one, so he had close the place down in the end. He couldn't find work in the area, I suppose educatin' is the last thing on people's minds when they're tryin' to keep body and soul together. He's travellin' to Adelaide as a carpenter. He has his indentures, trained for his skill as a young man when his parents were on their uppers, but he hopes one day to start his teachin', even if its tutorin' from home."

"God Bless him."

Bessie felt weepy. There were so many tales of people down on their luck but willing to pick themselves up by their boot straps. She hoped that their sacrifice of home and country would come right for them all in the end.

"At least we'll be goin' on a decent ship," Clarence said. "Finbar was tellin' me of the coffin ships that some of the landlords had clubbed together for to send their workers across to Canada. They were lured with promises of land, free accommodation and money, a paltry sum, but as much as a labourer's wages for the next five years. The ships they hired were leaky tubs, not even fit to transport cattle in and they were herded on with barely a place to rest themselves. They were made to pay a great amount for the little food and water that was tipped down the hold once a day, buckets were provided for a lavatory and there were dirty old blankets to wrap themselves in. Was it any wonder that fights broke out, dysentery and disease spread rapidly and there was hardly a soul who wasn't dead when they got there?"

"Jesus, Mary and Joseph."

Bessie crossed herself and without another word left him alone with his thoughts. He didn't tell her that Finbar had given him thirty pounds, which he could give back when he became a millionaire!

They were passing the entrance to Clew Bay, when he decided that he would return to the deck below, eat a little of the pie Sara had also put in the basket, then rest if he could as many of the passengers, including the girls from the orphanage, had swamped the upper deck, pointing out the coast in the distance where Westport and Newport lay. George Colmayne and his family would probably be finding it hard not to shed a tear.

It was six o' clock before they made the southern coast of Ireland. By this time it was raining hard as they sailed into St. George's Channel, there to steer along the coast of Wales across from Cardigan Bay. They would travel through the night, passing the mouth of the Bristol Channel and making landfall by the middle of the day.

The passengers were trapped once the hatch was closed for overnight safety. Some rested if they could, some talked between themselves desultorily, whilst the children who were hemmed into the confined quarters began to make nuisances of themselves. Molly watched, her thumb in her mouth, eyes wide as she looked at a few big boys tearing up and down playing tag with one another. Bessie's lips became even tighter as she witnessed the noisy scene. Once again, the thought of sharing her life with a mass of ill-bred people for the next six months, gave her the shivers and she felt like jumping ship. What a meanie she was married to. She knew that Filbey had stashed a load of money, as she had found it one day when he'd been over getting supplies from Ballina. There had to be more money than he had confessed to, from the days when his cattle had sold well at the market and from when his wheat had fetched a decent price. It wasn't as if they'd led an opulent life and there was still the rent to the landowner to pay.

She had searched through the trunk which he kept on the floor in the room where Grandad Filbey had slept all those years before. It was full of yellowing papers; ownership of goods, certificates of marriages and deaths appertaining to his ancestors. She had spent some time reading of the lives that had gone before them while sitting on the dirty lumpy mattress, which they had later given as a farewell gift to Maggie, their servant girl. She had moved the trunk, after she had got up to return despondently to her duties and noticed a crack in the floorboard, which upon investigation proved to be the hiding place she had been searching for. There it had been, all of her husband's worldly wealth sitting in a leather pouch under her nose in a small compartment. He must have put it there quite recently, of that she was sure.

It was misty on that November morning, when the *Bessie Belle* nosed her way into Plymouth Docks and anchored along the seawall. Her passengers had been up on deck since the hatch had been removed at cock crow, wanting to be one of the first to see the emigrant ship that they would be travelling on. There it was, the *Umpherston*, a 470 ton, teak built barque, moored in front of a low built building with an overhanging roof.

Bessie's heart sank, probably in common with a lot of other folk when they saw the mass of people down below; standing, scurrying, dodging horse-drawn vehicles, the broughams and hansom cabs, dray-carts, stevedores, sailors and well-wishers. All with business that day on the busy dockside. So, this was it then, six months of trying to survive alongside the would-be inhabitants of a foreign land in a hand to mouth existence. *What was more*, she thought,her heart sinking heavily, *they were never going to pass this way again in her lifetime.*

"Come on Bessie, chin up, grab your bag and Molly and we'll find our way to the ticket office. The trunks should be loaded on the *Umpherston* shortly." Clarence led them down the gangplank, whistling cheerfully, whilst Bessie, her shoulders slumped dejectedly and her mouth turned down, followed behind with Molly.

They were among the first to join the queue from the *Bessie Belle*. The line stretched from the door of the office to the two officials behind the counter, who were scrutinising each embarkation order that every passenger had to provide. Some were turned away which caused a lot of shouting, some passed the others in the queue looking solemn, others bright and cheery, but by the time the Filbeys reached the counter themselves, Bessie was feeling so wretched she felt like having a cry.

"Not much room now, Govner," the official was saying to her

husband, after Clarence had handed over the document and was about to count out the cash for their quarters. "Mid-ships is full, seems that the Commissioners have issued too many married couple orders. Your wife could travel with the single women and you with the men."

They looked at each other in disbelief. Travel apart for the whole of the journey! A whole five or six months, depending on the weather, living apart. Bessie felt faint, whether it was from what she had just heard, or because it was hot in the stuffy room. She leant against Clarence for support.

"We'll have a cabin." What had he just said? We'll have a cabin?

She looked at her husband in astonishment as he began to dole out sovereigns from the leather pouch she'd seen under the floorboard. Her legs went weak and she would have fallen, if it wasn't for the man who was standing behind.

"Two ships came in from Cork and Dublin before yours did," the official said by way of explanation as he gave back change, after charging Clarence twenty five pounds each for a second class cabin. "Must be the thought of all that fine weather in Australia." He smiled at his little joke, as he stamped the embarkation order and handed it back with a grin.

If she could have kissed Clarence there and then, she would have done! Bessie was so elated at the thought of not having to share a berth with the masses that her heels sprouted wings and she walked on air, clutching him by the arm in an effort to show how pleased she was. Molly looked up at the couple, wondering why on earth the woman was acting so happily; she had hardly ever seen her smile. In their flush of intoxication, neither realised that her name had not been recorded; there was no Molly Filbey written on the Ship's Register, nor was there likely to be.

The man, dressed in an unfamiliar uniform, welcomed them aboard at the top of the gangplank, taking a cursory look at their papers, which indicated they were to travel second class and, after assuring them that their luggage would be placed outside their quarters, directed them to cabin number four, which was halfway along the port side of the top deck. He didn't notice the little girl who had hopped over onto the wooden deck ahead of the couple and if he had, he would have assumed that she was a fully paid recorded passenger, though infants were free if they were under two.

They were followed by a large and bossy sounding woman who complained that having been allocated a first class cabin, she expected to be greeted by a servant, as that was what had been agreed. It was all very well, but they were doing Adelaide a favour by gracing the place with their presence.

The woman swept past, her crinoline skirts nearly knocking the trio over in her haste to get to her quarters. She was followed by a thin, nervous looking man. He was wearing a black, three quarter length jacket and black trousers that were pulled in at the waist, tight at the ankle and strapped under the instep of his black, slip-on shoes. He was carrying his black top hat in his hands. Obviously he was a man of substance if they had been put in First Class.

Their cabin, one of four, two berth and clean with a small table attached to the bulkhead, was not as big as Bessie had expected, though they had a narrow porthole to see through. Clarence, a bit put out now that he had less to spend on his purchase of land, the seed, some tools and a couple of cows to build a herd up with, wasn't in the mood to hear her niggles and from the look on his face she thought it wise to keep her mouth shut. There was nowhere to store their possessions, other than in their trunks that could be hidden out of sight in the space that had been created under the two single bunks. Bessie, used to sleeping in the big old bed in the farmhouse began to feel claustrophobic.

"Sure, it's only for sleepin' in," Clarence said, sensing her dismay and wishing for a moment that he was back on the headland above the River Moy, with the sea breeze wafting and a view of the islands in his sight. "There's the ship's bell ringing, warning those not sailing to go ashore. Let's take Molly and wave a fond farewell to the Mother country, then we'll have some of that cold meat that we didn't get around to eating before."

It seemed that all 112 passengers were up on deck, whilst the small crew was up in the rigging, unfurling the sails or undoing the hawsers for casting off. There were tears from those who had relatives waving from the dockside but most were stoical, as a better life was beckoning for them all. Molly stood alone, watching a flock of seagulls as they wheeled above and listening to the sound of a fiddle playing a haunting tune.

"So it's done now," Bessie said, wiping her eyes with a pretty, lace handkerchief that she had taken from her reticule. "No lookin' back for any of us, Filbey. Let's hope this distant dream of yours turns out to be a good one for us all."

✿

# Chapter Four

The woman, in her late forties and stern looking, who was to serve the second class cabin passengers during their six months at sea, was standing outside their quarters when they returned.

"Good morning, Sir, Madam," she said in a subservient manner, as that was how her superiors had told her to greet the second class passengers. "I am a member of the ship's crew and one of my duties is to bring along your food from the galley. I have placed a jug of water on the table for your refreshment. Shall I bring you your breakfast now? The cook has provided oatmeal with raisins and perhaps the child would like a little milk."

*Well, this was something I hadn't expected,* thought Bessie, quite liking the idea of having someone to serve her meals and wondering if the woman would also be willing to do her washing and keep the cabin tidy. "Of course," she answered graciously. "Thank you."

*Trades people,* Monica McFarland sneered to herself as she walked away, feeling slightly annoyed that she was having to stoop to this kind of employment and serve this type of person, just because the family she had worked for before as a housekeeper for the past ten years had lost their fortune. Though she had felt cheered when the captain, who she was beginning to feel a certain amount of attraction towards, had told her that second class passengers were far more generous with their tips than the first class ones were.

"Dinner at the Captain's table this evening, Sir, Madam," she said, after carrying in three bowls of porridge and a small bowl of raisins, with a jug of milk and dainty white cups and saucers balanced on a tray. "Eight o'clock forward and drinks will be served at seven-thirty." Still with an unfriendly manner, she picked up Molly's bonnet that had fallen from one of the bunk beds and replaced the offending article, with a withering look.

"What are we going to do with Molly?" Bessie whispered, after the woman had issued their invitation and walked away. "I didn't know that with you payin' for a cabin, the captain would be wanting to rub shoulders with the likes of us."

*Exactly my sentiments*, thought Monica, as she listened at the cabin door, before knocking for admittance on the next one.

"And what will I wear?" Bessie continued. "I've only got that velvet with the high neck that's good enough. Oh, I wish I'd known that we were going to have a cabin, Filbey, I would have been prepared."

"Give a thought to me," Clarence said. "I've no evening clothes, save my best jacket and trousers for when we went to church in Ballina, but talking of Molly she could be put with the orphan girls down below,; she seemed to like young Hannah."

"Well, that's one thing that can be taken care of, I suppose. I could take down some of the cold meat, an apple and a few leftover biscuits as a bribe."

The *Umpherston*, sails billowing in the gusting wind, the bow pushing along through the pounding waves, steered that day along the English Channel with the intention of making the Bay of Biscay by nightfall. If the going was good, the ship would strike out into the ocean, reaching the coast of Portugal in a few days time. Not that its passengers gave a thought to the nautical plans of the captain. Australia, they had been told by the government officials who had signed them up for emigration, was six months away at the bottom of the world. How you would get there, no one knew, unless you were a student of geography.

Bessie had no such thoughts as she left Molly in the care of

Clarence and climbed carefully down the wooden rungs to the deck that was referred to as steerage. She was glad she was wearing a simple gown, having not ever wanted to wear the latest fashions when she had lived on the farm. If she had been wearing a steel ringed undergarment which supported a mass of petticoats under a voluminous skirt like the ones that she had seen lots of women wearing on the dockside, she would have been in a dilemma. As it was, the bottom of her boots felt slippery and she was glad to feel the firmness of the wooden deck.

It was as if she had been dropped into some kind of underground cavern. No daylight came through any portholes, which made the interior look gloomy and Bessie feel trapped. Mingled with the pungent smell of sweat, there was the tear jerking odour from leftover urine, after a hundred empty buckets hadn't had a decent swill. There were battered tin bowls and plates, items of cutlery, a large pewter jug and small, thick glasses, sitting upon a long table made from planking with rough-hewn benches. Men sat around looking aimless, smoking pipes, playing some sort of game that involved flipping stones and sipping *poteen* from small stone bottles. Along the sides of what must have been a hold before it was converted to an emigration ship, a clever carpenter had constructed rows of two tier sleeping compartments which consisted of three single bunks on the bottom of the compartment and three bunks on the top. This was the men's quarters and these erections took up most of the aft wall.

The men looked up as Bessie peered into the gloom and one man stirred himself enough to ask her business.

"I'm looking for the single women's quarters." She faltered, as one of the men made a ribald comment that she hoped she hadn't heard correctly.

"Tis where they call for'ard Missus. Tis that way." He jerked a thumb towards the front of the ship. Her heart in her mouth, Bessie picked her way through bags and clothing, skirting the compartments which must have been the married couples quarters, as a few women sat on their bunks nursing their children, until she eventually saw Maura, who was sitting on hers with Hannah.

"Why, Mrs. Filbey," she said in surprise. "What brings you to our pleasant surroundings this fine morning?" Bessie hoped the girl wasn't trying to mock her, but perhaps if she was in Maura's place, she may have done the same.

"I thought I might have seen you on the deck with your young charges, taking the air." She smiled at the girls who were staring at her from their quarters, curiously. "I looked for you, so I did, but you weren't there. I hope you don't mind me coming here instead."

"You won't be seeing much of us," Maura said in a voice full of bitterness. "Steerage passengers are not allowed on deck while cabin class passengers are up there and will only be allowed to do so if the captain agrees."

"No," gasped Bessie. "Surely he's not allowed to keep you confined to your quarters? I've never heard such twaddle."

"According to the man who's in charge of the lot of us, it is for our safety. Her Majesty's Commissioners have paid for our travel, provisions and accommodation before we take up employment and we even have one of them travelling aboard to check up on us, or so we've been told."

Bessie shook her head in disbelief.

"I've never heard the like. What happens about your meals, surely someone has to go to the kitchen and here's you telling me you can only go up on deck with permission?"

"Each group has to appoint a mess captain. That's me in our case and I have to go aloft to the galley and bring our food back here. All mess captains have to be accompanied by a member of the crew." She shrugged. "It's no point trying to change it and if you tried to, they'd only put you off at the next port. Anyway, you haven't said why you've come to see us. Is it about little Molly? How is the little girl?"

"Would you believe we've been invited to eat with the captain this evening?"

Maura lifted her eyebrows at this.

"Yes, I know," Bessie hurried on. "We were surprised when the woman came with the invitation, but now I need someone to look after Molly, as we're not sure how she'll behave. She's only three years old and she could get sleepy."

"None of us would be allowed to come to your cabin; you'd have to bring her here. But would you want the little darlin' to be sharing a bunk with the likes of us?"

"Maura." Bessie did her best to sound reproachful at the girl's words, as the girl and her charges could be useful on such an endurance of a journey. "I'll bring some food along that you can share amongst the others. I've some cold meat, a bit of pie, some apples and a fruit cake."

"A feast compared to the rations we're expected to eat. I believe we'll be having a half pound of beef or pork each day and will that be in brine, I ask myself? Other than that we'll be treated to a bit of oatmeal, a handful of raisins, a small amount of rice, a slice of bread, pickled fish and three quarts of water."

"It's the same rations as we'll be gettin', Maura. You must have had the oatmeal and raisins for breakfast like we did." Bessie was not going to let the girl think that they were living in luxury. "And your blankets appear to be of the same quality as ours."

"Ah, but who empties your bucket? We have a rota system to carry the thing up top in steerage."

Bessie had no answer to that, seeing as they had a nice, porcelain chamber pot, so she shrugged her shoulders.

"I'm sure Filbey would do the honours if I were to ask him nicely."

The invited passengers who sat at Captain O'Neill's table, which took up the whole of the area allocated in the forward part of the ship, consisted of a Mr. and Mrs. Trowbridge, a pair in their late forties and three other couples.

Mr. Trowbridge was a stocky gentleman, clean shaven with the requisite bushy sideburns which were white in contrast with his full head of dark hair. He wore black, knee length breeches, striped, silk stockings, a white linen stock, a black, cutaway jacket and a pair of black, knee length boots. He announced at some point in the conversation that he was a renowned architect and had been invited by Her Majesty's Commissioners to help plan some of the architecturally designed buildings to be built in Adelaide. His pale faced, brown haired wife, dressed in a plain brown, empire line dress, seemed to be a nice woman. She was quiet, with nothing much to say for herself, though Bessie could tell she was a gentle soul.

A tall, thin, spare looking man who had difficulty with the height of the ceiling in the saloon and had to stoop a little, was introduced as the ship's surgeon. Dr.Foley was similarly coiffured and dressed to Mr. Trowbridge, though his breeches were brown buckskin and he wore black shoes. He and his wife Alice, who was dressed in a white, empire line dress in a lawn material, would make the trip to and from the colony and as Alice said to Bessie later, she didn't mind the journey, as sometimes she would be assisting her husband and so the time would fly by.

Mr. and Mrs. Dickinson, the husband being of stern eye and unbending views concerning the punishment of prisoners in penal colonies, and was fair-haired, clean shaven, of medium height and had a military bearing. He wore some sort of black uniform jacket with epaulettes, which befitted his status of a senior command in the police force. In contrast, his wife was small, plump and dark-haired, with a tendency to giggle nervously. She wore a magenta coloured bodice with a low neck and wide, elbow length sleeves and a violet, gathered skirt.

Then of course there were the Filbey's. They were a little awed at first by the grandness of their fellow passengers, but Clarence, dressed in his Sunday outfit; black, striped jacket, waistcoat and black, ankle length trousers, the signature of a working man's best, went to a great deal of trouble explaining how his family had owned a lot of land in a corner of Mayo, but as so many of their servants had left for pastures new, they had decided to make a new life for themselves. Bessie, wasn't wearing the clothes or jewellery that would testify that she was from a wealthy family. She had only been able to don her blue, velvet, long sleeved gown with white lace around the collar of the high neck, and arrange her hair on top of her head in a cottage loaf fashion, but she didn't feel out of place. None of the women were attired too splendidly or fashionably, except that they were all wearing long-sleeved satin gloves and she wasn't.

"Clothes might maketh the man," Clarence had said, as the couple prepared themselves for what they considered to be a "leg up" in their future position in Adelaide society, by rubbing shoulders with the other cabin passengers, but they knew that it was money that talked in the long run. They might not be dressed in the latest fashions, whatever they were, but his mention of owning acres of land in Ireland and his plans to purchase more of the same, would outweigh the fact that Bessie wasn't bedecked in jewellery or wearing a fancy gown. Of course, they knew they must try to stop dropping their aitches; it would be better if they could adopt a more refined tone.

The captain, a man who was more used to carrying slaves in his ship than members of the British middle class, wore a black, shoulder length wig from an earlier century. Being bald he liked to cover up his pate and his long, navy jacket with gold braiding and some sort of ivory toggle fasteners that he had chosen as his uniform, was on the grubby side. Black, flared trousers and plain, black shoes completed his outfit and he made a great show of welcoming them all aboard. He proposed a toast for a "safe and prosperous journey" whilst they all had a pre-dinner sherry, but was loath to mention in the presence of what he considered to be esteemed personages, that two of his guests were missing. His bosun, who he was using as a butler that evening, whispered a little something in his ear and the captain nodded his assent then shooed his man away. Five minutes later, the same couple who had swept past the Filbeys that morning, blew through the door like a sudden gust of wind.

"You'd think that with you being a representative of Her Majesty's Commissioners it would exempt us from having to eat our supper with the lower classes and we could have our meal served in our cabin instead." The woman's strident voice could be heard floating ahead of her and met the ears of her fellow passengers, which might not have boded well. "I had assumed that First Class meant we would be rubbing shoulders with *our* class of people, not plebs and artisans."

"You didn't have to come with me Harriet, I am quite capable of carrying out Her Majesty's orders on my own," came the meek sounding reply.

The woman had grey hair which was swept back and secured with elaborate combs. She was in her fifties and of medium height, looked like an angry wasp in a gathered yellow and black striped skirt, with a low, black, satin bodice, rows of jet necklaces and a white, silk, *pelisse* thrown around her shoulders. She swept ahead of her husband, clutching her black, sequined evening dolly bag as if her life depended upon it. Perhaps she stored her riches within, as the bag never left her wrist that evening, even when she was eating her soup.

She took out a pair of gold covered *lorgnettes* and peered through them at the waiting company, who were standing out of politeness, while she waited for someone to announce her and her husband, who was smartly attired in evening dress.

There was silence, broken only by a giggle from Mrs. Dickinson and suppressed by a frown from her husband and a not too gentle nudge, before the bosun whispered into the captain's ear urgently.

"Ah-ah. Sir Rodney and Lady Harriet," the captain said. " I beg your pardon, my lady. Welcome. Would you and Sir Rodney like to sit over there?"

He pointed to two empty places at the table, one at the bottom facing him and one to the left, next to Bessie. Her heart quailed as the woman flounced to sit at the end of the table. Sir Rodney, who nodded pleasantly, sat at the side of her.

The bosun brought two glasses of sherry on a silver salver, then he continued to ladle soup into white china, silver trimmed bowls. The soup was potato and tasted rather salty, served from a matching tureen placed on a small, separate, white table-clothed piece of furniture, which could have been a seaman's chest underneath.

There was a silence, except for noisy slurping or delicate sipping, while everyone assessed each other, wondering who would be the first to speak.

"Good grub, thank you Dunsty." The captain finished his soup and the bosun asked if he had enjoyed it, before taking the empty bowl away. He glanced around quickly, wondering if he had been too familiar with the man who was acting as his servant.

"Thank you, very nice." Clarence was also happy to praise the first course. Everyone followed his example, as none, except the First Class passengers, knew how to behave in esteemed company.

"A little too salty for my taste," boomed a voice from the top of the table. "Have the cook informed of it immediately."

"Yes madam," the bosun said and clearing all the bowls onto a large wooden serving tray, he left the saloon.

He returned with a wooden trolley, which was apt to roll with the swell of the waves if a firm hand wasn't placed upon it. He began to distribute silver edged dinner plates to each of the guests.

"And it's her ladyship, not madam," Lady Harriet said rudely, wiping her plate with her napkin after the bosun had placed it before her. "Kindly remember my title."

The bosun nodded politely and began to put tureens containing hot vegetables and two white serving platters, one containing slices of beef, the other of pork and two large sauce boats, one of them containing pureed apple, on the table. Once the lord and ladyship and the captain had helped themselves, so did the rest of the captain's guests.

It seemed as if conversation was destined to be off the agenda, no doubt caused by the brooding presence of the titled couple, until Mrs. Dickinson swallowed a piece of pork too quickly, resulting in her husband having to give her a good thumping in the middle of her shoulders. From where Bessie was sitting he appeared to be enjoying the opportunity. Everyone began to speak, relating their own incidence of choking, or of someone they knew who had nearly died, and suddenly the room was alive with the buzz of conversation.

Later, after a dessert of apple pie and cream, followed by coffee and a small, sweet biscuit, the ladies were asked to leave the table and adjourn to a small area provided in a corner of the saloon. The men were given cigars and glasses of port and sat at the table near the captain.

"So, what do you do?" asked Lady Harriet, who had decided she would chair a meeting like she would at the 'Ladies At Home' gatherings back home in Derbyshire. "What is your name, my dear?" She looked at Bessie, whose heart missed a beat. How was she going to reply on this occasion? It was like being summoned to the Big House back in Mayo, although she had only ever got to meet the housekeeper there. She swallowed and tried to speak nicely, reminding herself that she was not in the bogs of Ireland now.

"My name is Bessie Filbey and my husband is called Clarence and we had a farm near Ballina in Ireland."

"And?"

"Oh, we have left the farm as we had problems keeping the staff. Because of the blight, you know."

"So?"

"We're going to Australia to buy some land and carry on with the farming."

"Ah, so we have something in common, Mrs. Filbey. You and your husband are landowners as we are."

Lady Harriet turned her attention to Mrs. Dickinson, who answered her quick fire questions with a lot of giggling. It appeared that her husband was to be in a senior command position, helping to organise a police presence in the various townships that were springing up around Adelaide.

Lady Harriet dismissed the woman quickly as a woman

without a brain. Alice Foley, sometimes nurse in assisting her surgeon husband, was not cowed by the woman's probing questions and answered them briskly, leaving Lady Harriet in no doubt that if she was sick there would be no "flimflammery" in the treatment she would receive. This left Margaret Trowbridge, who answered brightly that her husband was to take up a position working in the city and it was something to do with constructing building there.

"So, it looks as if Mrs. Filbey and I will be the major landholders in Adelaide." Lady Harriet pressed Bessie's hand patronisingly. "We could go to the land titles office and stake our claims together, my dear."

Bessie flushed, muttering that it wasn't her place to make any major decisions about their future, wishing that a hole in the floor would appear and she could jump in. Then she smiled to herself, thinking that if she did that she could end up sleeping in steerage with Molly.

# Chapter Five

Molly was fast asleep in a top to tail position under the blanket in Hannah's bunk. She had enjoyed being with the young orphanage girls, especially Hannah, who with her dark hair and thin frame, reminded her of Maggie. All the girls had taken an interest in playing with the pretty little newcomer, who had arrived for her afternoon nap accompanied by a basket full of goodies. Molly didn't miss the woman, who had taken her from the cabin and washed her in a tin tub, though the man with her had been nice and she was beginning to like this little holiday at the bottom of a boat.

"I'm thinkin' that if the Missus wants a girl to look after her Molly when we get there, I'd put me 'and up" Hannah had said quietly that evening, as she sat with Maura on an adjoining bunk bed. "I'd even work for nothin', just me board would do. It 'ud be better than goin' to that place in Adelaide yer told me about."

"But that is why I've had my passage paid, Hannah, to take you girls to King William Street, where there is a place for orphan girls to stay before being hired out to the gentry."

"But can't you lose me, say I disappeared at one of the ports we'll be stoppin' at?"

"You're not so green as you're cabbage looking," Maura replied with a smile. "Where would you like to be dropped off then, a Canary island or somewhere in darkest Africa?"

Bessie didn't feel well the next morning. The ship was rolling at a frightening angle and she felt fragile from the meal she had consumed at the captain's table and a couple of glasses of wine and a sherry. She had told Clarence to see to Molly as she wasn't feeling up to it. The sound of others retching in the nearby cabin quarters didn't help her mood.

Clarence lurched along the ship until he came to the hold which housed the steerage passengers. The hatch was closed and sounds of crashing and lots of angry shouting came up from down below.

"Can't go down there, Sir," said a thick set, bearded sailor with a Liverpudlian accent, as he staggered along the deck himself. "Captain's orders, I'd go back to your cabin if I was you."

Clarence nodded. The wind was howling and he could hear the roar of the waves from where he was standing. He made his way slowly back.

"That was quick," Bessie said languidly, as she lay in her bunk with her eyes closed.

"I'll have to go later,"Clarence replied. "They've shut the hatch for safety's sake."

Down in the bowels of the ship which was taking more of a pounding from the elements than up aloft, people, mostly the men, cursed and swore as possessions flew off bunk beds, with utensils and food that they were trying to eat sliding down the table or onto the floor. Those who had taken to their bunks, feeling sick or after having thrown up the contents of their stomachs into the communal buckets, did a few rows of their rosary beads or sent up prayers of deliverance. Others sat morosely, or wide eyed like the orphanage children, who looked to Maura for reassurance that the ship wasn't going to sink.

"Tis the ocean we're travelling," she said kindly, patting Molly's hand, who upon waking had gone to use the bucket behind the curtain and found it so full of liquid she had wet her bottom using it. It had taken ten distressing minutes to calm her, as she cried in anguish for her sister. It was only a cuddle from Hannah that had soothed the sobbing child.

People around began to mutter uneasily, especially when

someone noticed that water was seeping through one of the planks nearby, and there was sounds of crashing as buckets were being overturned. One man, frustrated at the turn of events, began to stand halfway up the ladder, shouting.

"Will someone get their fecking arse down 'ere before we all fecking drown!"

There was no response, so a few of the single men took his place and started to hammer their fists against the hatchway door, then another brought his slane and began to knock against it violently, but still with no avail. They kept it up until one by one, tired out by their efforts to attract the crew's attention, they gave up the ghost and peace, as much as it could be, began to reign again.

It was two long hours before the sea began to calm and the hatch was thrown open, to the relief of all who sat below. The man in charge was a swarthy bloke with a bit of a mean streak, who went by the name of Jimmy and had sailed the seas with Captain O'Neill for a number of years having escaped from a squalid existence in the back streets of Liverpool when he was a fourteen years old. He couldn't quite understand how the inhabitants of the hold on *this* voyage, had to be treated that much differently from the slaves that had been transported before. Maybe it was because these people weren't black, or prisoners of Her Majesty. One of the crew had said that the queen actually wanted the English to sail to the new colony and was paying Captain O'Neill to get them there. He ignored their complaints and accusations, as one by one the bucket carriers came up the ladder rungs, by parroting the captain's words:

"If you don't like it you can get off at the next port of call." This seemed to keep the buggers silent as they meekly passed him by.

Clarence made a second attempt to see Molly that afternoon. They were passing the coast of France at that time, though the passengers were unaware that it was in the distance, as black clouds were still hanging low over the Bay of Biscay. He took along a share of Bessie's rations, his dear wife still feeling nauseous and confined to her bunk. He wondered how she would feel if he left her to go to the saloon again this evening for supper? According to Monica, their servant, that was where they would be eating their meal.

He thought back to the conversation he'd had with Sir Rodney, the evening before. He was a timid man to the onlooker, but a more astute man than Clarence was yet to meet. From an impoverished family distantly related to royalty, Sir Rodney had been encouraged to marry one of the daughters of a man who had inherited a great deal of land from his wealthy wool manufacturing parents in Derbyshire. The man had been only too glad to be rid of his waspish tongued daughter, Harriet, heaving a sigh of relief on her wedding day, as he walked her down the aisle. Not a man of handsome looks, nor having a charismatic personality, Rodney was happy to become the husband of the cranky Harriet, as with her came a pleasant house overlooking the Matlock Hills and the River Derwent and an allowance of one hundred guineas per year. There were no children resulting from their union, as Harriet had a distaste for all things carnal, so Rodney threw himself into becoming a valued member of Her Majesty's Commissioners, by involving himself in the Ordnance department in London, where several talented cartographers worked on survey maps for the colony of Adelaide. For the first time in his life, he had felt excited by a project, whilst dreaming of owning sizeable acreage in a distant foreign land. It was there for the taking, at a cost that was minimal, compared to the rising costs in London at that time and with a bit of luck, although that hadn't been the case unfortunately, Harriet might have been persuaded to stay behind in Derbyshire. Clarence had been promised a look at a copy of the maps that Sir Rodney had been charged to take along with him. It covered a township with the name of Willunga in the southern regions and all the land around. Sir Rodney had heard tell that the soil in that area was very fertile.

Down at the bottom of the ship, Clarence, like Bessie, was appalled by the confines of the passengers' accommodation, where the herding of so many souls in such a narrow area meant listening to a stranger snoring, breaking wind and any other noise that a body might make during slumber. It could have been them and he thanked the man above that he had decided to pay for a cabin in the end.

Jimmy, who was in charge again now that the sun was shining and the ship was sailing through calmer waters, had orders to let groups of ten steerage passengers at a time take the air whilst the hold was being swabbed and their bunks were fumigated. He had saluted Clarence as the man had asked for permission to descend the ladder, no doubt thinking that Clarence was the inspector sent by Her Majesty, who was rumoured to be travelling on the the *Umpherston*.

It was strange but the little dote appeared contented, sitting there on a narrow bunk as the girls waited for their turn to go on deck. She was playing with a knitted doll. She raised her eyes in answer when Clarence said her name, but there was no look of recognition, which strangely enough pulled at his heart strings.

"She's been asking for someone called Maggie" Maura said, after accepting his gift of a wedge of cheese, two thick slices of beef, a loaf of bread and a small pat of butter spooned into a hole in the bloomer. "She had a bit of an upset earlier and the poor little thing was quite distressed."

"Ah, she'd be askin' after her nurse," lied Clarence, " the girl who was looking after Molly back in Mayo. She was like a sister, but it was unfortunate that she went to England to be married before we came away. I'll take Molly up on deck and get her a breath of air. Mrs. Filbey is confined to her quarters and I was wonderin' if it would be too much trouble if I brought her back to you again?"

"Ah, she's no trouble, Mr. Filbey and she seems quite content when she's not after crying for this Maggie. Shall I come with you and watch her while you light a pipe?"

It was while they were on deck that Clarence met the man who he remembered was being called George Colmayne, whom he had talked to on the *Bessie Belle*. The man looked withdrawn, and was not answering the questions of his little boy, who was tugging on his coat tails.

*45*

"The top of the morning to you" Clarence hailed him cheerfully. "Looks as if we could be in for a spot of golden weather, according to the sky over yonder. I suppose it'll get warmer the further down the world we sail."

He seemed to have struck a chord with the poor weary looking fellow, who suddenly nodded brightly then told his son to join his mother, who was walking along with her other children further along the deck.

"Exactly what I was saying to the wife. I know we'll be into autumn when we land on the other side of the world, but the winters won't be anything like we have had in Ireland."

"Is she doing a bit of suffering like my wife is?" Clarence asked, after drawing again on his pipe because it kept going out. "Mine's taken to her bed, doesn't seem to be bothering with anything."

"It's being down there in our quarters that's getting to my wife." Clarence had the feeling that George was talking on behalf of the two of them when he said it. "She's used to the fresh country air, walks along the beach, looking out across to the islands at Westport and she liked to help me with the children I used to teach. Now she's got nothing and she's worried sick that I won't get a job as a carpenter when we get there."

"Of course yer will"Clarence soothed. "There'll be a thousand and one houses needing to be built for all the folk that'll be settlin' there in Adelaide and I've heard there's lots of townships springin' up all over the place. Have you thought about doing a spot of teachin' to these children whilst we're travellin'? Molly is only three, but I'm sure yer could help her count on her fingers."

George perked up considerably at his suggestion.

"Do you think I could? Oh, but I'd have to get permission from the captain and it's difficult trying to get past that Jimmy."

"Leave it with me" said Clarence, puffing out his chest at the thought that if he hadn't got the captain's ear, he certainly had Sir Rodney's. "And seeing as I like to be philanthropic, (he'd remembered his brother-in-law's use of the word) I'll chuck in a shillin' a week meself."

46

Getting permission for George to teach hadn't been difficult. It appeared that the captain had noticed the rapport between Clarence Filbey and "his honourable and honourableness" as he had privately named Sir Rodney and Lady Harriet, so when Clarence broached the subject in front of all the guests that evening, Bessie included, as she thought she might be able to keep a little something down, the idea had been roundly applauded.

"Can't have the children frittering away their time and getting up to mischief," Lady Harriet boomed. "What did you say the man's name was, Colmayne? I wonder if he's related to the Colmaynes from the Scottish borders? Their family originally came from Ireland. Westport did you say?"

Maura, plain of face but with the Irish beauty of auburn hair and green eyes that could change her appearance to attractive when she got around to smiling, was finding that she had a bit of a problem with Jimmy. She had taken the children up on deck one day and whilst standing there looking out towards the golden shores of southern France in the distance, her charges busy chasing each other around the deck excitedly, she was approached by the steerage overseer.

"So what's a nice girl like you trailin' across the ocean with a load of children in tow?" He had asked with fetid breath, not really interested in her answer, but he had to say something to get her attention.

"Oh, I'm taking them across to Adelaide, where they'll find domestic work with some of the settlers."

"And yerself?"

"I have the choice of going back to Ireland and perhaps escorting a few more lucky girls to seek a better life like these will have, or I can find myself a position as a children's nurse. The nuns have very kindly given me a letter of recommendation."

"And what do yer think yer'll be doin' then?"

"I can't say. I'll wait until I get there, probably get a job as a nursemaid for a couple of years."

"You could come with me." He lowered his voice, as if he

47

thought a spy might be listening. "I'll be jumping ship when we get there. I'm off to the gold fields in Victoria. I've heard you can make a fortune there."

"I don't think so. I'll be quite happy earning a living in other ways."

Jimmy leered at her as she had walked into his trap quite innocently. "I can arrange me cabin mate to go for a walk one night and you and me could see some action in me hammock. How about it? I could leave the hatch open tonight."

Being a Catholic girl, brought up by nuns and at one time considering becoming a novice herself, it had taken a while to understand his meaning, at first thinking he was offering her better accommodation with him and the crew. Of course to do that would be unthinkable and she was about to thank him and reject his offer, when the meaning of his words caused her to pause. She looked shocked and felt anger. Had he not been in the position he was in, she would have slapped the smirk from his face. *Who did he think she was, some sort of hussy, giving her favours to any horrid man?* She called for the children, gathering them together under a protective wing and turned on her heel, enraged.

# Chapter Six

As the ship continued on, the sea breezes pushing the billowing sails along the coast of Portugal and into the Atlantic on its way to one of the Canary Isles, life aboard the *Umpherston* settled into a routine. The weather was balmy and the cabin passengers took to sitting in wooden chairs that had been placed along the starboard side. Their days, when they were not resting in their cabins, were spent chatting, eating and playing some sort of deck game with a hoop, that the doctor appeared to have invented.

Sir Rodney, Lady Harriet and Clarence took measures to see for themselves how the makeshift school progressed, seeing that they'd had a hand in its creation. At first, parents were reluctant to have their children schooled in lettering and numbers, seeing it as a waste of time. Labourers and domestics did not have scholars for offspring, they muttered between themselves when the idea was first mooted by Mr. Colmayne at mess time one day but Lady Harriet, brisk and bluff, with a vision of how the colony could progress in the future, said attendance would have to be compulsory as the teacher was being paid. It soon appeared that the table, normally used for meals and recreation by the older steerage passengers, would not have been a popular place for the children to have their schooling, so the saloon where the cabin class had their supper, was pressed into service for a couple of hours each day.

It was a few days later when the *Umpherston* sailed into the harbour of one of the Canary Isles. The cabin passengers, up on deck to view the doughty ship's progress, were enthralled by the landscape that met their eyes. Volcanic ash had darkened the narrow beaches, a result of past eruptions from the distant mountain. Palm trees grew on the hillsides, where white washed buildings clung. As they neared the moorings, olive skinned, dark haired people were busily setting up a quayside market, laying out their produce on gaudy looking blankets, or selling their wares from a barrow or a cart.

"Bananas" said Bessie happily, turning to Margaret Trowbridge, who over the evenings spent together after supper she had found to be a little shy. "The only time that I have ever had a banana was when I visited Sligo and stayed with my husband's family."

"We usually had them at Christmastime" Margaret said sadly. "We bought them mostly for the children, along with a few oranges too."

Margaret's four children were grown up now with families of their own and all with professions as befitted an upper middle class, public school educated family. It appeared though that one of her sons was following in his father's architectural footsteps, and was considering a new life abroad. "I'm missing the grandchildren" she continued wistfully.

"You might not stay in Adelaide forever," Bessie soothed. "It could be that Mr. Trowbridge will return to England when all the new building ends."

"Let's hope so. I would hate to think that I would never see my family again."

She thought for a moment before saying "I haven't seen a lot of your daughter, Molly. The last time I saw her, Mr. Filbey was carrying her up on deck."

"Oh, that's because she is being taken care of by her nurse in steerage. Unfortunately there weren't enough cabins to go around. They seem happy enough and they are sharing accommodation with lots of other girls."

*Oh what a tangled web we weave when we first do deceive.*

"Look over there, Margaret," she said brightly, nudging her new friend in the hope of quickly changing the subject. "There's

Alice Foley and Lily Dickinson. Oh, followed closely by Lady Harriet. Perhaps we can disembark together and have a look around."

It wasn't as if she didn't like the child, Bessie justified to herself as she followed the chattering women down the gangplank, there to join their husbands who had exchanged British shillings with the captain for Spanish doubloons; it was because in their small cabin they would have difficulty in swinging a cat.

Down in steerage there was a muttering again amongst the single men. Fed up with being shut into the hold for what they considered to be long periods and not at all necessary in their eyes and with the ship having dropped anchor in a foreign country, where perhaps they could have stretched their legs ashore, one or two of them were beginning to consider mutiny.

Jimmy was tied up as he was helping to moor the ship and overseeing the taking on board of fresh meat, a couple of pigs, hessian sacks full of oranges, bananas, pumpkins and pineapples. He wasn't there to hear the murmuring which had begun after people had awoken and found that the hatch was locked against them again. The bucket carriers and the tray bearing mess captains who had been assigned to bring the breakfasts, were greatly put out. Johnny Healey was a pock-marked man that you wouldn't want to meet in a dark alley, having built up his muscles carrying heavy loads at the docks in Tilbury. He began banging his tin plate on the table, much as he would have done if he had been travelling on a convict ship and not one subsidised by Her Majesty's Commissioners. George Colmayne, urged on by his worried wife, who had asked him to go and talk to the man as people all around had begun to feel nervous, crawled out of his bunk then strode along to the men's quarters to see if he could help.

"They didn't tell us that it was one rule for us and one for them," Johnny cried, after George had asked if he could listen to his grievances. "They said that we would be free settlers. Free means moving around when yer want to, not stuck down 'ere

*51*

waitin' until someone bothers to open the hatch and let us out. We're all herded together like in a cattle ship."

George nodded sympathetically. He felt the same as Johnny did, but as it was free passage there was not a lot they could do.

"I'll speak to someone," he promised, looking around at the other men who had begun to form a group, fed up with their captivity, especially as there was still a lot of ocean to travel.

"Meantime" he said, looking over to a man who had been entertaining them over the last few nights, "give us a tune on your fiddle, Seamus and seeing as there won't be any lessons this morning, the girls can have a dance."

It was the middle of the day before Jimmy arrived, throwing open the hatch to allow the appointed to carry out their deeds. He wasn't prepared for the rush of people who knocked him to the ground in their haste to free themselves whilst George stood back looking on in horror. Jimmy got to his feet and raced off to summon help, bringing back three rough looking sailors armed with muskets who came racing along the deck.

"It was a show of solidarity" George, who had been appointed spokesman said when the men were taken before the captain in order to hear their punishment. "How would you like it if you had to spend your life in a cattle pen?"

His words were heard by not only O'Neill but Sir Rodney, who being Her Majesty's representative, had been summoned to the hearing as well. Being a compassionate man and having seen for himself the conditions that the free settlers were having to put up with and knowing that the captain had not, he asked for leniency and asked whether perhaps a little more freedom could be granted too? Captain O'Neill, well aware that there were many ships now in competition for the lucrative contracts awarded by Her Majesty's Commissioners, agreed that he would think about it, but for the moment the men involved would have to scrub the decks for a week.

It was the talk of the table that evening. Later when sitting with the captain, each of them eating a freshly cooked steak from a whole cow that had been brought on board to keep the cabin class fed until they reached Cape Town, Lady Harriet, briefed by her husband on the limitations of his intervention between the captain and the passengers' welfare, suggested that the ladies present should put their heads together and come up with some ideas to keep to keep the steerage dwellers occupied.

"The conditions are disgusting down there" she said to the ladies, when their husbands were on their port and cigars and they had retired to their corner to drink coffee. "I wouldn't be surprised if they all go down with dysentery and the smell – I was glad I had a handkerchief in my reticule."

Bessie nodded. She had been down there that day, taking a bag filled with fruit, the bananas and a few navel oranges especially for the orphan girls and hoped that their delight upon receiving the goodies, wouldn't cause too much jealousy amongst the other passengers. She was well aware of the conditions below deck and often wondered if she was being fair to Molly by leaving her there, though the child seemed content and never gave her more than a passing glance when she visited. Maura, wondering why this might be, reckoned that Molly had been a late baby, as Mrs. Filbey must be way past her childbearing years and was quick to speak of the child's cleverness in counting up to five.

They were all grateful for George Colmayne's tuition. Even one or two of the men had joined his classes, though many wondered why. Could it have been the walk around the deck and the biscuits and milk that were served to his scholars that attracted them?

"Well, I think that there should be a cleaning rota amongst the women passengers" said Alice. With her husband being the ship's doctor, she was aware that a regular scrubbing of the steerage area, instead of when one or two sailors could be spared, wouldn't go amiss. "Many hands make light work and I'm quite willing to oversee a group of women to see that things are properly done."

"I can sew" said Margaret Trowbridge. "I'm sure we all can and have brought a few things with us that can be used for mending tears or stitching hems."

"My talent is floristry" said Lily Dickinson. "I don't think there will be much call for floristry on board."

"I can crochet" said Bessie. "I have brought some crochet hooks and a few skeins of wool."

"I am sure you could all contribute to their welfare" Lady Harriet boomed. "Even you Mrs. Dickinson. I am sure you could help Mrs. Trowbridge to organise a sewing group. Splendid, splendid, we'll make a start after we've lifted anchor. Now I wonder what we can think up for the men to keep them occupied?"

By the time the ship had tied up at the docks in Cape Town, there was a happier atmosphere aboard the *Umpherston*. They were halfway through the voyage and to celebrate, the captain had allowed all passengers on deck to watch as the ship steered across Table Bay to a berth at the busy wharf.

Poor, crudely built shanties sat cheek by jowl with the granary stores and warehouses; black skinned workers loaded bales of wool, crates of fruit and tons of grain onto the many sailing ships that had come from the four corners of the world.

Farmers, their heads covered from the sun with floppy hats, were on their way to market, or heading back to their land in the far flung areas of the Transvaal. They drove laden covered carts pulled by teams of bullocks; whilst locals took advantage of the many travellers, selling worthless *gewgaws* as souvenirs. In the distance, in the taverns of the fast growing town beneath the shade of the Table Mountain, British and Afrikaner masters did financial deals on land and property.

This time, the cabin folk had been given rand in exchange for their shillings and were allowed to troop down the gangplank one by one, but as Johnny said to the men who stood beside him, who were muttering that they weren't allowed to go ashore again:

"We ain't got a feckin' shillin' to spend between us anyway!"

Whilst the loaded ship waited out in the Indian Ocean for favourable winds to hasten their voyage along the last leg of their journey, a woman gave birth behind the curtained area in the female quarters which served as the vessel's hospital and two children went down with a bad dose of "the trots." Lady Harriet swung into action; there was no way that sickness or infection was going to cause an epidemic on a Her Majesty's commissioned ship. Just imagine what people would say if they got to hear that the *Umpherston*, carrying carefully selected workers to populate the free colony of Adelaide, had been stricken with an onset of dysentery or a child had died because of it. It was enough to make her rally her cabin dwelling troops.

Bessie, who was in charge of Lysol and scrubbing brushes, scurried down to steerage to oversee the team of willing females who had already begun their quest for cleanliness, whilst all the men were banned to the decks. The two sick children were isolated behind the 'hospital' curtain in the capable hands of Alice Foley and the new mother and child were sent to rest in one of the cabins above.

Margaret Trowbridge and Lily Dickinson were given the job of distributing the contents of the many sacks of fruit. Bananas, oranges, pineapples and fat, round melons which had been destined for the captain's table and would have lasted the diners until they had got to Adelaide, had been purloined by Lady Harriet and no one would argue with that. She became the steerage passengers' hero, even if she did treat some of them as if she had a smell under her nose. Which she had, given that there were no washing facilities other than a few shared buckets and no baths to bathe in anyway and the stench could have got even worse if she hadn't intervened when she had.

"Do you know, Filbey?" Bessie said grimly, after she had washed Molly from top to toe then settled the child on a makeshift bed of blankets on their cabin floor that evening, Clarence having been concerned that the poor little mite might catch an infection if she stayed with the orphan girls. "Do you know, I think that Maggie's sister cannot speak. I've only ever heard her say the words, "want Maggie." How old is she? Three, four maybe? Sara's children were gabbling away at this age."

"You're forgettin' where she's come from, Bessie" he replied, looking down fondly on the sleeping child, whom Bessie had stripped of her dirty clothes and given them to their cabin maid for washing, with the promise of an extra tip. "A cabin dweller, with parents trying to make a living from the land that they tenanted. Hardly a family who would worry about whether she could talk or not. She'll be fine now she's got the other girls to talk to. You'll soon be telling little Molly to hold her tongue."

"Hmm, well just as long as we haven't taken on an imbecile. Our life will be difficult enough without that."

She was right, life in the future would get difficult, Clarence thought, as he rested on his bunk waiting for Monica to summon them to dinner. It appeared, after talking to Sir Rodney, that to own a substantial bit of land in the colony they were going to have to travel south. There were drover trails they could follow and stopping points along the way, but unless he bought a horse and cart to get them to this place called Willunga, which he had decided they were going to take a chance on, it was going to be a hell of journey with the two trunks and a child to carry along too.

He sighed as he mentally counted the sovereigns that he had left in the leather pouch which he kept on his person, except for when he had a wash. It had seemed a fortune when he had pulled the money from its hiding place, especially with the thought of his money from Colooney too. But there had been the extra cost of their passage and now the horse and cart it would seem they would need, plus the price of a bit of furniture if they managed to find some sort of dwelling to move into and accommodation on the way. He thanked God he had taken a loan from his brother in law, or he'd have been reduced to working for a master, which he never, ever wanted to do again.

Bessie, sitting on the other bunk, her hands busily crocheting a table runner for the table which she hoped to own when they got settled somewhere, was more concerned with keeping up socially with the other members of the cabin dwellers' circle. Wherever this Willunga place was, it wasn't going to be near enough to attend the soirees that Lady Harriet was planning, nor the six bedroomed house that Margaret Trowbridge would have as her residence, once her architect husband had chosen his piece of land overlooking the ocean, near the township of Glenelg. Alice Foley had been dismissed as a possible friend in the future as she would be travelling backwards and forwards across the oceans with her surgeon husband and Lily Dickinson, destined to live in whichever headquarters that her husband was assigned to. She would hardly be in a position to entertain.

It had seemed to Bessie that they might have had the chance of coming up in the world, now that they were rubbing shoulders with the likes of her ladyship, who would be mixing with the cream of the Adelaide social circle. According to Clarence however, Sir Rodney, someone who was in the know about the land that was available and had kindly shown him a map, had said that this Willunga place was quite a distance from the city. Much of the land had been bought from the Crown by settlers who had arrived in the colony a few years earlier. Houses had been built and there was an inn, a general store and a slate quarry. Sir Rodney had said that the area in the south was vast and there was still plenty of acres to be had for those who had the money and he had hinted that if Filbey needed a helping hand with anything to do with purchasing it, he only had to say.

But for now, in the planning stages of arranging a pleasant Christmas for the passengers and crew aboard the *Umpherston,* Bessie was part of Lady Harriet's 'do good' committee, and was feeling well content.

♣

# Chapter Seven

After just over four months at sea, with the final part of the journey spent cruising through the blue waters of the Indian Ocean, past palm tree covered islands in the distance and into the warm waters of the Southern Ocean, the heat below in the *Umpherston* became so unbearable that many chose to sleep up top, with permission from the captain of course.

Edgy tempers became the norm, parents screamed at truculent children, fights broke out amongst repressed men and Lady Harriet made a discovery that caused moral outrage amongst the privileged passengers on board. It appeared that a little bird had told her that members of the crew had smuggled aboard a couple of girls when the ship had docked in Cape Town. Both were mulattos and although hidden from view they had been passed around for the pleasure of the crew members and had been seen parading along the deck one evening after the Captain had ordered lock down.

Lady Harriet, conscious of her status as a member of the aristocracy and wife of Sir Rodney and his position as one of Queen Victoria's representatives, had made her way to Captain O'Neill's quarters, without consulting her husband. She had barged into the cabin, intent on insisting that the men be punished and the girls locked up for the duration of the voyage. She had been shocked to come face to face with a girl of tawny complexion with lots of black, curly hair. She had never seen the offspring of a white person and a negro before. She had of course heard of William Wilberforce, the man who had insisted on the abolishment of slavery, which had been made law in an earlier decade, but having only seen the "blacks" who had worked on the docks at Cape Town, this exotic looking woman who was staring back at her with a pair of startled, sloe coloured eyes, sitting as she was on the captain's bunk bed, mending a tear in the hem of her calico dress, came as a complete surprise.

Recovering her composure as was her want as an upper class lady, Lady Harriet sprang across and grabbed the barefooted girl, pulling her savagely through the door, across the deck and up the steps to where the captain stood at the wheel, looking down in disbelief at the scene before him. The girl, screaming in fright at being discovered by this fearsome looking white woman, brought the attention of Sir Rodney and his fellow players, as they were having a game of quoits.

"Now, now, dear lady" said her husband, puffing slightly as he rushed up behind his wife, who had now released the sobbing girl and was now sitting at the feet of the angry looking captain. "Has this person done something to offend you, or have we got a stowaway on board?"

"Stowaway, Sir Rodney, only you could come up with such a simple explanation. I found this creature languishing on the bed in Captain O'Neill's accommodation. She is one of the two women brought aboard for the entertainment of the crew, or so I heard from a very reliable source."

Lady Harriet, her face sweaty with nostrils flared, her grey hair having come out of its untidy bun and her plump body heaving with exertion, caused Sir Rodney to look upon the frightened girl with sympathy. Who wouldn't be terrified of his domineering wife?

"Captain O'Neill," he said, aware that as Her Majesty's representative he must be seen to handle the situation firmly but diplomatically. He also saw that he had an audience that was agog with the most excitement they'd had since they had come aboard. "Perhaps it would be best for all concerned if we adjourned to somewhere more private, the saloon perhaps, where the bosun could make us a cup of tea."

The captain, feeling that his position was a little precarious now that the interfering old bat had discovered one of the girls that he had actually ordered some of his crew to go and capture at their last port of call, was quick to dismiss his sniggering men as he felt his authority dwindling. Aiming a kick at his petrified lover, he strode ahead of Sir Rodney, wondering who the spy must have been. There had to be one, how else would the upper class besom have known about it?

Monica, who was looking on, felt a thrill as she witnessed O'Neill's humiliation. It would serve him right for spurning her, if he was stripped of being captain of this ship.

It was with joy and uplift that the passengers, steerage included, stood on the decks of the valiant vessel a few weeks later, looking across to the lush, green hills and dense forests in the distance, as the ship nosed its way towards its quayside berth.

Anchoring amongst the profusion of vessels which had journeyed from all over the world in the pursuit of commodities to trade, the sound of cheering from aboard the ship was deafening. *This was it, a new life beckoned.* Some were fulfilling a distant dream, whilst others who had been forced from their homes or come to work in the colony, viewed their arrival with a certain amount of trepidation.

Down below on the busy quay, bullock carts unloaded grain into the holds of cargo ships; fishing boats laden with their catch of the day sold fish by the barrel to waiting merchants; cattle boats, the animals squashed together akin to passengers in an emigrant ship, were under sail in readiness for a swelling tide and bales of wool stood waiting, ready to be loaded onto the *Umpherston*, her return cargo destined for the weaving sheds of England.

Agents in smart attire waited for the passengers, some of them carrying lists. These were Her Majesty's representatives, there to collect those who had been given free passage to work as labourers in the colony. A stout woman scanned the deck above of the newly anchored ship, looking for the young girls who had been sent to the colony by a couple of Irish orphanages. They would be good, Catholic, God fearing girls who would make decent servants for the cream of society already there. Maura, in charge of seven of these girls, dithered, as she looked down upon the woman, having promised Hannah a place with the Filbeys, if that was a possibility. She felt unsure now what the reaction of the Superintendent from the orphan depot would be.

The gangplank down, the passengers stood waiting, whilst two emigration agents scrutinized the embarkation orders which everyone had to show. Molly, standing with Hannah amidst the chattering girls, was lost amongst them and didn't turn a hair when the Filbeys, having had their papers stamped and now allowed to set foot on Australian soil, went ahead to collect their trunks. Nor was she noticed when Maura and the other matron's head count was taken as read and the excited orphans were chivvied down to the quayside.

"I'm sure it doesn't matter to me" Mrs. Manley, the stout woman who had been waiting for them said to Maura, after she had shaken the Superintendent's hand and explained that one of her charges may already have a place with one of the families who had travelled aboard the *Umpherston* and was looking for a nursemaid. It had been discussed as a possibility already with the Filbeys, as their daughter had got on very well with Hannah.

"Hannah Sweeney?" The woman took her pencil and crossed the name off her list. She felt thankful. The Irish weren't so popular as they had been when the settlement of Adelaide was new and any worker had been snapped up as soon as their feet hit terra firma. It wasn't just because they were Irish, but because there was a lot of them around. Institutions such as workhouses and asylums were opening their doors in the mother country, embracing the call for workers to populate the new colonies, in an effort to reduce the amount of mouths they'd had to feed. German orphans were popular now, snapped up by the farmers who toiled on their land in Hahndorf, whilst some of the girls from a previous British emigrant ship were taking up space at the depot in Pulteney Street and eating their heads off whilst they waited for a job.

"Now, I've organised a couple of carts. A bit of a squash, but I know from experience that they'll be used to that. You put your girls on that one, Maura and get what's her name, that other matron to load her girls on the other."

She walked across to where the Filbeys stood, Bessie insisting that they hire at least a bullock dray to take them and their luggage to Adelaide, where Clarence was to meet Sir Rodney at the land title's office. Having looked at the dry mud caked earth of the rutted track that people and vehicles seemed to be following, she didn't relish trailing a child and two heavy trunks. Besides, what would Sir Rodney and Lady Harriet think if they arrived in the city many hours later, tired and weary, running with sweat as the day was humid, with their clothes already threadbare with constant wear and boots covered with this red, dusty mud? They would know them for paupers and wouldn't feel obliged to help them at all. She began to wave as a black, open air *phaeton*, pulled by four brown horses passed by. Then she felt cross, when she saw that the distinguished couple had given a lift to the Trowbridges. What a sly cat that Margaret Trowbridge was; she had never said a word about getting a lift when they'd all said goodbye that morning.

"Bernardette Manley at your service, Ma'am."

The stout woman stood politely at the side of Bessie, fearing that she might antagonize this would be employer who was wearing a sour expression on her face.

"I understand that you would like us to release one of our orphans into your charge. I believe her name is Hannah Sweeney. For a small persuasion, or should I say *donation* to the welfare of these poor unfortunates, I am prepared to place her with you as a nursemaid."

Another call on his ever dwindling florins, Clarence looked at Bessie in askance. Surely *she* would be looking after the child?

"We'll take her." Bessie nodded vigorously, butting in quickly when she saw her husband's look, knowing full well he was about to argue. She scrabbled in her reticule for a couple of shillings, mindful of the need to watch her savings too.

"Hannah," she called quickly to where the thin faced child stood uncertainly between them and the other orphans. "Get your bag and as soon as Mr. Filbey gets our transport sorted, then we'll be off."

"So?" she said to Clarence, after the girls from the orphanages were loaded in the carts and Hannah stood with Molly, waving to them, as the drivers geed up their horses. "I'll have enough to do supporting you on this great piece of land you're after farming, without playing mother to Molly."

Back along the port, whilst Clarence was haggling a price to the town with the driver of a fly wagon, and a group of single women were being escorted to one of the buildings across the way, an altercation had broken out when three men from the *Umpherston* and a government official clashed at the bottom of the gangplank. It appeared that some of the men, destined to be ticked off his list and taken across the road to where their employer waited, had disappeared. He had pounced on the three, thinking that by the look of them, as none were wearing uniform, just navy guernseys and working mens' trousers, that they were the three that were missing from his list.

One of the men was Jimmy, the overseer of steerage, who had made up his mind to jump ship in Port Adelaide and head for the gold fields of Ballarat. The other two, members of the crew that worked in the galley, had been given leave by the captain now that their duties were over for the day. None had papers and the official, mindful of the dressing down that he would be given by his superior if he lost three would be farmhands and their employer was waiting in the building across the road to receive them, shouted to a colleague to bring along a trooper to sort out the men.

Jimmy, seeing his chance when the official then ran across the busy highway between the wagons, carts, bullocks and horses, as no one had heard him above the melee, headed towards the east to join the well worn track to Victoria, where gold was there for the taking in the many rivers and streams.

A group of aborigines looked on, watching the antics of these crazy people, who had now become established in their lands.

Waiting with their trunks and bags for Clarence to appear with their transport, Bessie suddenly began to feel overwhelmed with thankfulness. They had made it. Praise the Lord they had made it and had lived in veritable comfort compared with their fellow men. Instead of living hand to mouth, packed together like sheep off to the market and existing in squalid conditions, whilst waiting on the whim of Jimmy to open up the hold and what food could be sourced from the mess captains, they'd had comfortable bunks, a cabin maid, were very well fed and had commanded the ear of the captain and the honourables. Of course the creaking of the ship, louder at night, took some getting used to, as did learning to roll with the ship when walking along the deck and having to ask Filbey to leave the cabin while she used the chamber pot. But for most of the voyage the seas had been calm, except for one such time when a squall had pitched and tossed the boat for a couple of days and it had been a case of battening down the hatches and taking to the bunks. They were there now though, back on terra firma and only one man, bless his soul, had perished when he'd been swept overboard. Of course it hadn't been very pleasant when Lady Harriet had insisted that those trollops be flogged and put ashore at a small and desolated island, but then what could a girl expect if she behaved so flagrantly.

Bessie looked across at the row of wattle and daub cottages, where passengers from the *Umpherston* stood whilst waiting to be assigned to the many farmers, builders and households that were willing to take a migrant on. Carriages, wagons and drays, the horses or bullocks shifted impatiently, stirring up the dust with the pawing of their hooves. One of those couples could have been her and Filbey, working for a petty-fogging master, reliant on his spirit of justice and good will. She watched indignantly as a man and woman were left to walk behind a dray while their master whipped up his team of bullocks, although he had kindly allowed them to stow their trunk in his vehicle.

There was only one substantial building on the side of the wharf; a yellow stone, slate roofed dwelling named the Customs House. It was where the government officials held court and demanded tariffs from the import and export of goods.

A group of aborigines, wild and shaggy, caught her eye as they shuffled along the front of it, aping the dress of white men in dirty, cut off trousers and tatty looking shirts.

"I've never seen a black man, Missus," a small voice said at the side of her, looking over with enormous eyes, as the indigenous were shooed along by an officious person. "I seen a Romany once when she came to our farm to sell me mammy things."

"Did you Hannah?" said Bessie absently, watching George Colmayne and his wife struggling across the road with their bags and offspring. She wondered what would happen to the agreeable little family, At least he must have a bit put by now from the coins he had earned from his teaching.

"Climb aboard Bessie," Clarence shouted, as he jumped off a battered looking wagon pulled by a tired looking horse and driven by a dark skinned driver with a mass of curly hair whom he had managed to haggle a knockdown price with. It seemed that vehicles, grand or poor, were much in demand on the busy docks of Port Adelaide. "Hannah, you help Molly and I'll help the driver with our trunks."

"Couldn't you have found something a little better?" Bessie demanded as the wagon set off, she supposed in the direction of Adelaide. "I saw the Trowbridges travelling in a *phaeton* with the honourables. Margaret didn't say anything about that when she said goodbye before."

"Be glad you're not walking" Clarence growled, feeling hot and bothered as the day was warm and he felt the weight of what was to come sitting on his shoulders. "At least we've got some transport. Look at the poor beggars who are having to leg it."

"Molly wants to go" Hannah piped up as the horse began to trot along the dusty track towards the flat plain covered in bush land. Its steady pace caused Bessie to search in her reticule for a handkerchief to bury her face in under her large brimmed hat. It was not only the dust that was irritating, but pestering flies that they seemed to have attracted.

"Tut, that's all we need. Filbey ask the driver to stop at the side of those bushes. Hannah you can take her and make sure she doesn't get her 'loons wet."

She watched impatiently as Clarence helped the girls down, wondering not for the first time, why she had wanted to bring a child to this foreign land. She'd had no experience with small children other than her sister-in-law's when she and Filbey had been visiting. She hadn't the patience, nor a maternal bone in her body if the truth was known. In the early years of her marriage, a child would have been a blessing – someone to pass the farm on to and a worker to help them in their elderly years. Perhaps they should have left Molly behind in the cabin. One of Maggie's family was supposed to have been there.

"We'll not be bothering his lordship" Clarence said quietly, startling her out of her bitter thoughts as she reflected on having *two* more mouths to feed as well as her and Filbey.

"We'll be wasting his time and ours if we follow him to the city. I've made him think I've been a wealthy farmer, all this sitting at the captain's table and having the comfort of that cabin, but imagine his face when he finds I can only afford twenty acres of that land he told us about."

"Twenty." Bessie was scornful. "Twenty acres, after all that money you had in a stash under the floorboards?"

"Ah, it was you who'd disturbed it. I wondered. Thought it was Maggie, though she'd have never touched a penny if she had." His face looked red and Bessie wondered if he was going to make something of it. She braced herself, ready to give him a tongue lashing, even if the driver would be listening to them.

"Let them go, Bessie," he said quietly. "We're peasants not gentry, we couldn't afford to live their kind of life. I've asked the driver to take us to this place called Willunga in the south. His lordship told me it's a pleasant place, the soil fertile and a couple of miles away from the sea. We'll find a property, something like we had before but not a tenancy. I'll buy some tools, grow some wheat or barley and get a horse or perhaps a donkey. I don't want to spend all the money on land that we'll have to clear before planting. If things go well we can get a few more acres later on."

Bessie sniffed, her vision of rubbing shoulders with the gentry going up in a puff of smoke. She kept her peace, reluctantly accepting this new life in Filbey's distant dream, as whatever she said in the future, it wasn't going to change a thing.

It was late afternoon before they reached the Onkaparinga River. It was a place of honour and respect belonging to the Kaurna tribe, according to their driver, Silas, who looked as if he had a touch of the indigenous in his own bloodline.

Along the way, he had pointed out the places he thought would be of interest to a newly arrived settler's eye; the breathtaking view of the ocean from the incline that they had just climbed wearily after walking beside the wagon as the horse had stumbled along; the terrain towards the thickly wooded hills rising in the distance, where a few small farms had been established on the flat expanse of land. He kept the girls amused by pointing up the trees at little koala bears who sat up high feeding on the gum leaves, or told them about the kangaroos and wallabies that kept their babies in a special pouch. He warned them of the deadly snakes and spiders and the bushfires that were sparked by the heat.

Passing by a few small settlements, where dwellings which lined the highway were made from rough-hewn stone or stringy bark, they stopped in a place called Reynella, where a small tavern stood on the banks of a gurgling river. They rested with the horse and driver and ate a meal of bread and cheese, washed down by a brew of locally made ale. The girls drank juice made from the fruit of the lemon trees, which grew in profusion there. Morphett Vale was a settlement where the inhabitants appeared to have lived for a while, considering that the dwellings were more substantial and much of the land was in the process of being cultivated. Orchards had already been established, along with many vegetables for sale.

Later, beginning their descent down a rather steep hill, the wheels of the wagon held firmly in place by sturdy brakes and the experienced horse which was used to the road's uneven surface, they passed a half built church, a brewery where the steam rose slowly through the large boiler chimney and into a small hamlet with a blacksmith's shop. A stone-built cottage and a flour mill stood at the side of a tidal river, with a market square that bustled with cattle and stockmen, across the road from the Horseshoe Hotel. At the river they were faced with a long queue of bullock carts, fly wagons, people standing in groups carrying bundles and mothers holding the hands of children or carrying babies, whilst waiting to cross the narrow wooden bridge ahead.

"It'll be a bit of a wait until the carts from the slate quarry get over. They load 'em so high, it's a wonder they don't shed them. Bin a few accidents – we can wait over there," said Silas, as he looked over longingly at a small, weather boarded cottage where men, mostly labourers, stockmen and waiting travellers, sat sipping drinks on the wooden verandah. There was a horse trough outside and the flagging beast looked over longingly too.

"Well, just until the bridge clears and then we'll be off" said Clarence, conscious of the fact they must find shelter before it grew dark, though the driver had assured him that it didn't get dark until late as it was summer. "Bessie, do you want to take the girls to the *dunny*?"

He spoke proudly, the driver having given him a few words from the local dialect and he had learnt that a "dunny" was a small hut used for relieving yourself in. Another one was "ankle biter" for a young child, but he didn't see Molly doing much of that. The poor little girl had kept up well, though the sweat had been pouring off her and Hannah, dressed as they all were for an Irish winter. He took a swig from the canteen of water he'd been carrying, wishing that they could be soon away.

"My canteen is empty, Filbey". Bessie looked flushed and had taken her jacket off before she had joined him. She had seen plenty of women along their way who were wearing their long sleeved blouses rolled to their elbows and she couldn't see the need for keeping standards in this hot and dusty land.

"Fill it at the river" Silas said, pointing ahead as he loped past her and Bessie saw the sparkling water of the Onkaparinga as its waves lapped below the river bank. In the distance pelicans and black headed birds that looked a little like penguins stood and a flock of white corellas circled in the air before settling on the sandstone rocks. A couple of enterprising men could be seen fishing in the waters with sticks and another was selling his catch.

"Can we paddle?" Hannah and Molly had joined her whilst Bessie scooped up some water. "Tis terribly hot, Missus."

"Aye for a minute, though don't go getting your hem wet nor Molly's neither and you may as well take your boots off."

She watched as the two girls, Hannah hatless and Molly still with her bonnet on, stepped down the bank gingerly before standing in the water, not screaming with laughter or splashing like a small group of children further up, but watching solemnly whilst holding hands.

The carts came across and the people began to move again, as the sun began to lose its heat and clouds began to form.

♣

# Chapter Eight

At last they arrived at the migrant settlement, feeling exhausted even though they'd had the luxury of travelling in the wagon. It was at the top end of a small village, situated below a backdrop of densely wooded hills. They drove along a narrow street which had a few stone built dwellings and a couple of primitive cottages made from wattle and daub. Passing the Bush Inn with its shady verandah, men, who judging from their dusty appearance were workers from the nearby quarry, stood chatting and slaking their thirst after the heat of the day. Silas, who was taking them to stay at the Government Reserve, which was used as a tentage area for immigrants, told them that they were to mind the many venomous spiders which took many an unsuspecting person unawares and could kill you stone dead.

"Willunga, a place of green trees" he explained, having been very informative on their journey, once he had got over his initial distrust of Bessie, whom he reckoned was the boss of the little family. It looked as if she'd terrified her daughters, who hadn't said a word between them since they'd climbed aboard his fly. He told them that they had just travelled through the Vale of McLaren, a place named after a John McLaren who had surveyed the area in 1839. Settlers, mostly farmers, had begun to turn the land over to the raising of cattle and sheep, or the growing of wheat or barley, using the seed that they'd brought with them from their homeland. Now they were in Willunga, where most were employed in the slate quarry, as the fine grained rock which provided bluish purple roofing materials, was hewn to supply the vast amount of building in the city and surrounds.

"Boss man is Mister Ellis." Silas pointed to one of three single storey buildings set apart from a dozen canvas tents on a dusty piece of land. It was on a hilly incline, where gum trees, pines and golden wattle grew in profusion and overlooked the site. A couple of families sat around a campfire and one of the men had just put down his fiddle.

In the darkening of the evening, feeling so tired that it could have been the Devil himself who was in charge of the place, Bessie snapped that Silas should get their things from the wagon and then be gone. She was sure he would want to get himself back to the dockside to bring another poor family to such a God forsaken place!

"Bessie, there's no need for that" Filbey chastised her, embarrassed, as the man slunk off obediently, muttering as he went. "He'll need shelter for himself and stabling for that poor, tired horse of his. Besides, it doesn't look so bad here, seems they've made the best of the place."

Bessie sniffed and walked towards the building that Silas had pointed to, ignoring the nods and welcoming smiles from the other settlers and a little boy who had run to them excitedly carrying a large frog.

"Thank you, Silas," Clarence said as the driver struggled over with the wooden trunk. " Have yer got somewhere to stay yerself?"

"Under the stars, Master. Know a safe place back along the way, me and the horse'll be sweet."

"Well here's our fare and a little extra. Good luck on your travels, eh?"

The man nodded and went on his way, glad he wasn't saddled with such a wife. Bessie returned accompanied by a large bearded man, shaggy haired, tough looking and walking with a limp. He announced his name as Mort and said he was a government official.

"Yer can 'ave that one over there," he said, pointing to a small canvas tent a few yards away. "Dunny's there, creek's over yonder but don't forget to boil the water or it'll give yer the cramps. I'll see yer tomorrer then." He walked away towards the group that sat around the campfire. "Any of youse moving on yet?"

"Come on then Filbey, let's get the trunk and you girls stop that messing about with that frog. I'd like to be able to lay my head down in the next few minutes."

"The boy said they're cooking something called a wallaby, Missus" said Hannah, her tummy rumbling at the smell of the meat roasting on an iron over the hot embers. "His mother has said we can go over, so she did."

"Then do so" snapped Bessie, swatting away yet another fly that had landed on her hand, feeling pleased in a way that she didn't have to set about looking for something to feed them with, as all she wanted to do was lie down and die. Her head was thumping, she felt dizzy and occasionally the floor would feel as if it was coming up to meet her. "Filbey, bring the trunk and then you can join them."

"Tis a very nice place we've come to," said a man in his early thirties, who if Clarence had known the accent, he would recognised it as a Cumbrian one. "The name's Fred Dickinson. This is the wife Mary, my youngest is Tommy, our little Katy, Elizabeth and my eldest, Eddie. We arrived a few days ago from the city, though it took us a while to get here what with the pace of our bullocks and the dray being loaded as it was."

"Aye, a bit of a journey, we thanked the good Lord for his mercy when we got here," broke in the other man who had just finished playing on the fiddle when the Filbeys had arrived.

"I'm Joseph McVeigh. Me and the missis come from Bonnie Scotland, Glasgow way. Me boys are over there somewhere. John, James and Joseph, he's me eldest. Sadly no girls yet, eh, Fiona?"

His wife shook her head, solemn faced, then turned away to check on her pans that were simmering away on top of hot stones that had been placed in the fire.

"You're welcome to join us, we've plenty."

"Aye, we will and thank yer kindly." Clarence motioned to Hannah to sit with Molly on one of the long smooth rocks that seemed to have been placed there for sitting on. "I'm Clarence Filbey, recently of Mayo in Ireland. These are my girls, Hannah and Molly and me wife Bessie is having a lie down. I heard the man ask if yer were moving on? Is there somewhere better to move on to?"

"No, he was *codding*," said Joseph. "'e knows we're 'ere to look around for work. Fred and me are builders. We worked together in the city for a couple of years, after meetin' on the ship comin' over from Liverpool. The wife and I are from Glasgow and we were lookin' for a new life for the bairns. We were sick of the crime and the tenement living, but found it just the same in the city over here. Drunkenness, fornication, blasphemy, immoral livin' and that's without the brawlin' that goes on. I'm a religious man and don't want that kind of life for my youngsters."

"We're hopin' to set up a business together" Fred explained, after listening to Joseph who had gone quite red in the face after his rant against people who he reckoned had brought their Sodom and Gomorrah ways along with them. "Buy some land, build a couple of properties then sell 'em on. As far away from the city as we can get, barring travellin' over yonder to Victor Harbor, that is."

"'Ere, get this inside yer," said Joseph's wife, who had been busily carving chunks from the hapless wallaby. "Mary'll dish up the parsnips." She handed out tin platters to their guests who couldn't help but eat the food greedily. Though chewing the parsnips, which were not very tender, was a bit of an ordeal. "Will yer wife be joining us, Mr. Filbey?"

"Bessie? No she's worn out, poor soul, best that she gets her head down. Mmm, this meat's delicious."

"So what's your story?" Joseph asked, once everyone had finished the food on their plates and one of the children had gone to fetch the others for a second sitting. "Look, why don't we sit over there and let our wives see to the bairns."

73

He pointed to a shady tree which the three men walked over to.

"Well, as yer might have heard, another blight got the potatoes in Ireland. It's been happenin' more and more over the past few years, so people are uppin' sticks and leavin'."

The two men nodded; they had met a few sufferers on their own journeys.

"Aye, and it'll be the landlords that'll benefit, I'll be bound." Joseph's parents had been victims of the Highland clearances.

"So we decided to throw it all in and make a new life as settlers. Bessie's not so keen, but I'm sure she'll warm to the idea once we've bought our own bit of land."

"Ah, it's land that yer after then. Well yer've come to the right people if you want to know about things. Me and Fred 'ere have been to the land titles office, had a look at the map and 'ope to sort out a place for ourselves. Perhaps we can build yer somethin', Clarence. We've a ready made quarry just up the way."

"It would have to be cheap. I've only enough for ten or twelve acres as it is. Me money seems to be goin' nowhere."

"Hey Fred, what about that place we heard about on the road out of the village? Yer know the place where that man shot 'isself and left a wife and two little ones."

"Aye, they say the place is going cheap 'cos the wife wants to go to back to England and there's still a lot of clearance of the land. She'll be stuck 'til someone buys it, as they will have put all their brass into it."

"Oh I don't know, I don't know what Bessie would think. How much land is there that still needs clearin'?"

"I've heard about ten acres, but I believe there's enough bin cleared to run a market garden and 'e kept a sow and a few layin' hens. Or you could turn the whole lot over to growin' almonds. I 'ear there's a lot of profit in almonds and easy to grow round 'ere. If it were me I'd start with sellin' the produce that he's bin growin'. People need food and not everyone 'as green fingers, I know I haven't. Think it over; I can give yer the name of the place if yer want me to."

"It would be nice living on a farm, Mr. Filbey" Hannah piped up at the side of Clarence, whilst Molly sat listening to the chatter of an excited little boy who seemed to be of the same age.

"Yes Hannah." Filbey's face creased with worry as he listened to her words, hoping that the others hadn't picked up that she had called him Mr. Filbey, instead of Dada. Bessie had told him that she wanted them to be thought of as having a couple of daughters, or even a daughter with a nursemaid and she would go mad if Hannah spilt the beans.

"Do yer know how much she's askin'?" he said, a little voice inside him saying that if he could beat the woman down he'd have some money to put aside for a rainy day. "Though I'll have to talk it over with the Missis of course."

"Dunno, but it'll be cheap, bound to be if she wants to go back to her family."

All the settlers were up at cockcrow, which didn't seem much time from when Clarence had lain his body next to the sleeping Bessie, with the girls cuddled up together nearby and the filtering light of the day which had appeared between the shady gums. The tent was small; there was just about enough room for the four of them. It was meant for sleeping, as cooking was always done outdoors.

Bessie, still feeling groggy from the deep sleep that her body had put her in to, groaned when she realised that lying on the hard packed earth instead of on her downy bed in Killala was a reality and not Filbey's distant dream. Seeing that this could be her way of life for the very near future, she was more than willing to listen to all that had gone on around the campfire the night before. Not being a pioneer, nor even having the will to be one, she implored Clarence to make more inquiries over the widow's land. They could go that very day if it meant she'd have a proper bed to sleep in.

"It'll mean a lot of work though, Bessie. It'll be a tough existence and we'd have to hire men to help with the clearance of the rest of the acres."

"Has it got a dwelling built upon the land?"

Clarence nodded. "I believe of sorts."

"Then that's all I need to hear, Filbey. Anything has to be better than this wilderness you've brought me to. Now go and ask that Scottish person what we have to do about it."

The "Scottish" person, after Fiona, his wife had offered the family a breakfast of a chunk of bread made from hops and potatoes cut up and boiled together that she had cooked in the communal camp oven and a drink of weak tea with no sugar in a battered tin mug, directed them down the street until they would come to the same junction from when they had come down through the McLaren Vale.

There they were to cross over onto a wide dirt track which led to a place called Aldinga and would eventually take them all the way to the port if they were to follow it. They couldn't miss the place which was known as the Aldridge's, as it was within a clearing just beyond a narrow creek. There was a small cottage on the land and it was just a hundred yards past the place where the first few settlers had been buried, though that might change now that the church of St. Stephens had just had the laying of its foundation stone.

Mort, the government man, on hearing that the family were previously farmers and after he taken a note of their names and where they had hailed from, was enthusiastic when he heard of their intention and promised to find them good workers from the small community to help clear the rest of the land. Clarence and Bessie set out together, leaving the girls behind, as they needed clear heads for this decision that could may well affect the rest of their lives.

It was a warm, sunny morning and Bessie, wearing a long sleeved, ankle length dress, felt hot and sticky before she had even started walking. Flies bombarded her from all directions, sweat began to pour down her face and from her armpits and it wasn't long before she started to berate Clarence for bringing her to this horrible land. She jumped when a flock of blue mountain parrots sitting in the gums above, began their squawking and a kangaroo dashed out ahead from the scrubland, causing her to squeak in fright at its untimely appearance. By the time they had got to the junction, where across in a clearing men were busily laying the footings for a small church, her tone was bitter and Clarence heaved a sigh of relief when they began to follow a well-worn dirt track, shaded each side by overhanging gums, which would bring them to the Aldridge place.

"You must try to get her to sell you the place for a rock bottom price, Filbey," Bessie insisted as they passed a wall that a couple of stonemasons were working on, seemingly to enclose the new cemetery. "Don't be swayed by her tale of woe. It's a sin for a man to kill himself and she won't be able to hold her head high in the community because of it."

"Bessie, we don't know that her husband killed himself. There could have been another explanation for his death so don't be jumpin' to conclusions. Anyway we're 'ere now, for God's sake keep yer opinions to yerself and let me deal with it."

Bessie sniffed, tempted to start again with her complaining, but thought better of it as they came to a clearing and saw ahead of them a small, one windowed wooden dwelling, with a narrow verandah and a gable roof, surrounded by a roughly built picket fence. Attempts had been made to make inroads into the dense thickets of golden flowered acacia. There was bottle brush and tea tree shrubs with their long fingered tentacles, and an abundance of high growing weeds that might have engulfed the dwelling in time if left there. However, there *were* a sizeable couple of acres that had now been cleared of scrubland, where there was evidence of flourishing vegetables, a couple of young fruit bushes and a row of trees, their branches already heavy with almond blossom.

From behind the house came the sounds of a pig grunting, the cluck of a small flock of hens and a dog who had a deep throated bark. Two young boys ran along the newly laid path towards them and their young fair haired mother, wearing ballet type slippers and dressed in a grey ankle length gown over which she wore a white, voluptuous apron, stood in the doorway.

It had to be said that it was during those few minutes that Clarence Filbey, he who had been married to his barren wife for over twenty years, fell in love when he saw that the blue eyed beautiful looking young woman standing now on the verandah, was pregnant. How it happened he wasn't sure, because he had always believed that Bessie was the stuff of any dreams he had, if he was to think back to when he'd gone a courting. But this young mother brought forth a compassion in him so strong that his heart flooded with an overwhelming sympathy for her plight and he wanted to take care of her for the rest of her life.

"Good morning to yer, Madam," he said courteously, lifting his bowler in deference, leaving Bessie wondering why he was being so polite to someone in her precarious position. Expecting a baby when there wasn't a husband around didn't merit civility. "Clarence Filbey and me wife Bessie. I was told by someone at the government hut that you might be interested in sellin' yer land and property. I was told that your name is Mrs. Aldridge."

The young woman merely nodded and watched sadly as the couple, followed by her two solemn looking, tousle haired boys, came towards her. Clarence held out his hand formally as he walked up the three steps to where she stood. Bessie stood below, feeling cross as a bag of cats and a little jealous of the woman's beauty if the truth was known, flicking out at the persistent fly that she must have carried along on her shoulder.

"Do you want to come in?" The woman's voice sounded cultured as she opened the thin wooden door, more a plank really but it sported a brass handle, then kept it open for Clarence and a sour looking Bessie, to go in. The boys stayed outside, sitting upon a rough looking bench on the verandah, throwing pebbles idly over the edge of it, whilst they waited for the visitors to depart.

The two roomed dwelling felt cool, given that it was morning and the sun didn't penetrate until the afternoon. There was an earthen floor and wooden walls that were covered in hessian to keep the draughts out, a chimney with a hearth made of slate, but it had no fire under the iron bars that had been fixed across it. There was a rug made from tatted rags, a table made from logs, four rough-hewn chairs and an old horsehair sofa and, through the open doorway to the other room lay three straw filled mattresses.

78

"Can I get you a drink?" Mrs. Aldridge pointed to a glass jug of cloudy liquid that sat on the window ledge. "It's lemons, made from the fruit of a tree that my husband planted."

It seemed that his mention had brought tears into her eyes and she wiped them with a clean white handkerchief that she took from her apron pocket.

"I'm sorry, my tears are never very far away. What must you think of me? I can pour you a drink if you wish me to."

Clarence cleared his throat and Bessie wondered what the drink could be poured into as she couldn't see any glasses.

"No we're fine Mrs. Aldridge, we've not long had breakfast. I hope yer don't mind us callin' upon yer at this hour, it is rather early."

"No Sir, do sit down and you too, Mrs. Filbey. I'm afraid we only have the one sofa and Mr. Aldridge made the kitchen chairs." She sounded apologetic, running her hands over the bump beneath her apron as she spoke.

The couple did as they were asked and she stood by the window looking out to the yard.

"I was told there is around ten acres of land that may be up for sale, Mrs. Aldridge. I imagine that includes the property as well."

"Yes and the livestock, the horse and cart, the hut where William stored his tools and I suppose the furniture. I cannot see that it is worth transporting it back to Lincolnshire, although it has a certain sentimental value."

"Yer husband made it all," Clarence said, seeing the young widow searching her pocket again for her handkerchief.

"Yes, he was clever with his hands."

"So, yer intend to return to Lincolnshire? I take it that Lincolnshire is in England, although I couldn't say where. We're from Mayo in Ireland ourselves."

"I have decided to return to my husband's family, as I have none of my own now and I am sure his parents will find me a little cottage on their estate for the sake of the children. I haven't informed them of his demise just yet; I thought I would wait until I sell this place and we can be on our way."

79

Clarence coughed modestly, trying to be delicate in what he had to say next. Bessie dug him with her elbow, as if to say "don't you dare even think about it."

"If yer don't mind me sayin' so, Mrs. Aldridge, yer can hardly travel back to England in your condition. Being a family man I beg yer to reconsider."

"Ah, you have children." She ignored his referral to her condition, though it was quite plain to see, as she would have had a slender figure normally, taking into account the thinness of her face and high cheekbones.

"Two girls," Bessie chimed in, trying to coast her husband back to the reason they had gone there.

"Four years old and twelve, both very willing helpers if we should buy this place from you, which I think we will be if the price is to our likin', Mrs. Aldridge, though I question your foolhardiness."

"Mr. Filbey!" Bessie sounded harsh in her objection. "Surely that's for Mrs. Aldridge to decide when she embarks on her journey back to her relatives, not you."

"I am only sayin', Bessie. We could get Joseph and Fred to build another room 'ere for the time bein', until Mrs. Aldridge and her children move out, that is."

"At our expense? Mr. Filbey, I think we need to do some talking."

Bessie had noticed another door that must lead out to where the livestock still grunted, barked and clucked. Filbey obviously needed her guidance; he was getting above himself.

"We'll go through there." She pointed to a door and hustled him out of the room.

"What are you doing, Filbey?" she hissed, drawing him to the side of the cottage where the lemon tree stood dripping with its fruit and the banks of a slow running brook was evident "What are you trying to do? She looks as if the birth of her child is imminent and there's no way I could deliver it. Let her go to the government hut, there's bound to be someone who will help her. Give her what she wants and let's get shut. I don't want to spend another night in that smelly tent."

"Bessie, yer can't just throw her and her children out and yer can't just pay 'er off and move in neither. There will be formalities, forms to be signed, deeds to be had, probably there'll be a judge somewhere who'll want his palm crossed with silver. Then we'll need to see if we can help the poor things in some way. Don't forget the children are fatherless and she's just been made a widow."

"Nothing to do with the fact that she's pretty I suppose? You've always had an eye for a good looking young lady."

"Bessie, I object to that. I've always been faithful to yer and I'm tryin' to be fair to me fellow man."

"Or woman!" Bessie snorted and flounced around to the front of the house, whilst Clarence went back in again.

"We'd like to buy yer place, Mrs. Aldridge, if the price is agreeable that is, but we don't want to put yer to any inconvenience. Do yer have the deeds? Did your husband register with the land titles office? Have yer seen anyone, an official, about sellin' the place?"

"Yes, to most of that, Mr. Filbey, but not anybody official yet about selling the place. In fact my husband is still at the mortuary until a coroner gets around to an inquest, so I've not been allowed to bury him, although he has been dead for over a week. It appears that he might not have shot himself on purpose and why would he have done? According to the man who worked for us, we called him Jackie by the way, according to him, William was shooting at a kangaroo when a spider ran up along his finger. The shock of that made him drop his rifle as he was pulling on the catch and it burst into fire hitting him in the chin. Jackie carried him back here, then ran. Being an indigenous leaves him wide open to being accused of my husband's murder, so a judge is having a think of what will happen next."

"God Bless him," said Clarence and crossed himself. He wasn't a religious man but sometimes it was just a comfort to have a belief.

❧

# Chapter Nine

Her name was Aubretia and she was everything that Clarence would have liked to have had in a wife if he hadn't been married to Bessie. They walked along the dirt track to the police station together Bessie having walked off to the settlement on her own, feeling cross and wrong footed. He found that Aubretia was of good nature, loved her children dearly and was a well-mannered soul. She told the him that her father had been the master of an endowed school in a small village near Lincoln and that is where she had met William Aldridge. He had been the fourth son of a gentleman farmer who owned much of the surrounding land. Although she had known of William's existence, she hadn't been allowed to play with him as a child, but love had blossomed one sunny autumn afternoon, when the traditional Harvest Home celebration was put on by his family for the villagers.

It had been of little consequence as to whom might make a suitable bride for William, given his position amongst his siblings, but with his itchy feet and the knowledge that his elder brothers would be more likely to have a permanent place at the farm more than he would, he decided to head for one of the colonies belonging to the queen.

He had read a notice in a broadsheet that a new settlement was proposed in the south of Australia, where there was land aplenty for a man who could work the soil. Aubretia and William had emigrated there in 1839, one year after their marriage and before their children were born. Little had William known that his fateful decision would cause his early demise. Her children were delightful, rough and tumble as most boys are, but seemed obedient to their mother when she called them back when they raced ahead.

Bessie was cross because Clarence had taken upon himself to help this damsel in distress with any formalities regarding the burying of her husband, the procedures involving the buying of the property and his genuine desire not to abandon this young woman and her children in their hour of need. To the consternation of Fiona and Mary, who had just finished clearing up after all their brood had finished eating and were about to look through their cookbooks to decide on the ingredients needed to make the midday meal, she appeared in front of them demanding to know what had happened to her children, as they were nowhere in sight and she had entrusted them in their care.

"They've gone off with the others. It seems they're on the trail of a couple of wombats. Our husbands are with them, so they shouldn't come to any harm." Fiona, not fazed by the woman's angry words as she had lived cheek by jowel in the tenements of Glasgow with women just as bold, continued. "Would yer like me to make yer a brew or something cool to quench yer thirst this fine hot day?"

Faced with her kindness, Bessie let go and was soon in floods of tears.

"How do you put up with this God forsaken place?" she asked, from her position on the dusty ground where she had placed herself nearby. It was said between muffled sobs, as she had lifted the hem of her skirt showing off her not so clean petticoat. "I don't think I can stand it – the heat, the flies, the dirt. I wish I was back on my own little farm in Ireland."

"Starving to death, or so I heard," Fiona said gently. "Wasn't it in Ireland that the potato crops failed?"

"Well, yes, but we weren't too affected. Filbey and I could have sat it out, we didn't have to emigrate. It was his dream, not mine."

"But he is your husband and as such you must obey his wishes. Whither he goeth, then ye must follow. He will be doing this to give you and your children a better kind of life."

"Mmm." Bessie sipped at the water that Mary had gone to draw from the communal water well for her and poured it into a thick, white mug from a heavy, glass jug. "I don't know how you can bear it."

"We do so for the sake of our childer." Mary's voice was certain. "We can only do our best, ask the good Lord for his blessings and the strength to carry our husband's decisions through. Isn't that so Fiona?"

The other woman nodded, ignoring Bessie now, as there'd be more to come from the distressed woman if she were to show an interest and began to read through one of the recipes she had seen in her handwritten book. It had obviously been passed down from an earlier generation, by the battered look of it.

"We could make a soup from the bones we kept from the wallaby. We can use its liver and kidneys and add a bit of barley, some peas, an onion, we could get the *bairns* to collect a few mushrooms and I'll make dumplings from last night's bread. That'll take us on to tea time and you and I could walk to the general store in the village and see what we can put with that pickled pork we brought with us."

Bessie listened to the women's plans, feeling her stomach churn at the thought of eating soup made from yesterday's bones, especially as she didn't even know what animal a wallaby was. She'd always thrown the bones away if they'd had a chicken, or given them to the cat to lick clean, but there again, she might not even be offered a taste of this wallaby soup they were promising and might be taking a walk herself along to that general store.

Filbey was in his element. Though he knew he should be mourning the demise of a good man, just being in Aubretia's presence was keeping his old heart racing. He tried not to show his elation, as they walked together with her boys to the building on the reserve that housed the police station, but it was difficult to suppress this new found feeling.

William's body lay on a marble slab, whilst awaiting a visit from the district coroner, Mr. Archibald Pepper. The slab had been placed inside an empty shed away from the main building and was for the storage of the deceased of the community until burial. The coroner was due that day and according to the sergeant who was on duty, his verdict on whether the death was a suicide, a criminal act at the time, an accident or a murder by the family's servant, would rest on his findings. Retribution would be carried out accordingly.

Aubretia had already spoken before on behalf of the hapless Jackie, who hadn't yet been found, but by the virtue of being an indigenous man he was a likely suspect and wouldn't get much of a hearing anyway. She spoke to Clarence of her fears for the poor man's safety and he suggested that he accompany her and the children on a walk alongside the nearby creek for an hour or so. There was no point sitting around the place, given that she would probably be waiting for this official's arrival for a while.

"What will yer do when yer go back to England?" Clarence inquired, as the two boys ran ahead through the stand of trees that lead into a deep, dark forest.

"Be a mother to my children. Enjoy a life of leisure with a nursemaid and a round of social engagements courtesy of the Aldridge family. The children will probably be sent away to boarding school and life could become very boring."

"Perhaps yer could stay 'ere in Willunga." Clarence's mind had been racing as they walked, trying to come up with a good enough reason for Aubretia to delay her departure. "I mean, in your delicate condition it would be a difficult journey – if yer don't mind me saying so."

"I have been giving the situation due consideration Mr. Filbey, especially as I have to stay here to hear the outcome of my husband's inquest and to see that justice for Jackie is being done. There will be the funeral to arrange, and a place found to stay with my children if I were to sell the farm to you. I have a few weeks still before I will need a midwife's attention, so I thought I would seek accommodation in the city before my lying-in."

"You could stay on at the property. I'm sure I could arrange for someone to come and build an additional room for Mrs. Filbey and meself. It wouldn't be a problem." He could hear the words flowing from his mouth like a fast moving stream and wondered why he was saying them. Had he gone completely mad? Bessie would have his guts for garters when she heard his plan!

"Oh, Mr. Filbey." Aubretia, for all her outward toughness sounded quite flustered and had gone pink in the face with embarrassment. " No, I couldn't trouble you to go to such lengths on my behalf. You must put your wife and children's comforts first. It is quite uncomfortable at the settlement as I know from firsthand experience when we arrived here ourselves seven years ago. I shouldn't like to delay your family further from moving into a proper home and I am an adaptable character, Mr. Filbey, quite able to face whatever life has in store. In fact before we moved to this village we lived tooth by jowl in a squalid overcrowded building in the city, whilst William worked as a labourer there. Now, perhaps you should be catching up with your wife instead of listening to my troubles. I am sure she'll be wondering where you are."

He would have argued, taken her hands into his and pleaded to be given a chance to make her happy, if not for herself then for the sake of her children, but she was calling to her boys, seemingly astounded at his forwardness and desperate, it seemed to remove herself from his company.

"Please think about it, please don't act too hasty – you must think of your children and your unborn child. I'll walk back with yer, you may still need a little moral support."

"As you wish" she said reluctantly, still sounding rather embarrassed, but recovering a little after the boys had hurtled back along the track to join them. "Then you must go back to Mrs. Filbey. As I said, she'll be wondering where you are."

A small crowd had gathered outside the building that housed the police station, when they arrived. They were mostly white; some had come from the settlement and some from the locality, and a couple of Aborigines stood muttering together, seemingly waiting for something to occur.

"They got the Abbo" a man explained, when Clarence asked why people were standing outside the place, waiting. "The troopers brought him in, caught him at the port. He started running, so they shot him."

"Oh no," cried Aubretia, then hurried up the steps to the verandah and through the open door with little decorum, leaving Clarence to hold her children back from following her. Her face was ashen when she returned to join them and ignoring the questions from those who waited, she grasped the hands of her two worried boys and hurried down to the street. Clarence felt he had no option but to follow, though feared rebuff as she had taken off to the stand of trees again without a backward glance. He caught them up as Aubretia sat under the shade of a gum tree near the creek, crying into the handkerchief she had plucked from her reticule, leaving her children to pat and caress her shuddering body in concern.

"It wasn't Jackie" she said between sobs a little later, not looking up at Clarence, when he asked if he could help in anyway. "Though this poor man's had half his face blown off, I could tell it wasn't Jackie. Jackie was much younger, a boy really." Her two boys cried with her in sympathy, whilst Clarence stood there waiting, not sure what to do.

"They told me the man was running" she said after she got to her feet clumsily and walked to the edge of a creek in order to splash a little water on her teary face. "The shock of seeing the body prevented me from saying that if that was so, why had the damage been done to the poor soul's face? I saw that the man wasn't Jackie, but I let them think it was."

The older boy, whose name was Bertie, took his mother's hand protectively, as Clarence stepped forward to try to steady her, as looking weary, Aubretia leant against the trunk of an overhanging tree.

"I will look after my mother" the eight year old said stoutly, glaring at this newcomer's intrusion. "I will be the man of the house now my father has gone."

"If we had a house to live in, Bertie, darling," Aubretia replied a little bitterly, clasping the hand of the youngest child too, who was looking at them all in wonder. "We must go back to England and seek shelter with your father's family."

"But not yet," said Clarence, firmly. "I insist that yer stay on until your infant's born. I would be a cruel man to let it be any different and I am sure that meself and Mrs. Filbey can be of assistance to yer while yer there."

Aubretia nodded weakly and with hesitating steps she allowed herself and the boys to be led back along the track.

The two girls sat on the fallen trunk of a gum tree which lay in the scrub just outside the settlement. They were hot, sweaty and very dirty, but both were reluctant to show themselves. The woman would probably shout at the sight of them and Hannah knew it would be her fault for letting Molly get into such a state.

Hannah felt fearful of the woman with her nasty tongue. There had been one like her at the orphanage, no one could do right for doing wrong and only the favourite children went unpunished. The man was nice and was very kind to his daughter Molly, but she wondered what she herself was doing there. Had she been chosen to be their daughter's nursemaid? If so, she was in trouble, because a nursemaid wouldn't have allowed her charge to get so hot and dirty.

"Hungry" Molly said, looking trustingly at Hannah, hoping she had something to eat in her pocket. Her hair which Hannah had tied into a plait with a blue ribbon that morning, was hanging untidily after she had caught it on overhanging bushes when they had rushed along after the excited boys. Her white dress, which she hadn't been changed since they got off the boat, was looking very grubby. Was it part of a nursemaid's job to do the washing too? Not that Hannah made a pretty picture herself, as her shabby, green dress, one of two donated to the orphanage, was ripped in places around the calf length hem and one of her heavy, black boots had lost its laces. She hadn't wanted to rummage in her box in the shelter for a replacement in case the woman came back and found her there.

"We'll have to wait," Hannah replied, used to going hungry when it had been the strongest and the fittest who got to eat where she came from. She was anxious to spy out the lie of the land before she took her charge back to the settlement. "Let's play a game, Molly, shall we? Let's pretend we have to find the man who brought us here and not the woman. When we see him we'll tell him that you're hungry and he's the one who will give us food."

Molly nodded. She liked the man who had said he was her daddy, though she remembered that her daddy lived in a different place, in a different time, when Maggie was there and her mammy who lay on a *palliasse* in a corner. She had lain next to the body of her mammy until some people had come with a box and had taken her away.

A sudden whooping and screeching caused the girls to jump up from the trunk in fear, but it was just the boys crashing through the undergrowth, still energetic in spite of the draining heat. One of them carried a sack and whatever there was in it seemed to be struggling, although it didn't seem to deter its captor at all.

"Come, Molly." Hannah held out her hand and the pair started to run towards the settlement. By arriving together with the hunters and gatherers, it would look as if they had been with them all the time. The smell of cooking assailed their nostrils and they watched as a fat, brown wombat was tipped onto the ground at the feet of the waiting women. One of the boys hit the squirming animal across the head with a rock and it lay dazed for a moment until its heart stopped and was still.

"Where've you two been?" asked Bessie, listlessly, from her place on the grass where she had stayed whilst watching the two women prepare dinner. She hadn't offered to help, as she could see the pair worked in harmony. Her inquiry to the girls was a mild one; she couldn't summon up the energy to raise her voice. Her head was still hammering, her body clammy, she also felt a little shivery even though the sun was beating down overhead.

"With the boys, Missus" Hannah replied, whilst Molly hung back, having looked at the poor little animal lying there with a certain sympathy. She could still remember the staring eyes of the dead rabbits that her daddy used to hang on the back of the cabin door.

"Don't call me Missus. While we're in this god forsaken place, you're to call me Mammy. Go to the shelter and get me the big hat."

"Would yer like another mug of water?" Mary asked, coming over with a look of concern on her face at the red, sweating face of her new neighbour. "Do yer not have a better hat than that one? Yer need a shady one, not a bonnet and a straw one is better for you."

"She's gone to get it for me." Bessie jerked her thumb in the direction of the shelter. "I will have another water, my throat's gone dry with this heat." She just wanted to sleep. It was the warmth of the day that was causing her to shiver. It was going to take a day or two to get accustomed to it.

It was alright for these two women, already used to the hateful place, with its dirt and the flies and living a hand to mouth existence. Though if the widow was willing to move from her property in the next few days, she could look forward to a little comfort soon. *Where was Clarence?* She thought impatiently. *He'd get the run of her tongue when she clapped eyes on him.*

"I's hungry." Molly had walked over to Fiona who was dishing up stew to eager recipients, whilst Mary handed a mug of water to Bessie.

"Of course yer are, little one," Fiona said kindly. "I'll get yer a bit of something if yer mammy says yer can so. And what about yer sister? What are yer names?"

"She's Molly and I'm Hannah" answered Hannah, having dropped Bessie's hat into her lap obediently then followed Molly, seeing there might be a bit of food going for the two of them. It was obvious that the Filbey woman wasn't going to stir her stumps and make a bite to eat.

"And 'ow old are yer, Hannah, yer look to be the about same age as me eldest?"

"I dunno, twelve, thirteen mebbe, nobody ever said."

She watched with growing dread when she thought of the words she'd just uttered. The Filbey woman would kill her if she had let the cat out of the bag. The woman's face, looking sad because she always baked a cake to celebrate her children's birthdays, thought better of questioning her further. There was obviously a mystery surrounding these people who had recently arrived, but being a Christian woman, it wasn't her place to pry.

# Chapter Ten

Clarence arrived back at the settlement just as the two women were packing the dirty dishes into a woven willow basket and were heading to a nearby creek to give them a wash. There was no sign of Bessie. It appeared she had gone to the shelter not feeling very well. The two girls looked half asleep as they lay under a tree together, watching the other children playing a game that involved a lot of shouting.

"Has Mrs. Filbey fed you?" he asked, his own tummy rumbling and the smell of the wallaby stew still lingering in the air. Hannah nodded but told him that it was the nice mothers who had given them food, as *their* mammy was feeling poorly. Clarence smiled to himself when he heard her words; Bessie had suddenly become a mother to the pair of them.

"I saw a place that looked as if it were a grocery when I was comin' up the street," he said, thinking quickly that if he was to have a reason for leaving the settlement again, he could check on Aubretia at the courthouse. "Hannah, did yer get a bit of cookin' at the orphanage, 'cos I don't think Mrs. Filbey'll be up to it for a while?"

Hannah nodded. Hadn't she always been the one sent to help in the kitchen, even though it was usually to stir the pot of vegetable stew.

"Good, we'll go and buy a few provisions for our dinner from the grocery, then we'll take a little walk and look around. I suppose I'd best have a look at Mrs. Filbey."

He saw that Bessie was shivering under a blanket when he

crawled into the shelter. He waited for her tirade – hadn't he just spent some time on his own with the widow? He was going to get it in the neck from his wife. Instead she stared at him anxiously, as she had never suffered a day's illness in her life other than the ailments of a child.

"It could be the sweating sickness" she gasped, having worked herself up into a froth, her hand trembling on the mug of water that Mary had kindly packed her off with. "It'll be this horrible place yer've brought me to, full of flies and creeping things and a heat to burn the end of your nose off. It'll be the death of me, you'll see, Filbey."

"Nonsense. It's the heat that's causin' the sweats, Bessie, bein' you're not used to it an' all. Ireland was a place of mist and rain and mostly coolish weather. Give it a couple of days, rest and drink a lot of water and you'll be fine."

"I need a doctor. I need a priest to say the Last Rites over me. I'm hot and shivery and my body's on fire. You'll be sorry that you dragged me here when they're lowering me into my grave."

Bessie began to cry, making Clarence feel like he was the cruelest man on earth for making his wife suffer as she was. And there was him making sheep's eyes at that young woman while Bessie had been suffering so. Shame on him.

"See, I'll go and ask if there's a doctor. I'll send him along and whatever it costs I'll have him make yer better. I'm sorry Bessie. I thought you'd enjoy a new life in the colony."

She snorted and pulled the blanket closer and Clarence ran from the shelter for help.

"There's Doctor Poskitt along the street."

Clarence came across Joseph, newly returned with Fred from the forage for edible food in the forest. "It'll be the heat that's causing it, that and a lack of good food on the emigration ship. Ship's biscuits are not what they're cracked up to be, eh Clarence?"

Clarence agreed hoping that Hannah who was standing nearby, didn't put the man right, with her coming across in steerage and the Filbeys living in a cabin like lords.

"I'll get over there," he said, shooing the girls ahead of him in case he should have to lie.

"Yer can't miss it. The house is on the right of the street. It's a stone built one just past the Bush Inn and the general grocery; his plate's on the picket fence."

Clarence didn't know what the plate would be for. Perhaps the wife put out some bread for any beggars that were passing, a plate like they had in the Catholic church on the Sunday whip round, or maybe you put a coin upon it before knocking on the door. He found it to be a brass plate announcing the doctor's name, when he and the girls stood before the squat, one windowed building. Chimney pots stood erect upon either side of the blue slate roofing, the window pane twinkled under large, ornate, wooden eaves and a verandah built in matching limestone ran along the front of the house, which stood on a large plot of land covered with shady trees. *Impressive,* thought Clarence, looking back to where a couple of wattle and daub dwellings sat on land nearby that still needed a bit of clearance. *A bit of money here if I'm not mistaken, not a doctor who would treat the poor.*

"Can I help you?" A stout woman with a large white apron on, opened the heavy wooden door and peered down at Clarence and the girls, who after he had knocked at the door, had withdrawn respectfully to the bottom of the verandah steps. He felt nervous, not having had any reason to see a doctor in Ireland, being sound of mind and limb. Then he heard himself sounding like a nitwit, instead of a man soon to be a local property owner.

"Begging yer pardon Missis, tis the wife who's ailin' and in need of a doctor. We're recently arrived at the settlement. These are me two little girls, so they are."

*Why was he behaving like some farm labourer in the presence of his lordship at the Big House? He had just sailed halfway around the world in the company of the queen's commissioner for heaven's sake.*

"Ah, a fellow Irishman" the woman replied. "We came over here in '41, that is Doctor Poskitt and myself did. We had a place in Dublin, but what with all the bother of the dissidents and then my parents shifting off the mortal coil, we decided to semi-retire. We work and play in the colonies and I'm the local midwife."

Clarence could feel his inhaled breath evaporate, although the thought crossed his mind that they must have come over from the old country with a great deal of money, if they could afford to build this property with it being on quite a bit of land.

"The doctor will be back at a quarter past three. He's over at the Courthouse with the coroner. Some poor man has had his brains blown out, so he's there assisting the coroner with his report."

*Aubretia, poor Aubretia. Perhaps he should leave a message for the doctor to visit Bessie at the settlement. It didn't seem right that the poor, bereaved woman should be all alone when the coroner made his pronouncement.* He coughed and put his voice back to his assumed genteel one, the one he had used when talking to Sir Rodney. He was going to be a man of substance soon, maybe even brushing shoulders with these people at social events.

"I'll call upon him later then, Mrs. Poskitt. My wife will probably benefit from an afternoon nap and feel all the better for it. I'd hazard a guess that it is heat exhaustion. We've recently travelled ourselves from Sligo and as you know we've exchanged our cool climes for a hotter one."

Mrs Poskitt nodded sympathetically.

"It happens to most of the people who hail from Europe, especially if they left in winter and arrived here in the summer. Plenty of water will serve her well, that and plenty of rest, though I'm sure these two young ladies run her ragged. Leave your name and I can inform him of your visit when he returns."

Clarence nodded, gave his name, then taking the hand of Molly, then Hannah, he walked them through the picket gate.

"Are we going for a walk now, Mr. Filbey?" Hannah asked, feeling the need to skip and jump, now that this nice man was holding her hand.

"We are so and you can call me Dada now we're going to live in a nice house together and run a plot of land."

"And Mrs. Filbey?"

"Yes, Mrs. Filbey too. I'm sure she'll soon get better."

"And Molly? We're to be like sisters together and never go back to the orphanage?"

"Yes and Molly." Clarence squeezed Molly's hand affectionately and she smiled up at him hesitantly. "And you'll never have to live in an orphanage again."

He had noted the grocery store as he had passed it earlier. It was similar to the *shebeens*, the unlicensed houses that sold goods and liquor from the front rooms back home in Ireland. Not that he imagined that the place he had just passed sold *poteen*, an alcoholic drink made illicitly, as there was the Bush Inn to serve the thirsty, but he'd pay the place a visit later, on the way back to the settlement anyway. They'd need a few provisions to tide them over until they moved to the Aldridge place; they couldn't rely on the settler wives.

He saw Aubretia in the distance. She was hurrying, her boys clasping her hands, running beside her. She was at the top of the road to Aldinga by the time they had caught up with her and he could see that she was crying and trying to get away from prying eyes.

"We'll come with you" he said, his own heart beating like the clappers as he listened to the gasps of the girls who still hadn't become accustomed to the heat.

"You don't have to" she said, though her face said different and she didn't murmur when he and the children accompanied her along the road. She didn't speak, except to say a polite "hello" when Clarence introduced the girls as his daughters. They hung back and walked in silence; this was another situation to get used to in their young lives.

"It was the bullet from William's gun" she said later, as she took off her bonnet and slumped on a chair on the verandah, after asking her elder boy to keep his eye on his brother and take the girls into the yard. "The coroner recorded misadventure after I stood up for Jackie and told him how hard he had worked here and that he was a valued member of our family. There was no apology from the troopers for the shooting of that other man and neither he nor my husband will get a Christian burial."

Her tears began to start again and Clarence almost took her in his arms to comfort her, but knew she wouldn't want him to.

"The coroner has released William's body and they're burying him tonight in the cemetery when the sun goes down. We didn't know many people in Willunga and I can't afford to get someone to make him a headstone. I can't even afford the price of a coffin" she said, her voice muffled now as she had her head in her hands. "So they're putting him in a hessian sack, just like you would if it were an animal."

His heart went out to her as he gazed upon her trembling frame. He could afford a coffin for her husband if she wanted one, he wouldn't hesitate to help her in anyway he could, but somewhere in his mind was the possibility that the coroner had recorded misadventure when he could have recorded suicide had he a mind to. His verdict would avoid the family's ostracism, as taking one's life was a crime.

"Begging your pardon, Mrs. Aldridge." Clarence hated himself for bringing up the subject but Bessie would give him the length of her tongue if she didn't get to move onto the property soon. "Have you given any more thought to the circumstances?"

"The circumstances?" A tear-stained Aubretia looked at him inquiringly. "My husband's burial, you mean. No, I couldn't face watching him being buried like that."

"No, I'm sorry, if I were you I wouldn't want to neither, no I meant have you given anymore thought to letting me purchase this place?"

"I've done nothing but think about it, Mr. Filbey. I would like to stay of course, for the welfare of the boys and the birth of my unborn child. As you pointed out, it is a long way to travel with a newly born infant if I was to book a berth on an England bound ship, but I could be able to afford to pay for lodgings and a midwife in the city, once we have come to a fair agreement on the price."

"How much were you thinking?"

He waited whilst she struggled with the embarrassment of talking about money to a stranger, when it had always been her husband who had handled these things.

"I had heard from William that land is selling for one pound per acre. I believe that this would amount to ten pounds for the land we have here. I thought five pounds for our home, which would include what bit of furniture William made and any household possessions that we have accumulated whilst here, though it wouldn't include the livestock. Those and the horse and cart and the growing vegetables, I would need you to state a separate price for."

Clarence considered. *Was he to be like Coloney, taking advantage of a situation that could only line his pockets in the long run? Could he live with his conscience if he was to offer her a pittance, agree with her price for the house and the land, but a meagre amount for the rest?*

"Perhaps twenty three pounds would cover it," he heard himself saying. *What was he thinking, Bessie would go mad?* "But I still think you should take a few days to consider leaving here in a hurry. I can get a couple of men to build another room; it would be up in a trice if I'm not mistaken." He could hear himself. He was sounding too eager. Why would anyone put themselves out in this way for someone they had only met that day? She was looking at him curiously, before gasping a little, as a tiny foot or hand began to kick her in the ribs.

"See, there's another little life besides your boys you must consider." *Please take up my offer of taking care of you.*

"It might be wise to stay a little longer, Mr. Filbey. Yes, I think I'll agree and stay."

♣

# Chapter Eleven

Molly and Hannah huddled together in their shelter, whilst listening to the sounds that were coming from inside the cottage. It was dark, around two o' clock in the morning if they were able to tell the time and had access to a fob watch, but Hannah knew from a bit of eavesdropping from time to time, that there was another little soul beginning to make its way into their uncertain world. Uncertain, because the big woman, the one they called the midwife, who had arrived just as they were being shooed off by the mammy to their shelter, was heard to shout on occasions and the muffled cries of the nice mother – Mrs. Aldridge, they called her, who had been walking around with her hand to her back for the past few days, was beginning to terrify them both.

It had been a few weeks before when their dada had arrived at the settlement with a horse and cart and had loaded up the family's possessions. The mammy seemed cross, but she was always cross and to avoid a slap, which she was wont to dole out if you didn't move fast enough, they had stood hand in hand waiting for instructions. It appeared that they were going to live at the place where they had played with the boys, Bertie and his younger brother Ralphie. They had liked it there with the grunting pig, the squawking hens and the black dog that would lick you all over if you let it. It would be nice to be part of a family and live in a house together, or so Hannah had thought at the time.

It seemed that the men who had lived at the settlement, the ones whose wives had seen to the cooking, had been to build an extra room onto the cottage since the girls had been there. It was to be used by the Filbeys, according to the mammy, but not the girls as they were to have their own little place in the yard. Their own little place was what the locals would call a *kipsie*, a small shelter by the creek, which had a door to keep the draughts out and a large, lumpy straw mattress which the girls could cuddle on together and keep warm when the nights got chilly. Across the way was the *dunny* or so Dada had told them to call it, a wooden hut where they could sit on a wooden bench and let nature pay its call.

It was chilly that night as they listened to the cries of the newborn baby. Autumn had arrived, a time devoted to harvesting and the girls were feeling tired from their exhausting day. Hannah thought back to when that they had arrived at *Meant to Be Cottage,* that's what the nice lady called the place. Hannah couldn't read, but there was a rough carved plaque with the name etched into it, hanging on the picket fence.

The shouting had started when the mammy had got down from the cart, walked up the steps of the verandah and in through the front door. Mammy had murmured something in return to the lady's greeting, which had caused their dada to rush in after her and angry words were said. Bertie and Ralphie, looking scared, had joined them outside as they waited, hoping that the sounds of quarrelling from the grownups would cease. It seemed that it was the mammy that was causing holy hell and from that day to this one, the mammy hadn't spoken nicely to the lady at all. Every day had been full of back break for all of them. Even Molly was expected to do her fair share.

Their job was to clear the weeds from and around the vegetable patch, digging with a small flat pointed blade. The weeds were used for something called compost and had to be carried in a bucket to the muck heap which held the waste. Another of their jobs was to search far and wide for the eggs that the "chooks", a new name for chickens, tried to hide in the undergrowth. Today had been the hardest day, having to pick the little nuts that Dada said were almonds. To be fair, their jobs were easy compared to what the boys were asked to do. Bertie was used to clear the scrub, following Clarence and the cart, which was loaded with debris after he had used a hatchet to hack at the bushes and tall growing weeds. Ralphie was the helper, holding the horse's bridle whilst Clarence was sawing down a tree, or helping to stack the logs onto the top of the cart, which had been hewn in readiness for winter fuel. They all had to pick the fruit from the trees, the last of the lemons and the nuts, then the parsnips, potatoes, onions and a fat looking thing that Dada called a pumpkin from the vegetable patch. Bessie sold the things from the "veggie patch" from a table on the Aldinga Road. It appeared that the cottage had been built on the road which went to the ocean, where fishermen lived and slate from the quarry was sent from the port, to the rest of the colony by ship.

Their food was good. They didn't go to bed with empty bellies. If they didn't get to eat from the produce that was grown or any animal that could be caught in a snare or shot with the Aldridge rifle by Dada, he would drive the cart to the grocery and come back piled up with all sorts of things. The lady could make a tasty, filling porridge, a mash from fat, brown spuds and slices of chicken or meat that had been baked in the oven range. She was good at making bread and they ate it with a spread of meaty dripping and she had made them each a nightdress, whilst she sat in her room in the evening waiting for the baby to appear.

Hannah had been told by one of the helpers back in the orphanage whose sister was about to take ownership of one, that babies were found in a cabbage patch, but as they didn't have any cabbages in the vegetable plot here to look under, maybe the big woman had brought it today in her bag. Quite why the nice lady had been shouting was beyond her, you'd think getting a baby to love would make you feel happy.

The Filbeys sat together on their timber frame bed that Bessie had insisted they buy from a carpenter who had recently set up business in the village. She wasn't going to demean herself by lying on a straw mattress in the new room that they'd had built and had used her own bit of money to make the purchase along with a flock mattress. She was loath to offer the use of it when it came to the birth of Aubretia's child. *Why should she? The woman should have travelled up to the city, not be lolling about in the cottage that didn't belong to her anymore.* There had been hell to pay from Clarence, who had sympathy with the poor woman having to give birth in such a confined space and on a mattress and the boys having to sleep outside on the verandah, but Bessie shut her ears to it and was determined to have her own way. Just like she shut her ears to Clarence, ranting over the division of labour in what Bessie was now calling "the homestead". Aubretia would have to earn her and her boys' keep; they were not a charity case.

To be fair to Bessie, she had never really recovered from the heat exhaustion that had struck her down on those first few days. She had lost weight and was apt to suffer from depression, being quick to note that her husband had a penchant, a *liking* for this young woman, which caused her fits of jealous rage at times. Each day had become a struggle. Although it was autumn now, the weather was still hot and humid and her only relief was to find a shady tree near the nearly dried up creek. And tonight, another night when she couldn't sleep because of the damn woman's cries keeping the sleep from her, she made a vow to herself that it wouldn't be long before the Filbeys had the homestead to themselves.

Clarence mopped at his brow, more with agitation than the heat that had built up in the small dwelling, Mrs. Poskitt having insisted that the kettle was simmering at all times. He was desperate to go and help the girl – to hold Aubretia's hand, stroke her beautiful face and tell her he'd take her pain away if he could. So this was what it would have been like if Bessie had given birth to an infant. All the pain, the agony, the fear that maybe it would all be for nothing and she could have died in doing so. He was glad that he hadn't been born a woman; it seemed a precarious way to have to live your life. Find a man, marry him, depend on him for everything. He'd go and sit on the verandah, let the women get on with things in the house. Not that Bessie had offered any help to Aubretia; she'd been walking around in a bit of a huff all day.

It was cool on the verandah. The boys were sleeping, wrapped up in a blanket and sharing a *palliasse*. He looked upon them with sympathy, as they lay there looking grubby and unkempt, Bessie having declared that it wasn't up to her to drag out the tin bath and stick them in it. She had enough to do; there was the cooking and preparation of their meals, now that Madam had taken to her bed to bring forth another mouth for them to feed, besides having to man the stall outside by herself. He'd been cross when she had had referred to Aubretia as "madam", just because she spoke well, had a headmaster for a parent and had married into the gentry. She was a human being who deserved their care in her time of need, he had declared crossly, which had set Bessie off ranting again. If he was that concerned about his fellow beings, he should take himself off to the city and feed the poor and starving there instead. There was no talking to her. He sighed, looking up at the planet Venus that shone so brightly in the darkened sky, the twinkling of the stars as they hung above the horizon out to sea and wished not for the first time, that life could be different and that the child whom Aubretia was giving birth to and these tousle haired sleeping boys were his.

Though perhaps there was a way that he could still have Aubretia in his life, without it costing anything. He hadn't paid a penny to Aubretia for the land title, they hadn't been to the office to have the papers signed or his expression of interest recorded whilst searches were done, nor had he paid her any money for the rest of the estate. She wouldn't know to find someone from the legal profession to give her a bit of advice. She was a woman and had been dependent on her husband, who had signed any document, seen all the plans and sorted out legalities without consulting her. He could ask her to stay, pay to have another small dwelling built on the acreage and have his cake and eat it.

*But she trusts you*, his voice of conscience prodded him whilst he stood there pondering how Bessie would react if he put his thoughts into actions. *Aubretia is trusting you to do what's right and you are the master of her destiny.*

It was dawn when the first cries of William John Aldridge were heard by the occupants of the cottage. Bessie sighed thankfully. Now she could get some sleep. The boys slept on, oblivious to the fact that they now had a baby brother, the girls cuddled closer as the dog, sensing something was different began his barking and Clarence leapt up the steps.

"It's a boy," said Mrs.Poskitt, beaming from ear to ear, thankful that it had been a fairly easy birth and she hadn't needed to call upon her husband. "Fists like a pugilist and a good pair of lungs. Mrs. Aldridge'll need to rest now, make sure she drinks a lot of milk."

Clarence nodded and after the woman had tidied Aubretia, washed the baby, got rid of the debris involved with childbirth, then wiped the area down with Lysol, he was allowed to take a peek. It was a perfect scene and one that he would remember for the rest of his days. Aubretia looked exhausted but satisfied with giving birth safely to the babe in her arms, her face aglow as she sat upright against the wall where the midwife had placed her and Clarence, spellbound as he looked upon her, knew that even if he had to take the blows and curses from Bessie, he would aim to protect this woman forever.

It didn't take long before he had to prove that vow, as Bessie, envious of Aubretia's ability to produce three healthy boys that would have been an asset to the homestead had they been hers, was dismayed to be asked by Clarence to allow Aubretia to sleep in their bed. It seemed unfair to expect a woman just getting over a birth and having to stay in bed for the next two weeks or so and needing privacy to suckle the child, to carry out this duty in the same, small room which her sons had to share. They could sleep on the verandah, they would be warm enough together for a time and he and Bessie would sleep on the *palliasses*. He should have seen the signs, should have been aware that being barren all their married life, Bessie might see the cosseting of the young mother as being an insult to her womanhood, might have suffered from some inferiority that could have caused her to react the way that she did.

Things came to a head a few days later when Clarence, noting that the milk urn was nearly empty, there was just a jug or so left because Aubretia was drinking more than her fair share, according to Bessie, decided he would take the horse and cart along to the grocery and whilst there inquire if the owners knew of anyone who wanted to get rid of a cot, rather than have one made by the carpenter. Bessie was cross on two counts. Firstly because she had wanted to go with Clarence, as she liked to have a look around the shop that could have been described as an Aladdin's Cave, the place filled with all the goods that the grocer could get his hands on. There was smelly cheese that was provided by a Greek farmer down in Reynella, oranges brought along from a place in Echunga, slices of pickled pork, quinces, gooseberries, dried fruits such as currants and raisins, plums, apricot curd, beef or kangaroo steaks, bacon, locally made butter, flour, oats and barley, all sourced from the many settlers in the area or shipped in via the nearby port.

Clarence had given her his orders. He was becoming more and more like a petty tyrant each day. Somebody had to keep an eye on things, he insisted when she challenged him. The boys were to dig up a few potatoes to go with their mid day meal, the girls were to help in the kitchen or do some washing in the tin tub outside. It was a fine day, just the day for drying the clothes over the rope he had tied between the back porch and the *dunny* and there was a breeze coming across from the ocean, so they would soon dry. Secondly, Bessie was annoyed that Clarence was going to spend their precious savings on a cot for the Aldridge newcomer. She had tiptoed into her bedroom one day where Aubretia lay asleep on the dearly beloved bed and peeped at the child who was lying in his makeshift cot, the trunk that they had brought with them from Ireland. He was an ugly child to Bessie's mind and the thought crept through her head that it would have been easy to close the lid and let him suffocate. That would serve the young madam right. It would force Aubretia to take her boys and go back home to England, then she would get the attention back from her husband.

It had been the girls coming in with the eggs they had collected, which had startled her out of her reverie and for a moment she had felt quite ashamed of herself for wishing the little baby dead.

The tin tub lay in the yard, waiting for Bessie to add some water from the rain butt. A wicker basket stood alongside it, full of dirty clothes waiting to be washed. Of the children there was no sign. The boys had gone and supposedly the girls with them, then Bessie heard the high spirited cries of excitement coming from the almond grove.

She saw red when she heard the noise from them. Someone was going to pay for this, they all knew that they had jobs to do before they could play in the grounds. Her temper brimming over she walked between the rows of trees until she saw that the children had captured a small echidna, an animal like a hedgehog, which was trapped in a hollow beneath one of the trees. Bertie had a stick and was poking at the small creature and the girls were screaming with alarm as the frightened animal tried to escape. The boys, scared upon seeing the vexed looking face on Bessie, who came running out of the orchard ready to give them a cuff around the ear because of their clamour, escaped to the barn where they hid behind a haystack until the coast was clear, but Molly being the smallest and not quick enough to run for cover, found herself lifted in the air and tucked under the irate woman's arm.

Hannah, ever protective of her little friend, ran along at the side of Bessie, shouting that it wasn't Molly's fault that they weren't getting on with the washing, that the boys had persuaded them to go and have a look at the creature, strange so it was. It wasn't until they reached the yard that Bessie let go of her prisoner and did so with such a force to knock the wind from her. Molly stopped her screaming in distress, stumbled over the wicker basket and fell face down into the metal tub, hitting her head.

For a moment the two of them stood there feeling stunned, whilst Bessie stared in disbelief that the child was lying still and wasn't crying. Hannah, caught in the moment, waited for her friend to climb out of the tub and run to her for comfort, but Bessie went to lift poor Molly and cradled her in her arms. The blood that had been rushing from the head wound stopped suddenly and with a little sigh, Molly's life was over, never again to be a burden to the woman who held her, never again to be a little friend to the sorrowing girl who stood close by.

With tears rushing down her poor thin cheeks, her heart beating madly and her fists balled in readiness to give the mammy a good drubbing as payment for her crime, Hannah heard a familiar voice shouting across from the side of the cottage where Clarence was tethering the horse and cart.

"For heaven's sake, will yer stop pickin' on the girls, Bessie" he said, walking towards them with a scowl upon his face. "They can help me unload the grocery. I just got there before they sold out of – Jesus, Mary and Joseph. What in the Hell has happened here?"

He ran then, kicking out at the chickens that had rushed across the yard, thinking that he might have some scraps to feed them with, past the dog who was barking madly on the end of his rope and the pig in his enclosure, who was staring at the scene. He reached his wife, who was trembling with fear at what had just happened and where poor little Molly lay prostrate in her arms. The child was deathly white. Her eyes were closed and there was an ugly gash on her brow, her hair hung down in tangled tresses and she wore one boot. The other, the lace having worked loose (which had been a major factor in the poor girl's fall), lay abandoned in the grass nearby.

"She fell over the basket," Bessie whispered, her face full of anguish. She was feeling full of trepidation in case Filbey didn't believe her tale. She turned around to Hannah, with her hand out toward her in mute appeal. "I didn't hit her, did I? It was like I said, she fell over the basket and hit her head."

Hannah nodded, still feeling angry, still ready to put all the blame on this horrible woman who was nothing like the mammy she would have chosen for herself.

"But it was you who dropped her. Yer dropped her so hard that she tripped over the basket and fell into the tub. We were going to start the washin' and it wasn't her fault."

It was said in an accusing voice and said with all the bitterness that Hannah had kept inside her heart, because of their treatment. There'd been no love, no hugs nor kisses for her and Molly, which she had seen Aubretia give the new baby and the boys. They'd been made to work in the house and yard, until they'd dropped asleep exhausted every night, in exchange for their meals.

Clarence listened, his heart beating loudly at the thought that his wife may well have killed the child resulting from her temper. Not intentionally, but there had been a lack of kindness to anyone since they'd arrived on Australian soil.

His eyes brimmed with tears as he stroked little Molly's shoulder. She hadn't asked to be brought along to the colony. She would still be alive if she had gone away with Maggie or left to live in the hamlet with Aunt Tess, her relative. They had interfered and had snatched the child from her homeland, determined to bring her up as their adopted daughter. Now none of that was going to happen; Bessie had seen to that.

"It could be the end of a hangman's rope for yer" he said in warning. "Either that or yer make a run for it, before someone finds the body and calls the troopers in."

*Why had he just said that?* He wondered. *Was this his chance to get rid of Bessie and have Aubretia and her children all to himself?*

"No, Filbey, it was an accident. For God's sake tell him Hannah, it was an accident like I said." Bessie passed the body over to a dubious looking Clarence, as her arms began to shake.

Hannah stared back at Bessie, warring with her conscience and with loathing in her heart. *Who would believe the word of an orphan girl? She could say it was an accident, partly true, as Molly had fallen out of the mammy's arms and tripped over the basket, but the mammy had been cross and they'd been frightened, but wait, what was she hearing now from the dada, it seemed he'd suddenly had a change of heart?*

"We can't have the troopers stickin' their nose into what's happened here, not after what Aubretia told me about what they did to that poor bugger who was shot fer runnin'. We'll take the child and put her in the shelter and then we'll think on what we can do."

♣

# Chapter Twelve

*It had been strange how the Filbeys had just upped sticks, saying that they had a mind to go back to Ireland as Bessie hadn't taken to the new country and it was taking a toll on her health,* thought Aubretia, as she stared out of the window at her eldest boy, who along with his brother was dragging a hessian sack full of potatoes, newly dug up from their vegetable pit. She had been surprised that her son was capable of such ingenuity, but recently it had become obvious that he had learnt his skills from Mr. Filbey, who had been such a nice man.

It was a few weeks before, one afternoon when she had decided that enough was enough and it was time she stopped treating herself as an invalid. Clarence had stood in the doorway, gazing upon her and the baby as they sat on Bessie's timber bed. He was looking rather pale and agitated if the truth was told. She couldn't ask him in, it wasn't done unless his wife had been with him, but it seemed that the flint faced Mrs. Filbey had disappeared, along with Molly and Hannah. At least she hadn't heard any movement from them, she had only been aware of her boys that morning, when Bertie had asked if he could make some toast.

"Begging your pardon, Mrs. Aldridge" Clarence had said gently, wishing that he could hold this moment forever as he looked upon her. "As you probably know, the wife hasn't been 'erself, what with one thing and another. Now the youngster has gone down with somethin' and we've a mind to take her up to the city to see a doctor there. We'll find a place to stay until she's better, then we might hot foot it back to Ireland. It was my dream, not theirs, to make a new life here."

"Oh. Oh, I'm sorry to hear it, Mr. Filbey." Aubretia had felt startled when she heard his words. He had seemed so determined to have the place, giving her time to get over the birth before the formalities of ownership was required. "You were making such a good fist of things, you've cleared a lot of the land, tended to the growing of the produce, helped with the marketing and even the addition of another room. I had thought that your intention to buy the place would have set me free from my obligations here. Now I must make arrangements for mine and the children's future."

"No – No, you'll be right here, don't even try to sell the place to someone else. Bessie's built up a good little business on the front there, the grove is producin' well, the boys can keep it all goin' until you can get a bit of help. Don't go back to England. Take advantage of the work that's been done. Like yer said, there's the new room, the scrub we've cleared to make a paddock and there's enough logs in the shelter to see you through the wintertime. Stay at least until the spring, when the seed I've sown in the acreage will begin to grow."

*And perhaps I may pass this way again and you'll still be here, dear Aubretia.*

They might not have survived that winter if it hadn't have been for the money that Aubretia had found slipped under one of the *palliasses*, when she had shaken it to plump up the straw after the Filbey family had gone. There were five white pound notes, folded neatly underneath. With the money, the eggs from their hens, the pickled meat, the preserves of bottled fruit that Bessie had prepared and the pit which Clarence had dug to prevent the early decomposition of their vegetables, it had all sufficed to keep them going, though the winter hadn't been that severe.

She had taken the death certificate that the coroner had produced as proof of William's demise, to the land title office. It was more to stake her claim on the property as his widow, should she decide to sell it at a later date. She was approaching the decision to provide a living for her sons and herself at the property rather than becoming dependent on William's family back home. She had looked at the place with new eyes after receiving two offers from settlers who had recently arrived, especially when one man had said quite bluntly that a woman couldn't run the place effectively, which had spurred her on to think that she could. She had asked at the grocery store to see if they knew of a diligent worker, hesitant to employ an Aborigine again and hopeful this time for a married man, someone to drive the horse and cart if needed, with a wife who could help her with the children. The man could do the heavier work that running the place involved. She found her support in Bill.

Bill McMahon was a hard worker with a wife and three young children – boys of a similar age to Bertie and Ralphie and a little girl aged two. They'd had an itinerant lifestyle since arriving at Port Adelaide three years before from Liverpool, as Bill, a restless soul, always wanted to see what was around the next corner. He was a jack of all trades but had managed to support his wife and family through taking any work that he was capable of. It had mostly been labouring, in fields or on city building sites and he had once toyed with the idea of making his way to Victoria's goldfields, but his wife had soon talked him out of that.

It had been Mrs. Poskitt who had put out the word. Still visiting Aubretia, as was her wont after being the midwife at little William Aldridge's birth, she had felt dismay when the new mother had declared that she was going to run the place as a business and not go back to England, as formerly she had said she would. The couple, known as the Filbeys, the wife seemingly a delicate creature, had gone back on their word of buying the property and scurried off back to Ireland, which had left the poor widow in the lurch. There was no way that this young woman could cope with running the place, besides raising three children without the support of a husband, according to Mrs. Poskitt; someone must be found to give her a hand.

The McMahons had been living at the settlement, with the intention that Bill would try to get a job in the slate quarry. Failing that they would make the journey to Encounter Bay, where he could try his hand at making his living as a whaler. They'd had their possessions loaded on a handcart in readiness; a change of clothing, tin mugs, plates and a billy-can, their canvas shelters, floor mats and their woollen blankets.

Bill was a thin and gangly person, originally from Scotland, but had married a lass from Lancashire. He was strong as an ox and wore a permanent smile on his face. The fact that he had made it to the new country, with so many opportunities to be found for him and his boys and the love of his good wife and daughter, constantly amazed him. He presented himself one morning to the widow, having been told of the job by Mort, the boss man at the settlement, and found her to be a likeable creature. After searching the acres for somewhere to park himself and the family, he chose the ground just beyond the almond grove. It had shelter from a stand of red gums and was near the creek which was beginning to fill with water again, after a few downpours of heavy rain. His wife Dorrie, who was relieved that perhaps at last her husband might just put down some roots in this wondrous place called Willunga, was happy to assist the widow in anyway she could.

It was the following spring, when Catherine McMahon, a sweet little three year old who liked to go walk about, found the shelter where Clarence Filbey had decided to bury Molly's body. It was in need of a new support, having a tendency to lean whichever way the wind was blowing and Bill had meant to ask Aubretia if there was any point in keeping it, given that it wasn't used for storage.

Catherine crawled inside and sat on the old *palliasse*, watching in fascination as a small lizard ran up and down a branch that was part of the collapsed in roof. A movement outside caused her to peer around cautiously; it wouldn't be unusual for her mother to come looking for her.

Instead, her gaze met the blue eyes of another little girl who was standing outside. She was dressed in a white calf length dress, a pair of black boots with the laces undone and her long, brown hair, partly plaited, had a trailing blue ribbon.

"'Ello," Catherine said, in the Lancashire accent she had inherited from her mother, feeling pleased that she might have found a playmate as her two brothers were older and didn't have any time for her. "What's yer name?"

The little girl smiled sadly and didn't say anything.

"Would yer like to play tag?" It didn't matter that the little girl didn't speak; they could still play with each other.

The little girl nodded and soon Catherine was running around the yard, hiding behind the pigsty, giggling behind the hen house, whilst waiting for her new friend to follow. But she hadn't. When Catherine went back to the shelter, the little girl had disappeared.

"Just look at the state of yer", Dorrie, her mother had exclaimed, when a few minutes later she had appeared from the almond grove, looking around irately for her wandering offspring. "Yer look as if yer've been dragged through a hedge backward. That dress was clean on this mornin', it was supposed to last until Sunday this time. What are yer doin' anyroad, mankin' about, away from where I can see yer? Don't let it 'appen again, our Catherine, or you'll get a skelp around yer lug."

Catherine set off ahead of her mother. "A skelp around the lug" was what her elder brothers got if they crossed their mother. She wasn't keen on having a sore ear herself and she could always come and look for her friend another day.

The young woman who walked along the Aldinga Road one Febuary morning a few years later, was unrecognisable as Hannah, the girl who had been plucked from the Irish orphanage and sent across the seas to the new colony. The year was 1854 and Hannah, now seventeen, at least she thought she might be seventeen but she couldn't be sure as she didn't have a birth certificate, had her brown hair pulled back into a wispy bun, which helped to emphasis her pale face and high cheekbones. Slim now, rather than skinny looking, and dressed in a simple, brown frock and black boots as befitted a girl from the working classes, she was making her way to the property that had briefly been her home.

That fateful day all those years ago when the Filbeys had fled the scene, taking a frightened Hannah along who had also been in shock at what she had witnessed, had stayed in her mind like a nightmare. Seeing Molly, her forehead gushing, then white as a sheet when her spirit had left her, her grubby frock tangled up around her legs and one of her boots missing, could hit her hard when she wasn't thinking, causing her to shake and tremble at her thoughts. As the years had passed and had become a distant memory, she wondered if she had dreamt it all and Molly was alive and well.

Bessie Filbey had been quiet and very withdrawn for most of that journey to the city. They had been fortunate in that as they had emerged from the property early that morning and headed towards the village, a cart driven by a farmer who was taking his bags of wheat to a flour mill at Noarlunga, stopped and asked had they wanted a lift? He was only going as far as Noarlunga, but they were welcome to climb aboard, even if they were going further. Clarence, who could have gone to the settlement and asked if there were any wagons setting off for Port Adelaide that morning, leapt at the chance. Although Molly's little body had been buried under the shelter at the dead of night, he wasn't going to hang around the property longer than he had to.

They had arrived in the city later that day, early enough for Clarence to find a good class hotel on King William Street, where he had left a still scared Bessie with a still stunned Hannah in a bedroom there. He planned to find Sir Rodney and throw himself on his lordship's mercy, (explore all avenues in Adelaide first rather than having to throw the towel in) tell him that their daughter had died having been bitten by a venomous spider and that Bessie, grieving for their small child, was pining to go back home. The rest had seemed a bit of a blur to Hannah but a couple of days later, Mr. Filbey had taken her to the orphan depot. Mr. Filbey, somehow she could never have brought herself to think of him as her dada, had a long conversation with the superintendent. He'd said goodbye, told her to behave herself and walked away.

She'd been sent to work, first into the Catholic household of an Irish banker, who had a wife and four children and hailed from Dublin. She was sent to assist the nursery maid, whilst the lady of the house had her lying in. The work was hard, with unpleasant jobs, mostly the emptying of chamber pots, washing of soil cloths, keeping the children clean and tidying the nursery, given to the girl who seemed to have been robbed of her senses. Then one day she was no longer needed and she was sent to the depot again.

The superintendent, despairing that she was never going to place this child in a permanent position, a bit of a dolt if the truth was told and only fit to do the lowest of jobs, had sent her later to Willunga to join a group of Irish girls, presently accommodated at the government reserve, until they'd found a place of work.

Hannah hated it. It was reminiscent of the orphanage in Crossmolina, where girls, young as they were, had all sorts of cat fights. Picking on the weakest, jeering at a girl with a speech impediment, pointing fingers at a girl who perhaps had a deformity, with Hannah sometimes also at the butt of it, as she was as quiet as a mouse. There was a group of girls, young women really, who had been sent to look for work at the farms in the area, as due to the sudden exodus of labourers who were tempted to find their fortunes in the Victorian gold fields, the farmers were having difficulty with their harvesting.

The girls were a raucous lot, led by a flame-haired hoyden called Mavoureen. From the sounds of sniggering that came from the corner of the room where they did their chattering, some of the girls were already earning their money by lying on their backs. Hannah hadn't a clue what they were talking about, but there seemed to be one or two young fellows always hanging around the house.

That morning, the Matron, a gentle mannered woman who had her charges' interests at heart, was being berated by some member of the local council whilst Mavoureen, hands on hips,was using language that was most unsuitable. Hannah was able to slip away unnoticed in order to try to find a peaceful corner away from the heated debate indoors.

It was a cool day. There'd been a few spots of rain that morning and Aubretia was standing on the verandah, speaking to Dorrie. Both women were dressed simply in long sleeved gowns, the hems just above their boot laces, with Aubretia wearing a large hat trimmed with a few goose feathers, as she had just been into the township with her children. Her eldest boys, Bertie now fifteen and Ralphie a year younger, had been home schooled. She had been the one to teach them to read and write and add up numbers, seeing as she had been a headmaster's daughter before, but little William, now six years old and very bright for his age, was to be educated in a local school, run by a teacher who hailed from England.

The work at *Meant to Be* had increased sevenfold since the Filbeys had left and the McMahons had taken over, Bill having turned out to be an excellent worker, now he had settled down with his family. Aubretia, now unable to give her youngest her full attention, had decided her son would attend the Buckland Hill Academy in St.Luke's Street.

"I urge you to think of sending your boys there too, Dorrie" Aubretia was saying, full of praise for the place after looking in on the pupils and the teacher. "They're not too old to pick up a little reading and counting numbers. Mine would have gone there as well, had I not home schooled them myself."

Dorrie however, sounded rather reluctant.

"I don't think I'll be sendin' them and I'm sure Bill would agree with me. The boys are wanted on the land and what use would educatin' do for 'em, beside the cost of it all? Anyroad, they go to Sunday school, that's enough learnin' as far as I'm concerned."

"Perhaps they might get their own farms in the future."

Aubretia wouldn't be put off by the woman's negative words. "They'd need to be able to count at least, so that they could see how many cows or sheep they were buying or selling at market and Mr. Colmayne isn't asking a lot for his efforts."

"I'll think about it." The subject was closed as far as Dorrie was concerned. She'd never been educated herself so she couldn't see the need for her children. "Now, shall I get on and ask the boys to fill a few of those baskets and now that it's stopped its rainin', we could get some washin' pegged out whilst it's fine."

Aubretia nodded. Dorrie was a hard worker, all her family was, even little Cathy. It didn't matter that Bill liked his jug of ale now and again down at the Bush Inn, in the Willunga high street; the McMahons had been a Godsend at what could have been a very trying time for Aubretia.

She'd allowed Bill to build a little place beyond the almond grove and with the help of a couple of friends from the church that his family attended, he had erected a workman's cottage and a bunkhouse for the boys.

At the same time, Aubretia had employed a couple of builders to improve her property. Gone was the mean dwelling that existed in her husband's time. They built a new, stone built place, its footings made from local hardcore, with a verandah that stretched across the front of the property. It had two large rooms, a kitchen with a large cooking range, a scullery, and three bedrooms. All dwelt comfortably under a fine slate roof. It was an extensive undertaking, one large for a widow who'd had little income when the Filbeys had gone away, but Bill had been aware of the need to diversify, after a number of failed harvests of wheat in the area had occurred during the drought years of 1850-51.

The ten acres, initially under scrub, with dense, dark woodland on the perimeters, had made way for a field full of potatoes, another of oats, and an additional field had been purchased from the landowner next door, in order to expand the thriving almond grove. With pigsties, fowl-houses and a larger market garden area in front of a paddock, *Meant to Be* was doing well.

Her deceased husband, William, would have been proud of Aubretia's enterprise, even if she did owe a little to an Australian bank...Though perhaps he wouldn't have been too happy about that.

❧

# Chapter Thirteen

Hannah watched as the two women walked away from each other and the lady she remembered went indoors. She was trembling a little, suddenly scared that what she was about to do was perhaps a stupid thing. Surely she'd be recognised and if she was, what was her story? What could she tell the lady without getting the Filbeys into trouble? Perhaps it would be best to forget her plan to ask for some employment. It was just that she had been drawn to visit the place since arriving in the town.

"Can I help you?" Aubretia called after she had come through the door, still wearing her outdoors hat, and spotted Hannah hovering. Her voice carried over the fence, with its newly replaced posts and rails and the young girl nodded. *No going back now and she did need to find some work.* Aubretia beckoned in a friendly fashion and Hannah scurried down the path in an effort to obey.

"Do I know you?" Aubretia smiled, looking into Hannah's thin nervous looking face inquiringly.

"I don't think so, Missus. My name is Hannah and I only just come to Willunga 'cos I'm lookin' for work."

"Oh. It's just that you reminded me of someone that I met a few years ago. So what are you good at? Child minding, fruit picking, working as a domestic servant? There's such a shortage of workers at the moment, with everyone rushing off to the gold fields to try to make their fortune."

"I can do all them things, Missus." Hannah spoke eagerly, glad that she hadn't been recognised, at least not yet. "I can work cheap, just a few shillin' and me bed and board, if you've got a place for me that is, or I can bunk down at the depot in the village if yer like."

"I could do with extra help for the almond harvesting."

Aubretia considered, looking to see if this was a well young woman, not pockmarked or suffering from any disease. She looked healthy enough, maybe a little thin with bony features, but certainly capable and coming from Irish stock if she was not mistaken, given that her accent reminded her of someone else. Her memory stirred again. *The young woman definitely had a likeness to…* then a little boy with dark, curly hair pushed his way in front of her and the moment was lost.

"This is my youngest son, William."

It was said with pride. The little fellow was strong and handsome and the apple of his mother's eye. William put out his hand politely and Hannah shook it gladly.

"William is to start school next Monday and not a moment too soon."

She ruffled his hair and smiled at him fondly. Hannah felt a stirring of something akin to envy; she could never remember anyone doing a thing like that to her.

"I could take him to school for yer, Missus." She spoke quickly. "And pick him up after if you'd let me."

"That would mean I would have to offer you accommodation," Aubretia replied. "With my two older boys and the McMahons' two, I don't think that would be very wise."

"Oh." Hannah wondered what boys had to do with her staying at the homestead, but only having to sleep at the depot was a better outcome than before.

"However, you'll be very welcome to give us a hand from tomorrow onwards. It's all hands to the deck for the almond harvesting and then perhaps when that has finished I can find you something else to do." She stopped to consider something for a moment. "I suppose I could send my boys to the bunkhouse if you were to come and work for me permanently."

"Oh thank yer, Missus." Hannah felt relieved that she had found employment, even if it might be temporary for the moment. "I'll work terribly hard fer yer, so I will. Ah, before I go would yer allow me to use your *dunny*?"

"Of course you can. It's around the back, just across from the pigsties."

Aubretia walked through her front door, pushing William ahead of her, leaving Hannah to wander along the side of the property alone.

Her heart in her mouth, Hannah walked along the front of the verandah, turned to her left and looked across towards the creek, looking for the shelter which she had shared with Molly when they had lived there with the Filbey's before. The shelter had gone, along with all the buildings that used to be in that vicinity, because the house had been extended into the yard.

*They must have found the body, please God, had they found Molly's body and had she been buried in the local cemetery? She'd never know unless she asked about it and how could she ask about that now?*

"I remember, it's little Hannah."

The gentle sounding voice caused her to jump with alarm. She'd been recognised.

"You're Mr. Filbey's daughter."

It wasn't said in an accusing way, more said in delight, as Aubretia rounded the corner and looked towards her, having made her way to the back of the house.

"Where did you all disappear to, Hannah, dear? I thought perhaps you were going back to Ireland; that's what Mr. Filbey told me he was intending to do. Come into the house, I'll make you a drink and you can tell me all about it. Why didn't you tell me it was you that had come calling?"

Hannah was at a loss. She felt panicky; her heart was beating very quickly in her chest. *What to tell this woman, whom she had known as the nice lady who had been kind, had made Molly and herself a nightdress each and had given them slices of bread topped with tasty dripping. Some of the truth?* She blushed red, she couldn't help it, as she had been taught at the orphanage that she must never tell a lie. Following Aubretia, her mind was quaking as she cast around wondering what story to tell.

"Sit there." Aubretia pointed to a horsehair sofa opposite the mantelpiece where a warming fire kept the cold at bay in the large room. She bustled off to the kitchen and brought back a glass of milk which she put into Hannah's hand. Her little boy followed and sat beside his mother in a winged, upholstered chair, where he gazed curiously at the newcomer.

"You can tell me Hannah, I won't shout." Aubretia's eyes were kind. She had noticed the girl blushing and trembling since she had addressed her.

"I wasn't the Filbey's daughter. I looked after Molly when we came on the boat and I stopped with them to look after her. I came from Crossmolina, from the orphanage. I had a mammy but she died when I was three."

"Poor Hannah, but go on with your story. What happened to the Filbeys?"

"Molly fell over the washin' basket, hit her head on the tin tub and after that it was decided that we would go to the city, because the Missus didn't want to stay 'ere anymore. When we got there they took me to the orphan depot and I never saw them again." *Phew,* she'd managed to tell the tale without mentioning the horrible happening. She hoped that the nice lady wouldn't ask her more.

"And now you're looking for employment." Aubretia's tone was gentle as her heart had gone out to her. "Poor girl, you have had a precarious life, but perhaps from now we can change that for you."

So Hannah stayed on at the property as a live-in help. She became adept at running a household and helping with the harvesting, got to know the seasons and the surrounding terrain. Aubretia took her under her wing, treated her well and gave her a room to sleep in, but most of all she showed her how to run a home.

In 1859, the marriage of Albert Aldridge and Hannah Sweeney was announced from the pulpit of the local Roman Catholic church. Not that the couple were great attenders, as the homestead dictated their leisure time and now that *Meant to Be* had expanded into dairy farming, it was decided by the family to change its name to "Aldridge Farm," and not a lot of time was spent away from it.

There had been many changes since Hannah had arrived that fateful morning. The McMahonss had moved on, much to the dismay of Aubretia whose closest friend was Dorrie, but one of their boys, a young man now, had appeared before the magistrates' court charged with assaulting another, whilst "in drink" at the local Bush Inn. He had been sentenced to a spell in the city's gaol on Grote Street and with Dorrie being mortified, feeling she couldn't hold her head up high in the community any longer, and then deeply worried when her eldest boy announced he was off to dig for gold in Victoria, the family, along with young Catherine, had travelled north, to where a few enterprising men had begun a couple of fledgling industries.

The burden of running the place had fallen upon Bertie and Ralphie, with the occasional help from William, a would be academic not a farmer, to run their thriving business, with produce now sold from their milk cart to the settlers of Willunga and beyond. Outbuildings, including a dairy which became the domain of Aubretia and Hannah, were built to house the storage of almonds, potatoes, oats, hay for the animals and all the equipment needed for running a busy farm.

It had to be said that the marriage of Bertie and Hannah wasn't the product of a love match, it was more the joining of two people who were dedicated to the continuing prosperity of the Aldridge Farm for the generations to come.

The man who bowled along the newly laid Aldinga Road, in the smart, black, open topped *barouche*, pulled by a sleek looking piebald horse, looked every inch a man of substance, dressed as he was in a manner befitting his position in life.

Clarence Filbey, was a widower now as Bessie had thrown

herself into the River Torrens, having been unable to shrug off the devastating memories of her part in the death of Molly. He was in the area that day on business. Now Sir Rodney's right hand man, responsible for everything that came under the heading of his lordship's "investments", Clarence travelled far and wide around Adelaide, overseeing the tenants who rented acres on his lordship's extensive tracts of land.

He couldn't believe his luck, when on that fateful day after he had presented himself to Sir Rodney with his hard luck story of the death of his child and a pining Bessie, he was given tea and sympathy, a grace and favour residence, as well as a prestigious job. It appeared that his lordship had been let down by various rogues intent on deception and chicanery and was extremely pleased to be reacquainted with Clarence Filbey, an honest and hardworking man.

Clarence was in the area that day to represent his lordship at the fourth annual Willunga Show, as Sir Rodney was a member of the Agricultural and Horticultural Society. Clarence was taking the opportunity to see for himself how *Meant to Be* had fared. Perhaps Aubretia, she who had invaded his dreams on many an occasion since he had left in a hurry all those years ago, had removed herself back to England, along with her three young sons.

He reined his horse to a halt outside the homestead which was rather pleasing to the eye and now had a sign displayed above the picket fence that said "Aldridge Farm". Aubretia would never have had the wherewithal to have built such a prosperous looking place and yet it was called "Aldridge Farm", which began to cause a bit of puzzlement in Clarence's mind. As he gazed with interest at the handsome dwelling, sat as it was on a substantial looking site, surrounded by an extensive almond grove, it struck him that they must have dug up little Molly's grave when the place was extended. The thought didn't faze him, as who would connect the tiny body to such an influential looking man? He tied his horse to the picket fence and let it graze on some lush looking grass, whilst he ambled over to examine the contents of a couple of dog eared reed baskets, placed on a rickety wooden table nearby.

"Can I help you?" A man in his twenties, a working man by the appearance of his clothing, walked towards him along the unsealed drive at the side of the building. He looked with interest at the horse and carriage as he neared, no doubt wondering who the visitor was.

"Just passing by on my way to Aldinga" Clarence said nonchalantly, putting on a supercilious voice and playing with the fob watch that he had just taken out of his waistcoat pocket.
"I have business in the area and noticed your table with produce for sale."

"Anything you were wanting can be paid for in the Honesty Box," the young man said turning away, disinterested now he had ascertained the person's purpose. He was on his way to eat his dinner in the farmhouse, his mother having called him from the back porch a little earlier.

"It says Aldridge Farm on here," Clarence called, pointing to the sign. "I used to know a Mrs. Aldridge, when the place was called "Meant to Be". Does the family still live here?" *He'd never know if he didn't ask*, he told himself. *She'd been in his hopes and dreams for many a year.*

"Yes, Mrs. Aldridge still lives here." The young man turned back on his heel uncertainly and looked closely at Clarence, who had put on weight and had grown a lot of facial hair. "Do I know you, Sir?"

"You must be Bertie. You won't remember me, you were just a small child last time I saw you."

Bertie nodded politely, not sure whether to invite the man onto the homestead or leave him there.

"Give my regards to your mother."

Clarence looked at the fob watch and stared at it intently, wondering whether to turn his vehicle around and head back the way he had come. He could be stirring up a hornet's nest by staying. It was best that he should go.

"Who is it, Bertie?" Aubretia stood in the doorway, her voice impatient, as the food was cooling on the table whilst a stranger was chatting to her son. "Whoever it is, I'm just about to serve up dinner, perhaps you would like to come by a little later, Sir."

She paused for a moment, looking towards the picket fence, unable to believe who her visitor might be. " Mr. Filbey – is that you? Mr. Filbey – well I don't believe it – do come along in."

*She was still beautiful, a little lined in the face, but who wasn't,* he told himself as he sat with the family at her table in the cosy farmhouse kitchen. It was a world away from the poor dwelling that had existed when he had stayed there before. Her two elder boys who were both grown men now and young William, who was loud and boisterous, an annoying child, sat beside him as Aubretia, a little plump now and in her country woman's clothing, but still attractive as she had been before, served their meal. It was a simple meal, but very tasty, a vegetable stew served with lots of boiled potatoes and an apple pie for dessert with lots of cream. He had eaten the food hungrily, delicious compared to his housekeeper's efforts back in the city. Then after complimenting Aubretia on keeping hearth and home together, he told them a little of his life so far. He relaxed, lit a cigar, offered one to each of the boys, agreed to a tour around their fields and almond groves and accepted her commiseration on losing his loved ones.

He looked forward to meeting Bertie's wife, ensconced as she was in their cottage in the grounds, having given birth to a little girl a few weeks before. It would be a surprise for him, Aubretia had said, though Clarence couldn't see why.

*Yes, I could get used to this,* he thought, as he surveyed the land before him whilst standing on the back porch of the dwelling. The leafy almond groves, the produce of a fertile land; the tree shaded paddock with two fine horses grazing; the brick built outbuildings which he'd been told housed the dairy and almond storage and thankfully, there was no sign of the shelter that had been there before. The original dwelling had been given an extension and the narrow creek still ran through the property, bringing with it a natural water supply.

It could all be his if he played his cards right and married the comely Aubretia. Working for Sir Rodney might have brought him a steady income, respect from his lordship's many tenants and employees and given him a comfortable lifestyle, but he would give it all up for his love who resided in this pleasant corner of the world.

*Hannah, oh God, it was Hannah! What was she doing here? He had thought that was the last he would see of her when he had taken her to the orphan depot all those years ago.* Clarence felt alarm as he glanced towards the nursing mother, sitting as she was on an old horsehair sofa in the front room of the workman's cottage with her baby wrapped in a white, lacy, shawl lying contentedly on her knee.

Hannah looked visibly shaken as she recognised her visitor. Her face went white and her hands began to tremble and she clutched her baby to her in case it should fall. *Mr. Filbey. She had thought he had gone back to Ireland, taking his crabby tongued wife along with him. What was he doing back here in Willunga?*

"Hannah, we've brought Mr. Filbey. Of course you will remember him from when he employed you as a nursemaid." Aubretia sounded as if she was giving her daughter-in-law a treat in bringing the man into the cottage and Bertie looked gleeful, thinking that he was reuniting a former employer and his wife.

*So she had told them half a story, she had been the nursemaid and it looked as if that was all she had told them too.* Clarence let out a sigh.

"We wondered what had become of you, Hannah. I came back to the depot later to let you know that we had decided to stay in Adelaide, but they said you'd moved on. Mrs. Filbey eventually managed to come to terms with the loss of little Molly and I got a good job with Sir Rodney."

Hannah nodded politely, wondering where the Filbey woman was and thinking that the man was lying; he had never come back to get her from the depot.

"Do sit down Mr. Filbey" Aubretia insisted, pulling out an upholstered chair from underneath a cloth covered table. "Bertie has a few chores to do and I need to go back to the house to get a jug of milk for Hannah. I'm sure you two have got a lot to talk about. I'll bring some of my baking and a pot of tea."

"No, don't go to any trouble on my behalf, dear lady." Clarence fumbled around in his head for an excuse to depart the homestead. Being left with Hannah was the last thing he wanted to do, unless of course he could use the time to his advantage. "I must away to Willunga; I have some unfinished business at the show."

"But that is where we will all be going later, Mr. Filbey" Aubretia replied gaily. "Ralphie has exhibited some of our plump and delicious almonds there. Judging doesn't start until three, so you could spend a little time with Hannah before we go."

She didn't wait to listen for a negative answer, thinking she was doing them both a favour by leaving them alone to reminisce and bustled off, whilst Bertie ambled across the yard to check on one of his sows, who was about to give birth.

"So, Hannah. I'm sure yer just as surprised to see me again as I am to see you and I see yer've fell on your feet having managed to get yerself wed to a member of the Aldridge family."

His silken tones had gone and to Hannah's ears his words sounded menacing but as it was *he* who had committed the crime of burying Molly, why should he want to frighten her?

"I *am* surprised, Mr. Filbey" she admitted, her trembling having stopped, as the minutes passed by and she took stock of the situation. "When you took me to the orphan depot I thought that was the last I would see of you and Mrs. Filbey. I imagined that you had both returned to Ireland to cover up your wife's crime."

"Hardly a crime, Hannah, more of an accident – one of which you were witness to and thus an accomplice in any court of law." He sat back in his chair and watched as the colour drained from her thin features.

"But I…"

"Yes, Hannah, yer *were* an accomplice. You saw what happened and yer didn't raise the alarm, yer didn't go fer help from Mrs. Aldridge and yer kept quiet about it when we went to live in the city."

"But I was a young girl and I relied on you for everything. I was a stranger in a foreign land and I was frightened – frightened of authority and especially of Mrs. Filbey and what she could do." Her face took on an agitated look and she clutched her baby even closer.

"Hannah, Hannah." Clarence's voice took on a soothing tone. "Let's not peer into the past, lookin' for blame when nothing can put right from what has happened. My Bessie is dead now, taken her secret to the grave, Molly is in a better place and you and I have surely achieved everythin' we could have wished fer. You now belong to a loving family, with a child of your own to give succour to and I am the right hand man of Sir Rodney, well thought of and respected by everyone. It could all disappear like snowflakes on a sunny day if you went to the authorities, but then who would believe a *scut* of a girl like you?"

He waited for his words to sink in and watched whilst her mind seemed to be at war with herself. He smiled as he heard Aubretia calling to her son across the way.

"Yer wouldn't want to lose all this, Hannah, the love of yer husband and mother-in-law, not to mention that they'd take your baby away."

He stopped his persuading as Hannah nodded bleakly, then Aubretia made her way across the room, depositing the jug and holding her arms out for a hold of her little grandchild. It was a pleasant scene and Clarence knew that he had won.

The weeks went by and Clarence was a frequent visitor. It seemed that Sir Rodney's business interests stretched far and wide. Not that Clarence discussed the reasons for his calls upon the owners of the now flourishing orchards and vineyards that had sprung up around the McLaren Vale and the surrounding areas, but he always seemed to time his visit to coincide with Aubretia serving afternoon tea. He became a kindly "uncle" to her sons, though of Hannah he saw little, as she always seemed very busy at that time of the day.

One afternoon, just as Hannah was bringing in some washing from the yard as there was a threat of a shower in the air, he came hurrying through the almond trees with his red face wearing a scowl, either though through exertion or anger, Hannah couldn't tell.

"It'll be your fault, yer little schemer," he hissed, as he stood so close she could smell the stink of his breath. His Irish way of speaking that he had tried hard to get rid of in the past, was coming to the fore in his haste to get out his words. "She's told me she doesn't want a suitor, told me she doesn't want a marriage agin, suggests that I don't visit the homestead if that was what I was wantin' from 'er in the long run."

"How can that be my fault? I've never so much as mentioned to Aubretia about what happened on that awful day. You give me enough warnin' of what would 'appen if I did."

Hannah stood her ground. She couldn't understand why it was her fault that her mother-in-law had asked Mr. Filbey not to call at the farm again. "She has always vowed to never love another man, at least that is what Bertie has always said." It seemed that her stance took the sting from his anger. He had guessed as much, but needed to put the blame on someone else.

"Perhaps it's as well that yer don't come visitin', Mr. Filbey, then we can put the past behind us. I were doin' fine until yer came back into our lives again." Hannah turned to go, using the excuse that her baby wanted feeding, but not before she noted the slump in his shoulders and the sadness in his eyes. *The girl was right. He had seen the flash of desolation pass over the face of his beloved, before she had told him gently that perhaps it was time for him to go. He'd be wasting his time if he was after a courtship. Her heart had died along with William Aldridge, a fine man, the love of her life and no other man would ever take his place.*

♣

# Chapter Fourteen

Under the watchful eye of Grandma Aldridge, four year old Beth was discovering the delights and pitfalls of playing in the yard behind the homestead. Warnings, her grandma's gentle threats of what would happen if she chose to ignore her, rang through her ears as she picked a bunch of yellow soursobs for her darling mother. Don't go near the fast flowing creek that had swollen because of the last few days of heavy rain; don't put her hand into the pig pen where the sow was farrowing and don't go near the ferocious dog who was tied up on a rope in the yard. Flowers grew in profusion amongst the grassy undergrowth on the banks of the creek.

Hannah, now in her eighth month of pregnancy with her third child, was spending some time with her feet up whilst Aubretia in her element now that she was the grandmother of the couple's two children, took her grandson Matthew, inside the house to change his smelly cloths.

Life at *Aldridge Farm* had changed little since Clarence had made his departure and Hannah, now able to relax once more, was at her happiest producing babies, secure in the knowledge that she would have the love of her growing family for the rest of her days. She felt needed by her offspring and was the contented wife of Bertie, who was feeling fortunate that when all around him families were falling victim to poor harvests from overworked land, crop diseases, storms and terrible droughts in the summer, he and Ralphie, now married to a Willunga girl whom he had met at a public lecture, had heeded the call for diversification by the local agricultural associations, buying more land to expand their marketing to the residents of the area and beyond.

Hectares of maize, root crops and another market garden had been added to their acres of almond groves and with the improvement of the district's roads, the busy jetty at Port Willunga, the construction of many bridges and the transport of their goods to the city, townships and surrounding country villages, distribution of their produce was a lot easier than it had been before. There was a growth in population now in and around the settlements, all who were in need of fresh supplies of vegetables, butter, eggs and cheese.

William, Aubretia's youngest, now grown up and the brains of the Aldridge brothers, spent his life now at the city's university, where he was studying to become an agricultural engineer. He was also the instigator of starting the Aldridge family Bible. It was fitting, he said, to have a record of births, marriages and deaths of each family member, for the benefit of the generations to come.

This particular day was a cool one, the start of a summer which hadn't yet got into its stride. Beth was nonplussed when a little girl with long, brown hair, wearing a shabby, white dress and old black boots, appeared at her side and began to pick some of the yellow flowers too. It was unusual, to say the least, to see another little girl at the homestead, as Beth only got to see her friends when she went to Sunday school.

"Hello, where have you come from?" The little girl smiled sadly and shrugged her shoulders at the question and Beth noticed she had a mark on her brow. "That looks bad. I fell over last week and bruised my knees. See? Grandma said I shouldn't have been running. Did you do that when *you* were running too?" The little girl nodded and handed her bunch of flowers over, then turned away and began to walk towards the farmhouse. "Don't go," Beth called. "Stay a little longer and I'll ask Grandma if we can have a slice of her cake. It's an almond cake." But the child seemed to have a problem with her hearing and carried on ahead.

To say that Hannah was astonished after her small daughter

related the conversation she'd had with the strange girl who had appeared in the yard a little earlier, would be an understatement. At first her thoughts were ones of disbelief and she assumed that the child must have belonged to a family of itinerant workers who had been hired to help the brothers bring part of their harvest in. Then she remembered that Bertie had said he had paid them off and they were making their way to Aldinga, where a farmer needed help with his harvest of an early cereal crop.

It was when Beth mentioned the mark on the little girl's head and the fact that she hadn't spoken, that Hannah started having her suspicions and was dumbfounded to feel quite certain that it was Molly's spirit that her daughter had seen. It made sense. Beth had said that the girl had appeared from nowhere, hadn't spoken and was wearing a white dress and little, black boots which was exactly what Molly had been wearing on the day of her death. To say all this to her daughter could have been too alarming for the four year old dote, so instead she hugged her, thanked her for the flowers and hoped that Molly would rest in peace.

It was on her deathbed many years later, when still haunted by the visions of her dying friend, who would appear in her dreams from time to time, Hannah confessed to her youngest son, Bradley, a preacher by then who had changed his allegiance from Roman Catholic to the Wesleyan Church, of the part she had played in Molly's secret burial in the Aldridge yard. She asked him to write down her words so that Molly Mayo's memory could be kept alive in years to come.

It was a long time before Molly put in an appearance at the Aldridges again. Perhaps her spirit was always there watching, looking on at the successive generations as they played on the banks of the narrow creek.

The land around the homestead had flourished with careful husbandry. The Aldridge family, now using the modern agricultural machinery on their extensive hectares, began to reap the rewards of their endeavours, when many farmers had walked away from the uncertain climate, leaving buildings deserted and land in disuse.

It was one evening, when that particular winter had seen hail stones the size of pebbles raining down upon the poor cattle that grazed in the fields nearby, that the family of Matthew Aldridge, Hannah's eldest son who had inherited the homestead in 1893 after Bertie had passed on, was sitting in the warmth of the parlour, listening, along with Matthew's five other children, to Dorcas, his eldest, who was entertaining them with a rousing rendition of *Love Divine, All Loves Excelling,* a well known hymn by Charles Wesley and a favourite of the time.

Matthew's wife, Ellen, had just finished accompanying her daughter on the ebony piano amidst the scene of domestic contentment, when the sound of a child screaming could be heard outside. Matthew rushed to the window in alarm and from it, saw that one of the barns which contained a large haystack, had set alight, and a streak of something white was fleeing across the yard. Not thinking about his own safety, his only purpose being to save the child who had alerted the family with its yells, he dashed through the back door of the dwelling, to find that two of his workers from the farm cottages who had also heard the noise, were already armed with a couple of buckets and were filling them with water from the well.

There was no sighting of a distressed child, so Matthew rushed into the barn, hoping against hope he could save the little mite if was trapped inside. But the heat drove him back and the family watched with sorrowful eyes at its destruction, as well as a nearby pigpen which had been reduced to cinders. Luckily someone had rescued the pigs, but there was still the fear of finding the ashes of a body inside the barn after the fire had begun to die.

Heads were counted then scratched with disbelief when it appeared that all members and workers of the Aldridge Farm were present, including the yard cats that had stood around with arched backs as they listened to the barking of the ferocious dog.

An old man, a grandfather who lived with his family in one of the cottages, said he had seen this kind of thing happen many times.

If the hay had been damp, then it might have sweated in the middle of the stack and that could cause a problem and set the fodder alight. It could have been that someone in the village had a grievance, perhaps they saw that the Aldridges' were doing so well in a time when many people were finding it hard to survive. That suggestion was from a worker, who didn't dare say that it could be an act of revenge, as Matthew was mean with his money and would question each bill for the goods or repairs to the machinery for the farm.

So the fate of the child was forgotten as it could have been a frightened bird fleeing across the yard to the undergrowth. The barn and its contents lay in a heap of smouldering ash and Matthew began to reckon up the cost. As to who it was who may have started the fire deliberately, his finger of blame pointed to Pieter Olk, an unsuitable young clodhopper of Dutch descent, who lived with his widowed mother on a small landholding. The ne'er-do-well had set his sights on Dorcas, his eldest and they'd been seen in an embrace at a Sunday school picnic by a villager whose duty it was to inform the farmer of what she had seen.

Of course the girl had been punished, as Matthew had high hopes of Dorcas marrying into the Woodleigh family, who were making their money by exporting their wool to a Manchester mill. A couple of straps across his daughter's backside had caused her to reflect on her sins, as Matthew was a great believer in the adage of "spare the rod and spoil the child."

It was a source of puzzlement too when Mrs. Olk reported the loss of her only son to the troopers. It was assumed that he had joined the exodus of labour to the gold diggings and hadn't wanted to upset her with his plan.

In 1913, work began on the railway that would give a regular service to the city for passengers and transport freight from the area. It looked as if the wealth of the Aldridge family would know no bounds. There were two large houses now built on the land that looked across to the Aldinga Road. A warehouse, stockyards, barns and many outbuildings stood behind, along with a row of farm workers cottages, for the benefit of the men who were employed there.

The Aldridges had been lucky that in every generation since William and Aubretia had first settled at the place they had called "Meant to Be", there had been at least one male who the homestead could be passed on to. Most of them had inherited their work ethic from their ancestors. Some had been mean, some had been open handed, but all had, had the fortunes of the "Aldridge Farm" gathered closely to their hearts.

In this second decade of the twentieth century, there were four boys and three female siblings, the offspring of John and Hilda, Matthew and Ellen's elder son. One of John's brothers had died from brucellosis and two had died at the Relief of Mafeking in 1900. They hadn't needed to get involved in the Boer War in Africa, but had felt they had wanted to serve their queen and country and find excitement in their otherwise boring lives.

John's sons were all too young to get involved in this war when it was declared in Europe in 1914. Although sympathetic to the families who were having to say goodbye to a departing loved one, the Aldridges were happy to get involved with any fundraising for the good of the valiant men. They were eagerly awaiting the official opening of Willunga station, which would see their products being marketed far and wide. Already using the transportation of their goods by road and shipping, John had agents waiting in readiness, to go out near and far and clinch more deals.

But that was until the drought of that summer, which put paid to some of the crop yields. It was very expensive to buy in fresh water and the brook and the creeks on the property had all run dry. John made the best of a bad business by investing in a new type of irrigation that involved lots of tubes being laid on top of the ground. It was thought that when the rains came again that winter, the tanks would be full to their capacity and the tubes would mean a more controlled watering of the land.

When the railway was officially opened in January of 1915, there was much ado made of the occasion. There were luncheons and speeches made by the great and the good and a sense of excitement felt by young and old alike as they considered their new found mobility. The city beckoned, further education could be gained now at the universities, there was a chance for better wages and more of a social life than just dances at the village hall or having a drink at the many inns that had sprung up in the area. Now the locals could visit their city, which many hadn't been to before. The Aldridges could send their wares to Adelaide and they would arrive in a couple of hours.

One afternoon, John was driving to the homestead in his truck, as he came back from a luncheon that had been given in honour of the governor, who had travelled to Willunga by train. He had imbibed a few glasses of a rather delicious, fullbodied red wine, courtesy of a McLaren Vale winery that had supplied the bottles and he was feeling rather full after a satisfying five course meal.

If he was swerving a little as he ambled along in his newly purchased Ford, it didn't much matter, as the road was bare except for a flock of seagulls that were circling over something in the distance. His mind was full of the praise that the committee he belonged to had been given for their unstinting supply of comforts to the troops.

As John entered the entrance to the homestead, his foot fell onto the accelerator and not the brake. Through his windscreen he glimpsed two figures; one was his daughter, Edith and the other a little girl he didn't know. The little girl, dressed in a white dress with dark, brown hair growing onto her shoulders, seemed in his view to rise above the bonnet of the truck in very slow motion, only to fall back down across it again. Pulling the handbrake on, he threw himself from behind the wheel, as the vehicle lurched to a halt, the tyres making a terrible screeching noise as it did so. His body shaking and eyes filled with tears from his distress, he went to help the injured girl, only to find his daughter shaking like a leaf and being comforted in the arms of his wife, Hilda. Of the girl that he had thought he had run over, there was no sign.

After being lectured upon the evils of drink and being told that he should be more careful when coming through the entrance into the busy yard, in case there might be livestock or children too, he declared to his very angry wife that he would sign the pledge and never take a drink again.

As the Aldridge children grew into maturity, the four fine young men and three dumpling daughters, John was faced with a problem that he had never thought he would have. His eldest son, Samuel, who would be heir to the Aldridge hectares when his father died, decided he didn't want to follow in his ancestors' footsteps, rather he wanted to join the army and see the world a bit. His plea to join was echoed by his younger brother Joseph, who was seventeen. Then Albert and Thomas, twins who did everything together, voiced an opinion that living on the farm was boring, so they wanted a more interesting type of life. As they had been tutored at the local Bassett College which had produced a lot of academics over the years, they thought that they would like to continue their studies at a university.

John felt hurt and angry. In all the generations that had lived on the farm since William and Aubretia, this way of life had run through their very veins and he couldn't understand his four sons' objections to it. At first he tried to cajole them, then offered them a wage whereas before their labour on the farm had only attracted pocket money. He tempted them with a bigger say in decisions and offered them their own accommodation. Finally, he swore to cut them off without a penny as one by one – stubborn Samuel, then a strong willed Joseph – left the farm, leaving the twins to reflect on where their futures lay.

His daughters, he knew, would find husbands when they came of age and would leave the homestead, going off to support their spouse in whatever line of work they were employed in and the twins would eventually go to the city to live. None could have known that there would come a time when John would be grateful for his sons' lack of interest. When the years of the Depression hit the world's economy, it caused a severe strain on the finances, with hectares lying fallow and precious fruit dying on the trees.

♣

# Chapter Fifteen

It was after the Second World War that the Aldridges saw a resurgence in the family's fortunes. Financially that is, as Samuel was to die leading his platoon into battle and Joseph was invalided back to the farm. John and Hilda, getting on in years and now in poor health, but still holding on to what was left of the hectares that hadn't been sold to a small housing developer who had built a row of plain looking houses on one side of the Aldinga Road, did their best to market the produce from the dairy, the eggs from their poultry and a small variety of vegetables, as the twins had gone onto work as doctors at a hospital in Adelaide and many of their workers had died in the war.

Joseph, after enlisting early on in the war and losing an arm at Tobruk when a shrapnel wound became infected by gangrene, was still able to operate a threshing machine and drive a tractor once he had made his recovery. With a loan from the local bank, the family had tried to restore their prosperity by planting a hectare or two of grain. It also helped when Joseph, a good looking man and popular amongst the spinsters of the parish that he met whilst attending the Wesleyan church, announced his marriage to Maureen, the daughter of a man who had built an industrial site in the area. It was a depot where large amounts of produce could be stored in two large warehouses before its distribution via road or railway, now that the transportation of goods from Port Willunga had ceased.

Kathleen, the youngest of John's three daughters, was to

remain a spinster, as many eligible men from the district had enlisted after the announcement on the wireless of the Second World War. Here was their chance to see a bit of the world, even if the returning soldiers of the earlier war had warned of the perils of hasty enlistment, which was bound to end in tragedy.

No, this time the war would be over by Christmas, said the new generation, full of fervour. Hadn't the *Boshe* been given a bloody nose last time they went to war?

So Kathleen, a plain faced, plumpish, brown haired girl, became heavily involved in a local branch of the Red Cross and was kept busy in those war years, stolidly knitting socks for the warring warriors, packing up boxes with food for the troops and making an appearance at any of the fundraising events. She worked tirelessly on the homestead, living with her cats in a farm worker's cottage, which had been kindly donated rent free from her brother, Joseph, now that there was less demand for permanent workers because of modern machinery. She helped Maureen with the children that the couple later produced and attended the local church on Sunday to pray for the welfare of the servicemen.

Kathleen had a keen interest in genealogy, though at that time she didn't know it by that name. Most old families then could boast a record of their family tree, with the names of those who had departed for their heavenly reward listed in the family Bible.

In that quiet time, after she had put her small nephews to bed, she would sit in the homestead parlour, reading her favourite gospels from the big black book, whilst saying a few heartfelt prayers for the valiant young men whom she had known from attending the village school. Most of them had joined the Australian army and were fighting in the Middle East. There were letters and sepia photographs of the Aldridge family in a small, wooden box, with lots of the photos having the names and dates of birth of the forebear written in pencil on the back. An unsmiling family of five stood outside the picket fence of one of the cottages, the girls in their Sunday best pinafores, and standing to attention were well scrubbed boys. Another was a photo of John and Hilda on their wedding day and some with various chubby babies taken throughout the years.

There was a picture of a farm cart piled high with hay and pulled by two patient looking horses and one of a solitary boy standing on the banks of a river, fishing with a stick. Behind him stood a little girl in a white, old fashioned looking dress watching. That is, it looked like a little girl standing there watching, but it could have been a shadow, as the early cameras were renowned for their cloudiness.

It was the letter, written on behalf of her Great Grandma Hannah by someone called Bradley, which had always held Kathleen's interest. It was a sad little letter, asking for forgiveness for not speaking up about the accidental death of a small child called Molly. She assumed that the girl had not been related to Hannah or the Aldridges, according to the lack of an inscription in the family Bible, but had been brought over from Ireland, from a place called County Mayo, along with Great Grandma Hannah. How that could possibly have caused guilt in the dear old lady, Kathleen was at a loss to know, but there again times would have been different in those days and all a bit of a mystery.

After the cessation of the Second World War, whilst rationing of food and shortages of housing still existed in the ravaged cities and towns of Europe and returning heroes found that their homelands were certainly not fit to live in anymore, many men decided to up-sticks and seek a better life for themselves and their families in a different land. Canada and America were favoured but many chose to migrate to New Zealand and Australia, tempted by the promises of accommodation and jobs.

In 1947, Calwell's great immigration drive began in Australia, re-population being the agenda of the post war government there. Once again orphanages and children's homes across the length and breadth of Great Britain and Southern Ireland, opened their doors to send their unwanted inmates across the seas, to settle in the new country as they had done in the century before. These were children like Patrick, a dark haired, undernourished twelve year old, whose parents had fled to Liverpool from Ireland to escape the slings and arrows of a narrow minded parish priest. A German bomb had fallen on the couple's rented terrace house in Bootle, leaving a bewildered Patrick lying injured in the rubble, whilst his unfortunate parents left this mortal coil.

He was sent to work on the Aldridge Farm, Kathleen having chosen him from the wan little group that had appeared in Willunga one day. The children were the product of a committee she had been serving on which had been formed to find a home and some work for the orphans locally, and would help in the re-population of the area in the future. Patrick, dressed in short, black trousers, a navy blue blazer and wearing a crumpled, grey cap, his knee length socks, one up and one down, clutched tightly to the only possession he had, a small, fibre suitcase which held a change of underwear and pair of striped pyjamas. He was to fulfill the maternal instincts that Kathleen, thanks to Hitler and the war, would have otherwise not had satisfied.

Inspired by her thoughts of Great Grandma Hannah, who had been Irish as the day was long like Patrick, she took up her new role with relish, teaching the child the rudiments of reading and writing, before sending him off to the village school.

In all the ups and downs and vagaries of the harvests that the Aldridges had withstood during and after the Depression years, their one constant had been their almond groves. The area had always been suitable for their production, but in the early 1950s, Joseph and his two sons who were nearly adults and Patrick who was treated as one of the family, set about increasing their growth. The demand for wheat had diminished once the world had found its feet again and countries began to work on their own production of the grain.

One evening Patrick, now more nourished and his once stick-like body growing more muscle with each passing day, walked along to the farm worker's cottage that he shared with Kathleen.

It had been a hard day working as a tree shaker in one of the almond groves and he decided to sit for a moment on the grassy bank of the brook that ran alongside the perimeter of the farm. He had felt the urge to sit with his memories and ponder on the vastness of the oceans that separated Adelaide and Ireland, whilst wondering if he would ever be able go back to his homeland again.

He had loved those early years near Ballina, where they had lived in one of the fine row of cottages, which stood across from the farm where sometimes his mother had gone to work. Their cottage had lattice windows and a grey, slate roof. The walls inside were whitewashed and there had been a black range for cooking on. He had loved the sounds of the country as he lay in the warmth of his bed, waiting for his mother to call him from his slumber in readiness for the delights of his day. He would run down the track past the Giant's Tub, a pool full of clear cool water, where in the summer, he and the other small boys from the area would jump in naked as the day they were born, or they would sit as a dare in the eerie Round Tower that overlooked the River Moy.

He brushed back a tear as he remembered when the priest had come. He had been a fierce, authoritarian man, not like the gentle Father who had the living in Killala before. Patrick had been walking along the headland from the little school that he attended in Ballina that day and had wondered, as he cut along by the side of the farm yard, why the dog cart that Father Cronin drove around the parish in, was outside his parents' home? He saw his mother had been crying after she had spotted him when he came bounding through the cottage gate and she had ordered him, white faced, to his bedroom up the stairs. There'd been angry words between the priest and his Dada and the sound of his mother arguing tearfully with both of them, whilst Patrick shook with terror as he listened from his little bed. Then a few days later his parents had started packing, with the three of them making the long journey overland to the port at Dunleary, where they had sailed on a boat which was bound for Liverpool, where a bomb dropped by the Luftwaffe, had ended the lives of his beloved parents. Then had come the time he had spent in the hated children's home, where he found to his dismay that his accent was a source of amusement, causing him, to his distress, to wet the bed. The boys there had called him Paddy. They knew his name was Patrick Mayo, but seemed to find it funny to call him "Paddy Pee the Bed."

There was a cool breeze coming in from the ocean, causing the gum trees above to rustle as Patrick pulled his boots back on after resting his tired feet. He sniffed the air in appreciation of the roast chicken dinner that was about to come. Kathleen was the finest of cooks and he would love the woman forever for choosing to take him in. Others, he knew, were treated far worse at their billets. One or two had run away and never been heard of again and it was rumoured that one poor girl had been sent to a mother and baby home in the city, though Patrick didn't know what she could have done.

*The little girl who still hadn't gone into the spirit world, still hadn't laid her troubled thoughts to rest and had hung around the homestead for a century, watched from her place behind the trunk of an overhanging gum tree. Was this the boy that she had been waiting for? Was this the boy who had sailed across the oceans just to find her, his own kin, his own family, come across from Ireland to take her back again? Was he the one who would take her back to her homeland, back to the green fields of her hamlet, the sparkling river that ran down the side of the hill and the little church which overlooked the crashing waves of the sea below? Would she meet her beloved sister either there in her native Killala, or in the spirit world of the dead?*

One winter's evening, Kathleen and Patrick sat together on the sofa in front of a cosy log fire, curtains drawn against the chilly air, feeling full from an excellent hog roast dinner and all being well in their little world. Kathleen, curious about the lad's sad past, especially because his surname was Mayo, which she had learnt from the family Bible was the county in Ireland where Great Grandma Hannah had come from, hoped that her words wouldn't cause too much unhappiness as she asked him to tell her about his life in his homeland.

Patrick was seventeen now and a young man – a handsome, dark, curly haired young man with eyes the colour of cornflowers and muscles that rippled under his collarless shirt, the result of the heavy work that he did. He was happy to confide in her. From frightened child to a confident man, Kathleen felt she had made a good job of his upbringing.

He was hesitant when he spoke of his parents, though bitter that religion had caused the parting of himself from them. No matter how Kathleen had tried to coerce him to join her at the Wesleyan church, he had refused her, blaming all churches for their inflexibility. After all, it was the same God that all were supposed to be worshipping, so he didn't think that his parents had committed any sin.

Inspired by the stories that his father used to tell as a small child as Patrick had lain tucked up in his bed, he told Kathleen the tale of his seafaring ancestor, Bernard Mayo, who had run away to join a ship in Sligo in 1843. This Great Uncle Bernie had also travelled across the world as Patrick had *and* had found a little gold on his way, coming back to settle in Killala and living comfortably. There was also an aunt, the seafarer's sister, who had made a fortune across the sea in England, through buying land and property, but had given it all up for the love of her life, a man called Johnny. It was a romantic tale, one that Kathleen in her maiden state could only dream of and after that evening, she felt that she was closer to Patrick than she had ever been before.

It was in the late 50's that Joseph decided that changes must be made. John and Hilda, his parents, were now buried in the yard of the Wesleyan church, his sons were of an age when they should have been married and the patter of little Aldridge feet should have been heard around the farm. His thoughts were on the future and the young man with his feet under his sister's table would have to go. It was time that Patrick moved on.

Joseph saw his chance of making big money for little effort, spurred on by the increasing amount of city dwellers who were buying up the local land. Places like the nearby coast were within easy reach from the city as a holiday destination and Sellicks Beach and Aldinga saw a number of holiday shacks springing up above the shore as weekend retreats. Willunga, with its history firmly rooted in the past; its annual show, its Almond Blossom Festival, its quaint old buildings, creeks and native scrubs and the nearby proximity of the McLaren Vale wineries, had begun to attract those who wished to enjoy a quieter life. With this in mind, Joseph planned to rent out the farm workers' cottages, with their uninterrupted view of the Gulf of St.Vincent, that's if you climbed up a tree. Kathleen could move back into the more modern homestead, to share with him and Maureen. His boys could take up residence in the original house that had belonged to Aubretia all those years ago.

*But first he had to tell his sister of his plans and Kathleen could be a formidable woman if challenged.*

"So what is going to happen to Patrick if you ask him to leave the homestead?" Kathleen had demanded, when Joseph had spotted her going into the dairy on her own one day. Her tone didn't bode well as she asked him and her manner was like a protective mother hen who was shielding one of her chicks. "This is the only place he's known since arriving in Australia. What has he done to deserve you saying he has to up and go?"

"Needs must Kathleen" Joseph wheedled, wishing he had asked his wife to have a word with his sister, as Kathleen could always make him feel wrong footed if he ever argued with her. "I'll give him a reference, say what a hard worker he is. After all we have to think of the future of our family. What if the boys were to find themselves wives and we've more mouths to feed at the homestead?"

"Though you won't take into account the needs of your sister. Patrick has been like a son to me and in my unmarried state, there is no possibility of me ever having children."

Joseph scoffed. "There are plenty men out here who would jump at the chance of marriage with you. Look at Frank Lucas, he's had a crush on you for years. You're too damn picky, Kathleen."

"One eyed Frankie, married twice already and I had a lucky escape the last time he asked me, before he married the poor woman who died."

"You're only thirty seven, still time to have a family and I've my mind up anyway. Patrick is going, Kathleen, whether you like it or not. I'm determined to turn our cottages over to holiday homes, there's a lot of money to be made from doing it too. You can move in with Maureen and me and that'll be the end of it."

"Then if he goes, so will I." This was his sister's parting shot as she strode out of the dairy, crashing the creaky old door behind her as she went.

❧

# Chapter Sixteen

Patrick strolled down the road from the village of Aldinga. He had spent the afternoon walking along the coastline, where the beach was thick with layers of washed up seaweed and lined with hilly dunes. He had wandered first through the nearby scrub, which had always been a source of attraction. There was a wildness about the scrub, this bush land, where dense thickets of native gums, colourful flowers and foliage, all grew in profusion amongst the grassy undergrowth. Reedy clumps invaded the swampland and the bracken. Some of it was as high as the height of a man and was home to all sorts of birds and wildlife. He would often sit there quietly, listening to the rustlings of the many little animals that called the scrubland home; the clicking sound of insects and the screeching and squawking of the green and red parakeets as they flew in and out of the trees. He imagined himself back in Killala, the place where he'd far rather be.

It had never gone away, this great desire to return to his homeland and if it hadn't have been for the fact that he was penniless, he would have jumped on a ship and gone. He knew he should be courageous, take a chance and walk to Port Adelaide, where a skipper might take him on as a deck hand and he could work his passage back home, but deep down he had to admit he was a bit of a coward. Kathleen had made his life too comfortable and he didn't want to give it up. He whistled "Danny Boy" as he loped along, hoping that the family were attending an evening service at church, so that he could end this peaceful day with more serenity. Joseph's boys liked nothing better than to egg him on to spend an evening drinking, but he would only have to ask for money from Kathleen and that was something he didn't like to do. Oh, she clothed and fed him from the pittance that Joseph paid her for her work in the dairy, but he hated to ask her for anything for himself, though he supposed that really Joseph should be paying him a bit of a wage as well. He worked the same as everyone else and was now a man of twenty two.

The almond trees were awash with blossom and Patrick looked on appreciatively as he began to pass the Aldridge groves, with his thoughts going to the forthcoming Almond Blossom Festival, a big event in the Willunga calendar, along with the local agricultural show. He was a solitary young man, hadn't really fitted in with the local boys, didn't attend the youth groups, sporting events or the village dances and couldn't be persuaded by Kathleen to attend the Wesleyan church, but he loved the carnival atmosphere of the festival, the crowds and the excitement in the air.

He felt hungry. The sea air had given him an appetite and he liked nothing better than Kathleen's Sunday roast. She would have left his dinner warming on top of a saucepan if she was attending an evening service, he could be sure of that. He heard the angry voices as he passed the homestead window. Not an unusual event, as Joseph liked to speak his mind to members of his family and Patrick felt sorry for whoever it was that was on the receiving end, but then he heard that it was Kathleen's voice that was raised and sounding anxious and if there was one thing in life that Patrick had learnt to hate, it was the woman who had taken the role of his mother being badly treated or spoken to disrespectfully. He stopped in his tracks. This wasn't the first time that this beloved woman, who worked her fingers to the bone for her brother, served on committees for the benefit of others and had taken him in and treated him like her son, had run foul of this dictatorial man.

As the years had gone by, Joseph plagued with ill health and never really getting over the trauma of serving in the Second World War and coming back a cripple, had become something of a despot.

His word was law, whether you liked it or not. Many a time Kathleen had been taken to task for not "cutting off the orphan's apron strings", but she'd been resolute; Patrick was her adopted son.

"What do you want, bog dweller?" Joseph asked nastily, when an irate looking Patrick stood before him in the parlour, where Maureen sat like a statue listening to the ranting of her husband and Kathleen was standing over by the window, staring into space. She turned when her brother used the derogatory tone, seemingly ready to commence battle again judging by the clenching of her fists and her angry countenance, when she saw it was Patrick that her brother was speaking to.

"I come to find out what all the shouting is about, Mr. Aldridge, Sir" Patrick said quietly. "I was on me way back to the cottage when I heard it."

"None of your business, lad, other than you can pack your things and get off back to where you come from. It's time that you were gone. You're a man now and it's time you weren't hanging on to my sister's petticoats."

"Joseph, that's enough. Just because you want to use our cottage for your holiday homes, doesn't mean that Patrick has to leave the farm. He's a good worker, I've heard you say so yourself. He can have a room in the homestead with me." Kathleen's tone sounded pleading, but it seemed that even belittling herself to him was of no use.

"I've made my mind up. There won't be any work for the lad once the harvest's in, only enough for my boys as it is. Martin's courting and will be bringing another mouth for us to feed once he's married, along with any children they may have. Jimmy's already having to work up at the Alma to bring some extra money in, now that he's got himself that motorbike. Maureen and me could do with taking things a bit easy and she can have the job of cleaning the cottages after the people have gone."

"Which leaves me." Kathleen had a note of sarcasm in her voice which didn't go unnoticed.

"Yes you, my spinster sister, who in the terms of me father's Will I have to look after until I die – my spinster sister who could have found a man to marry her if she hadn't been so picky, someone else to support her until her dying day."

"That's not fair. I do my share on this farm and if it wasn't for a twist of fate, I could have been the owner of Aldridge Farm *and* run it better."

"Kathleen," Patrick said, trying to rein in his own temper and keep the peace. He saw that Joseph was very red in the face after Kathleen had alluded to his return from the war, and noticed that Maureen had gone white as a sheet with the shock of all the discord. "Let's go back to the cottage and talk things over. I can pack up me things and go, if that's what Mr. Aldridge is wanting."

"Never," said Kathleen. "If you go, so do I, so put that in your pipe, brother and smoke it!" She stalked to the door, leaving Patrick not much choice but to follow. "The cheek of the man" she muttered, as she hurried along to the cottage, with Patrick trailing her closely, not sure what he should do. Perhaps it was time he put his plan in action. He couldn't stay at the farm forever, especially now that he wasn't welcome. "We'll have our tea, then we'll start our packing" Kathleen said, as she opened the cottage door and strode firmly into the kitchen, leaving Patrick open mouthed on the doorstep after hearing her words. It appeared that she really meant it.

"But Kathleen, you don't have to leave just because Joseph wants to be rid of *me*. Where would we go, what would we do for money? I'd be better off making me way alone."

"You're going nowhere on your own, Patrick. We'll travel. I've a mind to see the world before I die and don't you be worrying your head about money, I've got plenty."

"But I thought…"

"You thought I was dependent on my brother for my living. So do lots of people, but my father put money in a Trust for me, in case I didn't find a suitor. It wasn't mentioned in his Will, but I was called to the office a few weeks after the funeral and the solicitor told me. If I didn't marry by thirty five the money was mine. Of course if I'd married sooner I would have had to hand it over as a wedding settlement, but I'm thirty seven now Patrick.

Yippee! This is my chance. I can travel around the world if I want to and not be dependent on any man."

"Oh" was all Patrick could respond with, looking across at this stolid looking woman, dressed in a shabby, knitted cardigan and a loose, calf length dress, who was giggling now like a young girl as she rustled up a couple of plates to serve their meal on. It was only an hour ago that he was wishing he was back in Ireland and now it could be true, if Kathleen was willing to accompany him there. *She might have other plans.*

"Eat up, dear Patrick, this could be our last good meal for a long while," she chuckled, after she had put down a plate of roasted chicken, potatoes, lots of leafy vegetables and gravy in front of him at the table, then gone into the larder and brought out an apple pie. "What a shock he'll get in the morning when he finds us gone and no one to work in the dairy. It'll serve him right, though I can't help feeling sorry for Maureen."

"Kathleen, are you sure this is what you want to do?" Patrick poised mid meal, suddenly thinking that this was all his fault and that Joseph was right to get rid of him. After all, he'd been an orphan not a member of the family and Kathleen, a Christian woman, may have only seen his upbringing as her duty.

"You mean give up my boring life, a life of servitude to my brother and the community, when I've the chance to go places along with you? *I'm* going to think of myself as the Aldridge pioneer, an independent woman like Elizabeth Blackwell or Emily Pankhurst, a freedom fighter."

"Steady on, Kathleen" Patrick laughed, suddenly seeing this normally dour woman in a different light than he had seen in the past ten years. "You've only said you'll leave the farm. You won't be changing the world, you know."

"Ah but I'll be changing my world, Patrick and hopefully we'll be doing that together. Now what is it that *you* would like to do?"

He didn't have to plead for a job with a sea captain, rather he was treated with the utmost respect as the nephew of a lady passenger who had booked two single berth cabins on the RMS Arcadia for their voyage across to Tilbury. There had been the option of travelling across to England in an aeroplane, as after the war the Commonwealth had set up the Trans-Australia Airlines, but early planes had to refuel on a regular basis and Kathleen, initially excited by the idea of being the only person in Willunga who had flown to the other side of the world, soon realised that the cost would be prohibitive. She would have to conserve her money, for the time being anyway.

The morning of their departure had been distressing. Maureen, under the thumb of her husband, had sneaked along to the cottage after Joseph had set off to check on a sow that had just given birth to a glut of piglets. She had implored the pair to stay, especially as it was only eight weeks away from Christmas. She said that it was the war that was responsible for Joseph's quick temper; he would feel very guilty once they had gone away.

"It's my one chance in life to do something with it" Kathleen answered, enthused now by the thought of her adventure, wondering why she hadn't thought of it before. Why shouldn't a woman travel the world, see the sights that might only be dreamt of if she had stayed living her life for the benefit of others? This was providential. With Patrick being ordered to leave the homestead, there was no reason now for her to stay.

"I'll miss you, Maureen" she murmured, touched by her sister-in-law's genuine distress at her leaving. "I'll write. I'll send postcards from all the places that we go to. I promise that I'll come back to see you one day."

"You won't, I know it," Maureen said, mopping at her tears with her apron. "You'll meet a man who'll sweep you off your feet and you'll have a ruck of kids with him."

"As if," Kathleen said gaily. "But if that happens you will be the first to know. Patrick," she looked up at the young man who had been in her life and heart for the past ten years, after she had glanced at her gold watch, a present from her late father. "Can you take our bags and wait by the gate for Mr. Evans to collect us? He said he'd be here by half past when I telephoned."

"Where will you go?" Maureen sniffed, seeing her sister-in-law's determination, as Patrick set off carrying his small, fibre suitcase which he had been given at the orphanage all those years ago and a large tapestry bag that belonged to Kathleen.

"Well, first we'll go to the city and spend a few days there having a look around; buy a few clothes in Rundle Street when we have decided on our destination. Warm clothes or light clothes, the world's our oyster as they say. Oh, I'm so excited. Sorry, Maureen. I will miss you, you know."

"We'll all miss you too, Kathleen. I know that the boys have drifted a little now they're grown, got their own interests and dare I say it, Joseph can be a pig headed swine, but if you change your mind, you can come right back again. It will be easy enough to speak to you now that Joseph has put in the telephone."

"And have Annie Pilling at the telephone exchange tell everyone in the village of my whereabouts? It'll be all over Willunga that I'm going to the city today. No, I'll send you a letter if I'm on my way back home."

"God speed then, Kathleen. May He watch over you until we meet again."

Kathleen nodded in agreement, then walked away.

# Chapter Seventeen

Arriving in the city a couple of hours later, after riding in a comfortable Holden car in which Mr. Evans made a living as a taxi driver from, they took a room at the South Australian Hotel in North Terrace. It wasn't an opulent haunt of the rich, but it was adequate for their needs until Kathleen had made the necessary arrangements with the firm of Thomas Cook, once they had decided on a mutual destination of course.

Patrick was eager to return to his birthplace. A fish out of water since he had arrived in this unfamiliar country, he wanted nothing more than to feel the cool of the Irish mist on his face, see the lush and green land in and around the town of Ballina and look across on a clear bright day to the distant Oweninny Hills. Kathleen though was thinking of a holiday, somewhere exotic like Singapore. It was free to visit since the Japanese had been routed after the war and she had the rest of her life, if she wanted to, to trail around the world.

"We could toss for it" Kathleen said, as they sat on one of the beds in the hotel room that she had just paid for. "Heads we go to Ireland and tails we go to Singapore." She took out a shilling and threw it in the air and closed her eyes in anticipation as it landed on her counterpane.

"Heads" said Patrick gleefully, as he got to it first and whether he had flicked it round to his advantage, no one would ever know. "You'll like it in my homeland; it's full of history which goes back to when St. Patrick first put his foot on Irish soil. I'll show you where I used to live and the beautiful loughs and the Oweninny hills."

"I'd quite like to visit Dublin, see the Trinity College and look at that Book of Kells."

"Then you shall do" Patrick's heart felt full with nostalgia and he began to sing. "I'll take you home again, Kathleen."

The next day, after a visit to Thomas Cook where Kathleen had gleaned the information that if she was quick they could catch a ship called the *Arcadia*, which was returning to Great Britain in a few days' time, arrangements were made for an overnight train ride to Melbourne on the *Overland* from Adelaide and an essential visit to John Martin's department store. The pair returned to the hotel exhausted, laden with bags and two large suitcases in which to carry their new clothes. According to the man in the travel shop, even if they *had* opted for tourist instead of first class on their voyage across the 12,000 miles to Tilbury, there was an expected standard of apparel that must be worn; evening wear, day wear and swimwear if they wanted to use the pool that was available for the passengers. Patrick, unused to wearing anything other than his working clothes, which were mostly hand-me-downs from John's sons or homemade courtesy of Kathleen, strutted in front of the mirror like a model on a catwalk. Then Kathleen, staring at herself in the evening gown of lilac satin, decided she needed a more modern hairstyle and a bit of makeup on her face.

The city of Adelaide was a very busy place, lined with fashionable shops and cafes in a place called Rundle Street. There, a profusion of double storied verandah buildings and a long, wide street saw a multitude of cars and lorries trundling up and down. Kathleen and Patrick, only used to country ways and the one high street in Willunga, stared in wide eyed wonder on that first day, as they ventured forth onto the crowded pavements, where many creeds and foreign tongued people passed them hurriedly by. Nervous of the hustle, they chose to drink a coffee first in a small place called Kindermann's Cafe. This was a milky tasting beverage that they had never tried before.

With a couple of days to cool their feet, Kathleen decided that they would spend some time looking around the city. With five parks to visit, many churches and a beautiful cathedral to wander around, the hours sped by and it was soon time to board the *Overland*, or *Melbourne Express* as the locals called it, late one afternoon. Kathleen dressed in a light weight, calf length dress, brown, peep toe sandals, a long, brown jacket with a half belt and her newly permed hair crushed under a white, pudding basin hat, hailed a taxi to take them and their luggage from the hotel to the Adelaide Terminal. Patrick had never felt so dapper, dressed as he was in a light brown, single breasted suit with a waistcoat, a fine, white, linen shirt, brown polka dotted tie and shiny, brown lace up shoes. His hair was cut neatly into a short back and sides and he carried a three quarter length coat as well as a dark brown trilby, as his head might get hot and sweaty with the city being so warm and humid that day. His heart soared as they were driven along in the taxi. He was on his way home to Ireland and he couldn't wait to get there.

A white hull and superstructure, two masts and a yellow funnel with a red ringed top and boasting seven passenger decks, the ship met their gaze as they stood on Station Pier, looking up in awe at the *RMS Arcadia*. Built by the John Brown shipyard in Clydebank in 1953, she was on her way back to Tilbury after a three month voyage.

After a good night's sleep in a roomette, a single sleeper that Kathleen had booked for each of them aboard the mauve liveried compartment train to Melbourne which was pulled by a steam engine from Adelaide, they were looking forward to embarkation. It would be a relaxing sea voyage and, according to the brochure that the travel shop had given Kathleen, there would be lots to see and do on board and exotic places to visit on the way.

Kathleen had paid for a single cabin apiece on C Deck. Both had a bunk bed, a chest of drawers, a small table with a chair placed underneath, a wash basin with an overhead cabinet and a porthole to look out onto the ocean. At £120 per passenger, some might have thought it was a costly expense, but Kathleen, ever mindful that this might be a trip of a lifetime, didn't want to share her cabin with anyone.

Once aboard and after having their papers checked by an official, they were shown to their quarters by a pleasant mannered steward who was rewarded with a tip from Kathleen. Their luggage stowed and with a quick wash to freshen up for each of them, they made their way up the many steps to take a look at the public rooms. The tourist class dining saloon, which was separated from the first class dining saloon by the galley; souvenir shops where dolls, ashtrays, silver spoons all with the ship's emblem engraved upon them and toiletries and knick knacks could be purchased; a library with a quiet room; a swimming pool, a cinema and places for entertainment were all discovered that afternoon.

It was when they were passing the souvenir shop that Patrick noticed a girl amongst the flurry of a group of young, fluttery beings who walked in front of them, reminding him of the Silkie chickens that he had looked after at Aldridge Farm. Most of the girls had fair or golden hair but this one stood out amongst them with her dark brown tresses and beautiful, deep blue eyes. Judging by the clothes the girls were wearing – shorts, lightweight blouses and plimsolls, they were on their way to check out the sporting facilities on board. She smiled at Patrick as she passed him, showing off pearly, white teeth and dimples. There was something in her eyes that he recognised. Whatever it was, a shifting in some unconscious memory perhaps, was lost as Kathleen asked him if he would like to take a walk upon the upper deck.

"Is this seat taken?" asked a man who appeared to be in his late forties, judging by his weather beaten face, the white streaks in his once dark hair and his paunch.

"It appears that there are not enough deck chairs to go around for all of us, so I hope you don't mind."

"Not at all, join us. My nephew and I were just saying that everyone's taking advantage of the sunshine, before the anchor is lifted and we set off on our journey." Kathleen smiled up at the man and liked his sad but kind eyes.

"Harold Cooper." The man shook Kathleen's hand, then sat beside her.

"Kathleen Aldridge and this is my nephew Patrick," Kathleen replied.

"How do you do, Patrick." Harold stretched across to where Patrick was leaning over to shake the stranger's hand. As Harold did so Kathleen could feel his breath on her face, which caused her to shiver in the warmth of the sun. "So, Tilbury. Far to go to your destination when we get there? Oh, sorry, I don't mean to be nosey, we've only just met and I'm being rather forward."

"No, no, don't worry." Kathleen liked the way his face suddenly flushed, obviously embarrassed at asking his question when they had only just met. His accent too was rather charming, easy on the ears for listening to.

"So that isn't an Australian accent I hear? You're from England if I'm not mistaken." Kathleen tried to change the subject, understanding his discomfort.

"Lincolnshire, on the east coast of England. I've been working with a cousin. We have a small building company in Melbourne, but my parents, back in Blighty, are elderly and so I felt the need to visit them again."

"Ah" said Kathleen, ready to continue the conversation by saying that *her* family had come across from Lincolnshire all those years ago, when William and Aubretia had set sail for the colonies, but it seemed that Harold had said enough and was anxious to leave her.

"Oh, is that the time?" He glanced at his wristwatch and just after he said it, the ship's horn started booming. It was time for the crew to mobilise and any visitors to go ashore. "I must dash. Perhaps I'll see you at dinner." With that he was gone, leaving her wondering if she had said something wrong.

"Come on Kathleen, let's watch the ship set off." Patrick got up from his deckchair, looking forward to the excitement of it all.

Once out into the calm waters of Port Phillip Bay, it was time to dress for dinner and head along to the dining saloon, where they were shown to their table of eight by the maitre d'. He was a pleasant faced man, who looked as though he hailed from one of the Pacific Islands. He was smartly dressed for the occasion with a winged collar, dicky bow tie and black evening clothes. Their companions, four elegantly dressed older ladies and two well-groomed elderly gentlemen were quiet at first, until after their bottle of wine had been poured and sipped and pronounced palatable. Kathleen ordered a glass of juice and a glass of beer for Patrick. It seemed from their companions' muted conversation that they had embarked at Sydney and had already settled in.

Kathleen pulled up her white, spindle-backed, leather upholstered chair a little more, as their waiter, a fresh faced young man with a ready smile, handed out the menus decorated with acanthus leaves. The Corinthian themed murals on the walls, which had been painted by various artists on commission were the theme for the menu's illustration.

"What are you having, Patrick?" Kathleen asked in a subdued voice, glad she hadn't come alone, as up to now, no one had acknowledged their presence, which she thought was rather impolite of them, though she supposed she could have introduced herself and Patrick if she had thought about it.

"The lamb, no starter. I can imagine if we eat too much each day we'll be fat as pigs when we get there."

He glowered over to the women who were ordering soup or a selection of *knackwurst,* salami and *mortadella*, fillet steak with onions and fried potatoes or a rump steak. All were wearing dresses that accentuated their plumpness and Patrick wondered whether they would fit into them at all at the end of their voyage.

"I'll have the same, no starter, but I must have some of that pavlova later which is over there on the dessert trolley. I have only ever seen it in a magazine." Patrick smiled indulgently, Kathleen had always had a sweet tooth.

His ears were drawn to the sound of high pitched giggles from the foyer outside, as the group of girls who had earlier passed them by, presented themselves to claim their reservation, as it was a two sitting dining system there. They swarmed into the saloon, following the maitre d' who was smiling with good humour, as the girls all dressed in the latest fashion of many layered petticoats under a calf length dress with a nipped in waist, pulled his leg at his assumed pomposity.

All of them wore court shoes and had piled their hair up into fashionable *chignons*, except the girl who had caught Patrick's eye and if he had to be honest, had been in his thoughts since spotting her. How that had happened he couldn't be sure, as he had never been attracted to any girl since reaching puberty and had shunned the offer of introduction to a local girl by one of Joseph's sons. Perhaps he was shy or perhaps he instinctively didn't want the complication of finding a wife so early and settling down.

"Patrick." Kathleen shook his arm, just as the girl glanced over and caught his eye. "Patrick, do you want fried potatoes with the lamb or boiled? The waitress has asked you that question two times?" He watched as the six young women were joined later by a couple of fellows around their own age and felt a twinge of jealousy, as he wished he was sitting there too.

The Orpheus Room was full. Each table that surrounded the polished floor of the entertainment area was occupied and Kathleen and Patrick had scanned the daily newsletter that the ship provided for the pleasure of their passengers decided on watching a variety show. There were just about to leave to look for their second option, which was to watch a cowboy film in the cinema.

"Kathleen, over here." They heard a voice nearby and to their surprise it was Harold Cooper, whom they had met on the upper deck that afternoon smartly dressed in evening clothes.

"A favour for a favour" he said smiling amiably, as he stood to attention beside a small round table that was surrounded by four spindle back chairs.

"Oh, thank you" replied Kathleen, suddenly feeling a bit shy now that a man was making an effort to be in her company. "I looked for you at dinner but I couldn't see you anywhere."

"I was there" said Harold, frowning as he pulled out a chair for her in a gentlemanly fashion and gestured to Patrick to sit next to her. "I like the way they have a Greek theme throughout the interior, Olympus or Mount Olympus, a heavenly abode for the Greek gods."

It was then that Kathleen realised that Harold was a first class passenger, as the theme in their dining room was Corinthian. She felt uncomfortable. He must be loaded to have booked First Class. *Why had he invited them to sit at his table?* There must be plenty of other nobs that could join him instead. She hated ostentation and deplored the fact that class and status still existed in Australia, though not as much as it had before the war. She saw that Patrick felt the same, as he had raised an eyebrow in response to hers.

Too late, the entertainment had begun. A small band started to play the theme tune from *Cafe Continental* and a scantily clad show girl began to dance.

"What can I order for you?" Harold asked, when during the interval, a waiter came to ask them what they would like to drink.

"Nothing for me" replied Kathleen, wondering if it would be rude of her to make up an excuse so that she and Patrick could make tracks to the exit.

"I'll have a beer" Patrick replied, knowing that Kathleen felt that she had been deceived and didn't want to rub shoulders with Harold, but he was hoping to catch another glimpse of the dark haired girl.

"Kathleen, do let me order you a drink" Harold implored. "Perhaps I could order a bottle of something that we could share."

"A bottle of champagne, Sir?" asked the waiter, anxious to be off as the bloke was dithering. He only had ten minutes of interval time to serve his side of the room. "Yes, a bottle of champers, just the ticket. Forget the beer, Patrick, you can help us drink the champagne too."

After a turn by a banjo player, a comic and a singing duo, the band leader invited his audience to take to the floor. Harold, spotting his chance, asked a reluctant Kathleen to take a waltz with him and one glass of champagne seemed to have loosened her reserve towards him, they danced to the strains of "When I Fall In Love" by Nat King Cole.

"Hi there, how's it going?" She was standing by his table, her eyes sparkling with mischief at her daring and his disbelief as he saw her there. "Care to jitterbug?" *A jitterbug? What was a jitterbug?* Patrick hadn't heard that the rhythm of the music from the band had changed.

"*I'll* show you, it's like rock n' roll, just follow what I do."

She dragged Patrick by the hand, until they found a spot near to where the band was playing "Rock Around The Clock". Ignoring his protests about how he hadn't got a clue of how to dance to modern music, she told him to stand close by and watch her. It was easy, nothing to it, just tap his foot to the music and she'd show him what to do. Quickly she pushed off her hand from his hand, drifting back from him in a zigzag motion and then walking back to him again, where she took his hand and guided him through a swing move.

"See, it's easy" she shouted, although Patrick stumbled against her when she went to go under the arch that he had made with his arm.

"Sorted" she said, as the band finished playing and out of breath, they ran back to where Kathleen was sitting watching in amusement. "He'll make a dancer yet" she said, smiling triumphantly, then left them as she walked back to her friends.

♣

# Chapter Eighteen

It appeared that the young lady was having too much fun on her travels to be bothered with a gauche Patrick, whose eyes searched for her every day from breakfast to dinner hoping for a smile or a word. Kathleen sensed that her adopted son may have fallen in love, at least perhaps he thought he had, but he was far too young at twenty two, in her opinion, to be getting a permanent girlfriend or a shipboard romance. She tried to keep him occupied.

She involved him in the time that she had begun to spend with Harold, who was very attentive to both of them, seemingly uninterested in pursuing one of the pretentious, diamond jewellery clad first class female passengers who could be heard issuing their orders from the comfort of their privileged first class club. He had demoted himself to eating in tourist class with Kathleen and Patrick, insisting that maitre d' provide them with a table just for the three of them, though he hadn't given up his luxuriously appointed cabin on A Deck. Hours were whiled away learning to play whist, baccarat, quoits and attending lectures on marine life, mountaineering and the history surrounding the lands that they would be passing by. It was a pleasant way to spend their days, made even better by the mild temperatures as the ship cruised along the Southern Ocean on its way to Fremantle. Already tanned by the unrelenting sun, which Patrick had endured through his teenage years whilst working at the Aldridges', he had no inclination towards lying on one of the wooden deckchairs as most did, preferring instead to gaze into the distance to the horizon, imagining his joy when he saw the land of his forebears once more. It was little wonder when a hearty slap on his shoulder caused him to jump in alarm, shaking him from his reverie.

"Penny for them." The girl was standing beside him, grinning from ear as she saw his stunned face after he had looked towards her. "I said penny for them. My, you were lost in your own little world for a minute, weren't you? I'm Mel by the way, pleased to meet yer. How's it going?"

"Er, I'm Patrick Mayo." He stuttered a little as he shook her outstretched hand, wondering why she had singled him out to talk to when her friends, both male and female, were lying about on chairs along the deck. Not only that, she was wearing a navy blue, one piece swimming costume which showed off her ample figure and long, tanned legs. He decided to look instead into her beautiful eyes, the colour of cornflowers and fringed with dark lashes, rather than stare at her attributes like a slobbering idiot, which was how he was feeling just then.

"You should come and join us" she said, waving her hand towards her group, where one or two of the other similarly clad girls were regarding him with interest. "We're all taking a gap year. Well me and Sue are, the others have fathers with fat wallets who are paying for their sabbaticals. Me and Sue are doing Europe, but we'll have to sing for our suppers on the way."

Patrick nodded. It was all he could do at that moment, he was so tongue tied. Never having been used to a girl starting a conversation, especially one who had introduced herself so forwardly, he was at a loss to know to react to her.

"Cat got your tongue?" She grinned again and in that instant he didn't want the moment to ever end. It was like the time when he had stood in line with the other orphans in the community hall, anxiously waiting to see if he was chosen by someone who looked to be kind and Kathleen had taken him by the hand and led him away to warmth and security. This was something he hadn't felt, as a child without parents, for a long, long time.

"No" he said haltingly, staring across with dread at the bright young things, who had probably never put in a hard day's work as he had, knowing that he would never fit in with that circle in a million years. "I promised my aunt I would accompany her to a lecture on the history of Fremantle, she likes that sort of thing."

"Poor you. Well never mind, perhaps we can meet up later. G'day to you, Patrick, you'd better go and join her then."

He watched as she turned away. Signaling a passing waiter to get her a lemonade, she joined her carefree friends.

Meantime, Kathleen was sitting with Harold in a small corner that was reserved for taking afternoon tea or whiling away a few hours in the sunshine. She had begun to warm to Harold, who always seemed to be hovering, seemingly wanting to give her his attention at every opportunity. He had explained to her, in a moment of brutal honesty, that it had been his daughter who had purchased the first class ticket on his behalf, after receiving a letter from his sister in Lincolnshire, telling him that his elderly parents were losing their hold on life and that if he wanted to ever see them again it would be wise to make the journey home.

"I went into a bit of a tizz when I read her letter" he had explained. "You never think that the day will come when you'll be one of the older generation. They were always in their sixties in my mind – active, spritely, well able to run the farm at Nethercote without much help. They would always be there to give me a home if my money and luck ran out." It had been the mention of the farm that had sparked Kathleen's curiosity, why would he have left it to make a new life in Australia? He soon supplied her with an answer.

"It was after the war. I did my time, dodged the bullets, killed a few *Jerries*, then returned to "Civvy Street" to find that our land was certainly not fit for heroes. All I had was sixty pounds and a demob suit to show for my pains. I had a wife and two growing children and one day the wife said she thought it would be a good idea if we took up the government's offer of a ten pound passage to Australia. There'd be work and accommodation guaranteed and the children could grow up in the sunshine. My parents, though upset, didn't want to stand in my way and they would always have the support of my younger sister anyway. She lives in the same row of cottages as we had, with her husband and two sons. So off we went and I met up with a cousin in Melbourne and we set up a business together. We did rather well, even if I do say it myself."

It appeared then that he felt he'd said enough, as his eyes misted over and Kathleen could sense that he was reluctant to tell her more. He urged her instead to tell him her story and listened as she told him there wasn't much to tell. A spinster with the care of an orphan, she had worked all her life on her brother's farm. She was treating herself and Patrick to a trip around Europe, but that was as far as she had got with her plan.

"Certainly not a wasted life and one to be commended, doing things for others. I remember when Joan, that was my wife, I remember when she had wanted to adopt a little orphan. Just as well we didn't in the long run. Can I get you another beverage, dear lady, or perhaps an orange juice to take your thirst away?"

"Fremantle in Western Australia" the speaker boomed to her audience of interested people, who had gathered in one of the public rooms for a talk on the history of their first port of call.

"The settlement began in April 1829, when the *H.M.S. Challenger* arrived in the waters of the Western Australian coast at the mouth of the Swan River. Captain Fremantle formally took possession of the lands, previously known as "New Holland", on behalf of King George 1V of England. Later, a Captain James Stirling arrived from England to begin the Swan River Colony of Perth. With him came 400 free settlers, including, a harbour master, surgeon, bricklayer, blacksmith and a boat builder, their wives and over twenty children."

The woman paused for breath and took a sip from a glass of water that had been placed on a nearby table. She saw that she had the peoples' full attention and gave out a little sigh.

"By 1832, 1500 people had settled there, but they found that the land was hard to cultivate as the vegetation was tough to clear and the soil was poor and sandy. Times were hard and in the

Depression of 1843, many people decided to leave to try their luck in the gold fields of Victoria. Man power was badly needed to build vital communications, transport and an administration framework if Fremantle was to survive, so the Secretary of State for the Colonies back in Great Britain, sent out a gang of convicts solely employed for this public work.

As you can imagine, the free settlers were rather aghast when they heard the news, but the convicts kept on coming and by 1868 over 9,000 had arrived. Luckily, all were men who had nearly completed their existing sentences and were more than willing to finish their punishments there. You can see the products of their labours when we anchor in the harbour just off Rottnest Island, as the colonial building named the Round House, the Boys School and the Lunatic Asylum are still standing to this day. Any questions so far? Can you hear me at the back? Young lady, you seem to be showing a profound lack of interest in what I am saying to the other members of the audience. Perhaps you and your friends would like to find another venue where you can chat amongst yourselves."

"Is that the young girl who got you up to dance the other evening, Patrick?" Kathleen asked in a disapproving voice, when all heads turned to see who was causing a distraction. Patrick nodded. Her presence had surprised and discomforted him. She and her friends didn't seem the type to enjoy a lecture on history, so he hoped that they hadn't come along in an effort to embarrass him. He felt relieved, when taking note of the authoritarian voice that the woman had begun to use in an attempt to restore order, and with the possibility that she could have had them ejected anyway, the group moved on, laughing and joking as they went.

"So to continue. The economy of Fremantle was based on wheat, meat and wool and in order to market their goods, the railway line from Perth was built in 1881. In 1887 there was the erection of gas lamps on the main thoroughfares and the telephone exchange in 1888. By 1890 there was a water supply to all the town's dwellings and public buildings and by 1897 there was a hospital. Then in the 1890's, Fremantle had its own gold rush. This brought a surge of immigrants to the area, which in its turn brought an increase in agricultural output and created new businesses. Stylish buildings such as the Esplanade Hotel sprang up, which attracted the rich and wealthy. And to finish my lecture, which I hope you have enjoyed, even with our earlier interruption, in World War Two, Fremantle had the largest submarine base in the Southern hemisphere, quite a feather in the cap for those employed there."

"And I say amen to that" said Harold, as the three of them wandered out of the room to settle on some chairs from where they could order drinks from the waiter. "It helped to win the war against those pesky *Japs*, who thought that they could rule the world just like Hitler tried to do, but we showed them. Once the *Yanks* came in they never stood a chance and the world is all the better for it."

*Except I don't have my parents,* thought Patrick, feeling bereft as a pang of longing for those two people that had given him life struck him, knowing that they wouldn't be there when he got back home to Ireland.

"So, dear lady, any thoughts of what you would like to do when we get to Fremantle? Patrick? If it is not too presumptuous I could show you both around Perth. It is only twelve miles away from the port and can be reached by rail, or we could hire a taxi. Fremantle of course, has fine buildings and plenty of history as the lecturer has just informed us, but perhaps you would like to venture further afield."

"Well" Kathleen was at a loss as she listened to his invitation. She was tempted to seek his company, but what if it lead to something – well perish the thought, more than she expected from this voyage of independence with Patrick? Friendship, romance – he was still good looking in a rough diamond sort of way. But didn't he have a wife, or hadn't he had a wife? Hadn't he said that it had been his wife's idea to move to Australia?

"You go, Kathleen. I'm not bothered about trailing around

places that I don't really want to see. I'm happy to stay on board and perhaps have a look around the library. I keep meaning to see if they've anything on Ireland, even a map to consider would be just the thing." Patrick didn't want to be a gooseberry.

"If you are sure." Kathleen's heart leapt a little at the thought that just for once, on the arm of a man like Harold, she could indulge in a little role play, pretend that she had a husband for the day.

"I'm sure. Now let's get ready for dinner, I'm starving."

It was eight o' clock in the morning when the ship tied up alongside the wharves and warehouses of the Long Jetty. "When in Perth Shop at Borns" shouted one large sign on the side of a commercial building. "Welcome to Australia From Fortuna Fabrics" said another. The dockside was awash with humanity. Trucks, trolleys, cars, dockworkers, sailors and officials dressed in navy suits, all could be seen below by Patrick, as after breakfast he watched Kathleen and Harold descend down the gangway to the pier. It was warm already and he felt glad that he'd decided to stay aboard, rather than go sightseeing. What did he care about how Perth was built, its economy and if it had been a free or a convict settlement? His only wish was to tread the soil of his beloved Ireland and learn of the trials and tribulations of his own country's history. He waved as the couple turned to look back upon the *Arcadia*, then reddened as he saw that the girl named Mel was waving up at him too.

As the ship nosed its way through the calm waters of the Indian Ocean, its next of port being Ceylon, many passengers took advantage of the sporting activities on board and the less agile drifted along throughout their days. Kathleen and Harold, finding themselves to be kindred spirits when it came to all matters appertaining to the various card games that were on offer, spent many hours in each other's company, leaving Patrick at a bit of a loss about what to do with his time. He had read most of the books that the library had on Irish history, could probably walk blindfolded across from Dun Lagaore, to Ballina, having studied most of the maps that they'd had on offer and was finding it hard to fill up the hours until another day was over and it was bedtime. As for the girl who might have invaded his dreams, had she been shy and less juvenile than she appeared to be when walking around with her peers on the vessel, he had hardly caught sight of her, because he avoided the places where he thought that she might be. Dancing had no appeal, an occasional pint of Guinness was enough to satisfy and as he had never indulged in any recreation that involved a ball, other than the odd kick-about with the Aldridge boys, his time was spent moping about or watching films at the ship's cinema. Decked out in classic Greek style architecture with plaster gods and goddesses, and the installation of a big screen that had opening and closing curtains, Patrick became enthralled by "The Rats of Tobruk" starring Peter Finch and a colour film called "Jedda", a story which starred an aboriginal girl in the Northern Territories.

Then one morning, not far off Ceylon, which was the next port of call after sailing from Fremantle ten days before, Mel was sitting alone in the refreshment area, sipping an iced tea from a long, frosted glass and staring into the distance. Patrick dithered. She was sitting in the same spot that he liked to sit each morning whilst he waited for Kathleen to come and join him after they had breakfasted. He tutted. Now he would have to hang around outside Kathleen's cabin, until she had finished her ablutions and changed into her day dress. There was no way he wanted to be in this kind of girl's company and to have to endure her cheerful conversation of all things. He turned to walk away, but it was too late, as sometimes fate decrees a happening – the girl had seen him and waved across for him to join her and it would have been churlish not to have done.

♣

# Chapter Nineteen

She was wearing a long, pale, pink cotton wrap, the type of garment that most women on the vessel wore to cover up their swimwear. He saw that it was so as he joined her at the table, as the heat of the morning had made her figure visible through the thinness of the material. It caused Patrick to concentrate on the blueness of her eyes again.

"Going to the equator party?" she asked in a nonchalant manner, as if she was continuing a former conversation. She smiled at him engagingly, which made him want to hold that moment in his heart.

"I hadn't planned to" Patrick said hesitantly. "It's not something I would enjoy. I've heard it's all about getting drunk and being thrown into the swimming pool. I don't swim that well."

"Oh, you'll love it. Tell you what, if I promise to come to the rescue if someone tries to drown you, will you sit at a table with me? My friend Sue, who I share a cabin with on Deck C, has got herself a boyfriend – one of the crewmen would you believe. That's why I'm sitting here on my own. And to be honest, I'm getting heartily sick of some of the boys in our party; I could do with some decent company."

"I don't know, I'll have to see what my aunt and Harold want to do this evening."

"Are you all joined at the hip?" She looked at him, frowning slightly. "Surely you're allowed off the tether now and again. Talk to me, will you Patrick? You always look as if you're ready for the off."

"Kathleen has done a lot for me. I can't very well abandon her when she's paid for my trip to Europe."

"Well, she doesn't look abandoned to me. Look over there – she's on the arm of the person I've heard you call Harold."

Indeed she was. Kathleen was walking along the deck, her head thrown back as she laughed at something that Harold was saying.

"So, no excuses, sit with me and I'll tell you a bit about myself and then you can tell me a little about you."

It transpired that Mel was the daughter of a man who had a small winery in the Barossa. The eldest of five children, she was taking a gap year before commencing her studies into European history at the University of South Australia.

"Long term I would like to become a lecturer on the subject, but for the moment I would like to put names to the places that I'll hopefully see."

"Such as?" Patrick felt buoyed as he listened to her dreams and aspirations. He was relieved that she wasn't a silly young woman with cotton wool in her brain.

"Well, seeing that my ancestors come from Southern Ireland – my Dad had found out that he's third generation Irish by the way and so he gave us kids Irish sounding names, mine's really Maolisa – I thought I would make a start with Dublin. I've read a remarkable book that tells of the turbulence of Irish history via a storyteller and that, combined with tales told to me by my dad when I was a youngster, has been enough to make me want to investigate my roots. Then maybe I'll take a trip across to Paris; my mother is descended from French nobility. Think chateau in the eighteenth century and the name Molyneux. She's always ragging my father. She says that if his wines are fruity little numbers, it's her influence."

"Oh." Patrick felt embarrassed as he heard her speaking about her mother in that way, though he was heartened to hear that Mel was from Southern Ireland. It might even make them related if they were to go back into the eons of time. "And whereabouts in Ireland does your father's family come from, do you know?"

"I believe they were from Galway. At least an aunt who lives in London and is interested in the tracing of our ancestors believes so. She made a trip to the area in 1953, visited a few Catholic graveyards, found a few "Devines", "Devaney's" and "Devereux" and decided that we were descended from stonemasons who worked on the little cottages round about. One of them, whose name was Cornelius Devaney, made the trek from Galway across to a place called Westport in the 1830s, but then unfortunately the trail went cold. His wife was called Moirin and they had three sons and that was as far as my Aunt Edna got with it. She thinks that the family probably emigrated to Australia during the famine years."

All this time, Patrick's mind was a jumble of astonishment, hopefulness and a yearning that this girl would never disappear from his life. He saw them settled down and raising a family, he would work on a local farm and love her forever more. Then his spirits sank, as this vision quickly passed and he realised that she would want to follow her dreams of becoming a lecturer and living in a place full of sunshine, not settle in a wet and misty land.

"And from the lilt you have in your voice Patrick, I'd say you were also from the old country."

Mel's beautiful eyes stared into his keenly as she waited for him to tell her of his own ancestry. He nodded, loathe to pick at the wounds that he carried within his heart.

"Not more than a generation though, didn't come over on a leaky old ship like my forebears had to do."

Then suddenly, there he was, beginning to tell her his tale. He couldn't stop himself. He wanted her to know of his pain and anguish, about the country that he'd had to leave behind because of a priest's stuffed shirt morality and how he had lost his parents in a stupid war, which being Irish, they hadn't even wanted to be a part of. He found that he was shaking; his body, his limbs, even his face was as the tears ran down his cheeks, as he recalled that night when he had lain injured amongst the rubble of the house, after it had collapsed upon the three of them. The terror he had felt as he heard the screech from another bomb nearby and the following explosion, the groan of the next door building as it tore from its footings and crashed into the road. His desperation and grief stricken heartbreak when the man who had lifted him from the ruins, had told him gently that his parents hadn't survived the blast and carried him to hospital through the devastated streets.

Suddenly embarrassed, as he noticed the look of concern from a fellow passenger who was sitting on a nearby table, he rejected the hand that Mel held out to him in sympathy, got to his feet and rushed away.

"Hi". She was hunkered down on the wooden deck outside the gentlemens' toilet, where Patrick had dashed when the embarrassment of the occasion had caused him to hide his unmanly tears.

"Sorry, I'm not usually a blubberer…"

Smiling gently, she got to her feet and linked her arm through his. "Let's walk around the ship a bit. Let's have a look at that island in the distance that they call Indonesia. You know, dear Patrick, that we may never pass this way again."

It was a magical time for the two of them, a shipboard romance with all the trimmings. The stars shone brightly, evenings were spent together staring at the golden moon as the vessel continued on across the ocean to Sri Lanka. Two young people who began to share their hopes and dreams. Gone was her frivolity of youth, as Mel began to spurn the company of the girls with whom she shared a cabin and the arrogant boys who made up their group, as she sought Patrick's company instead. She even managed to get him to the King Neptune party, which celebrated the crossing of the middle of the world. It was a fun night, with the female entertainment staff dressed as mermaids and a giant plaster model of the Ancient Ruler of the Seas. There was diving for treats, races to be the first one to get to the finishing line with a borrowed item, forfeits which involved a lot of merriment and a lot of riotous dunking of people who had never crossed the equator before.

Kathleen, becoming increasingly worried when she saw that Patrick was becoming involved with a most unsuitable girl, who in her eyes was a "flibbertigibbert" and not the kind of person he should be friends with, tried to keep him close, as Patrick, having never been used to mixing with the youth of Willunga, preferring to shun most of the social life such as drinking in the local pubs or dancing at the assembly rooms, was not used to flippancy or sometimes thoughtless adolescent ways. Harold, now a daily presence in her life, advised her to loosen her apron strings.

On this particular night, as the ship drifted along towards the port of Columbo, most passengers having made their way to their beds, with just a group of young men making a racket by the swimming pool, Patrick and Mel, both still dressed in their swimwear as it was a balmy night, held hands in the shadows as they lay side by side on two wooden chairs. Kathleen and Harold had been to a lecture that day, this time on the history of Ceylon, now named Sri Lanka and the ship, needing to top up on fuel and provisions would be anchored along the wharf for a short time the next morning and the passengers would be allowed to disembark.

"Kathleen said they're going to have a look around St. Paul's Church first, then visit a couple of old colonial buildings. They suggested that we might like to walk along the Galle Face Green promenade together. She told me that it is at the side of the Mount Lavinia beach and lined with palm trees."

"Hmm – romantic, didn't know she cared." Mel purred with contentment.

Patrick stroked her hand, feeling relaxed after drinking a few dark beers.

"She's getting used to me and you. Don't forget I've been a big part of her life for the past ten years. Anyway, she was telling me that the British took over Ceylon from the Portuguese in 1848, something to do with swelling their empire at the instruction of their then Queen Victoria. It would have been the usual thing, forcing their religious beliefs on them, governing with prejudice and injustice, just like they did when they gave our land to the English lords centuries ago."

"You sound bitter."

"I blame the British for the Catholic evictions and the loss of our traditions and our Irish law. My dad told me of the struggles, the famines, when even then Ireland was exporting grain to England and our people were dying in their thousands on the roadside. Then there was the Easter Rising in Dublin. According to my dad, his father got caught up in a skirmish and was sent to the city's jail. My grandad, who I can't remember well as I was a small child when he went to Heaven, was supposed to have shouted as they lead him away in manacles. *Beidh la eile ag an bPaorach.* "We will live to fight another day". I miss them, Mel – even now I miss my mother who would sit me on her knee and sing old Irish lullabies and Dad would say a prayer or two as I settled down in my bed. He took me shooting for rabbits, fishing for salmon in the River Moy and my mother's cooking was – well she was a dab hand at cooking. She made everything taste delicious, especially her rabbit stew. Sometimes me, Billy and Brendan Hanley would splash buck naked in the "Giant's Tub" nearby."

Mel leant over and was about to kiss poor Patrick on the cheek in sympathy, but shrieked when she saw what was about to happen, as two men came out of the shadows and began to lay about him.

"Another bloke trying ter pinch one of our girls, eh Paddy? Get him Rick, let's throw the bog trotter in the water and see if he sinks or swims!"

He was hurled off the chair by the two young men who had crept up behind them, whilst Patrick had been engrossed in his memories. He struggled to be free as they dragged him by his arms to the side of the nearby swimming pool, where he slipped on a puddle as they let him go. The last voice he heard was Mel's. She stood there screaming, as his head went down upon the concrete trim.

*The little girl who still hadn't gone into the spirit world, still hadn't laid her troubled thoughts to rest, watched as the boy who was to take her back to her homeland, back across the oceans to her own kith and kin, lay on the floor below her with his forehead bleeding. He was there to take her back to the green fields of her hamlet, the sparkling river that ran down the side of the hill and to the little church which overlooked the crashing waves of the sea. Would she meet her beloved sister, either in her native Killala or in the spirit world of the dead?*

He groaned, as through the mist that swirled above him he saw a little, dark haired girl who was dressed in a long, white dress and frowning down at him from a pair of cornflower eyes.

"Patrick, Patrick, thank God you're still alive." He heard someone shouting and he saw that it was Mel who was frowning down at him, the girl he had begun to love.

# ♣ Chapter Twenty

Columbo, was the political capital of Sri Lanka, with its large harbour in a strategic position along the East West trade route, the Jami Ul-Alfar Mosque, a recognised landmark for sailors as they approached the port and the Old Columbo lighthouse to guide the ships in. It had been independent from the British since 1948. Here at this busy port, where the *SLNS Rangalla* formed the Sri Lankan Naval Base, containers lined the dockside, where a ferry liner could be caught to take passengers just across the Gulf of Mannar to Tuticoran on mainland India, or ride on a coastal train to Galle and Matara and where auto rickshaws waited for the passengers of the *Arcadia* to disembark.

It had been the sick bay for Patrick and the "brig" for his two tormentors. Kathleen, summoned by the commotion from where she was having a nightcap with Harold, had demanded to see the captain, insisting that the two young men were put off the ship at Columbo as their punishment. Nursing a sore head where a piece of a broken glass that hadn't been swept up at the King Neptune party had caused a gash which needed stitching, Patrick went in and out of wakefulness. He dreamt he was lying on a beach in Aldinga, with the rippling sound of the tide nearby bringing pleasure to his ears. He felt free from pain. He was comfortable; nothing mattered at that time. The little girl whom he remembered seeing before he had regained consciousness, was standing on the sand dunes and when he waved she disappeared, leaving him to wonder who she was.

He saw Kathleen, as she sat by his bedside, bemoaning his meeting with the girl called Mel – it was her fault that he had been set upon. Of Mel there was no sign, no doubt having been warned off by Patrick's "aunty", but he found he still dreamt about her. She was standing by the "Giant's Tub", near the cottages, watching two small children as they splashed about in the river below.

After the *Arcadia* had weighed anchor, cruising into the Arabian Ocean on its way to the Gulf of Aden, Patrick who had been given the all clear by the surgeon once the glass had been removed and the wound sewn up with a couple of stitches, lay quietly besides Kathleen and Harold in a deck chair, as a couple of recent painkillers he had swallowed began to take its hold.

With Kathleen feeling unable to leave Patrick's bedside whilst the ship had been berthed at Columbo, it had been down to Harold to disembark and report back on the sightseeing that he had done on her behalf. There was a description of the church and the national museum that held many local artefacts and he had even managed to take a walk along the promenade where happy children flew their kites. Patrick lay half listening, feeling down because his hopes of a romantic stroll with Mel had been dashed by the bullies who'd been marched away by two burly crewmen. The next morning, after giving the young men a warning of what would happen if they got into trouble again, and the order to apologise to their injured victim, the captain had set them free from their captivity.

"So, I was thinking. When –" Kathleen stopped mid sentence, as the person who was standing above her, blocked out the afternoon sun. "What do *you* want, young lady? Don't you think you've caused enough trouble because of the behaviour of your male followers?"

"Kathleen, that isn't fair" Patrick protested, his heart beginning to beat quickly as he saw who was standing there. She was wearing a white, short, puffed sleeve blouse and a dark blue, dirndl skirt and her eyes were downcast as she acknowledged her blame. "Mel didn't know that they were going to pounce on me, did you Mel? Come here and share my chair."

"Let's go and get a coffee, Kathleen" said Harold, seeing that Kathleen's feathers were becoming rather ruffled as she tried to shelter her chick. "Leave the young ones to sort things out." He looked at his wristwatch. "Ooops and it's nearly time to dress for dinner."

Kathleen walked straight backed as she followed Harold, but declined to comment either way, though she knew deep down that she had lost the fight of keeping Patrick close to her. She had to remember he was now a man of twenty two.

"I'm sorry Patrick, I should have seen it coming. The guys were jealous because Sue had begun seeing this bloke who works in the engine room, another of our group got chatting to one of the waiters and then when they saw us doing a spot of canoodling, they thought they would teach you a lesson. It was the drink of course, none of them are used to it, nor being let off the leash by their parents and being responsible for themselves. They said they'd come over and apologise if you'll let them." She put her hand out and touched his cheek, looking closely at the padding that the surgeon had covered the wound and the bruising with. "Does it hurt much? Thank God you didn't have far to fall with them still having a bit of a hold on you. Oh Patrick, I couldn't sleep last night for worrying and your aunty was like a sentry on the door when I asked could I see you this morning."

"That's Kathleen for you, ever the mother hen." Patrick smiled wryly, as he acknowledged her concern for him. "It's because she loves me, doesn't want anyone else to have a look in."

"I know, but she has to let go of you some time, you're not a little child anymore. I say, why don't you see if she will let me join you for dinner and perhaps we can start over again?"

Thoughts were being directed towards the coming Christmas celebrations, which according to the weekly newsletter that was pushed under the door by a member of the entertainment crew, would be full of great jubilation. A Christmas Eve dinner dance, Midnight Mass for those who wanted to worship, a Christmas lunch with a visit from Santa and an afternoon tea with festive fayre. In the evening there would be a production of the pantomime *Aladdin,* a character from *Arabian Nights;* the cast would be members of the officers and crew.

The recent unrest in the area, due to the continuing posturing of certain governments, mostly the British and French, who were insistent that they owned the Suez Canal, was now over and President Nasser, head of Egyptian rule, ensured that more ships were given access to the shortcut to the Mediterranean, instead of taking the long way around as they had before. The journey, with favourable weather, could be cut down by at least ten days, whereas during the Suez Crisis and before the canal was built, vessels would have to voyage around the Cape of Good Hope.

To be fair to Kathleen, she did make a monumental effort with her attitude towards Patrick's girlfriend, for that was who Mel had become. Shaken by the incident and the scar on Patrick's forehead that constantly reminded her of the part she might have played in it, Mel had realised how much he had come to mean to her and hoped that this time they were spending together, wouldn't become a distant memory. Kathleen too had come to terms with the role that she must now play if she wanted to be part of Patrick's future. It had to be one of support, not criticism, as this young lady may one day become his wife.

For her, gone were her thoughts of touring the world, the pioneer of the Aldridge family, living an independent life and finding a job somewhere. In the short time that she and Harold had become acquainted, they had found themselves to have similar interests and certain values in life. She felt compassion for the man who she now knew had watched his wife as she died from terminal cancer. Harold in turn, had begun to feel a certain attraction to this kind-hearted woman, who had spent her years in unselfish duty to Patrick and her brother's farm. His heart was touched and although he could see that they may well settle down with each other in the future, there was still a lot of ocean to travel before they could make any plans.

Opened in 1869, the brainchild of a Frenchman called Ferdinand de Lessep, the Suez Canal was a heavily travelled shipping lane – 101 miles long, 984 feet wide, many lives had been lost in its construction.

With the Christmas celebrations over, strange though it had been to some to be experiencing the festive season in glorious sunshine, instead of seeing snow and robins, it was time to dock at the Port of Aden at the beginning of the Red Sea. The place was full of volcanic dust. It was smelly, dirty and not the type of location where a tourist would wish to sightsee, unless they wanted to wander through the narrow streets where market stalls had been erected to sell the unsuspecting a souvenir or two, or be taken for a short ride on a camel led by a fez adorned Arab. The three hours allocated to taking on fuel, water and other supplies was enough for most passengers to stay on board. The Suez Canal, though, was an impressive sight and sailing along it was an experience that many would boast about for years to come. Most of the canal was not wide enough for two vessels to pass, so several passing bays had been created to keep the shipping moving. There were no locks, which is common in European waterways, because the Mediterranean and the Red Sea are at the same level and vessels could only drift at low speed, to prevent the banks of the canal from eroding.

Patrick and Mel, standing together arm in arm on the promenade deck, watched wide-eyed at the vast sand dunes disappearing into the distance, a military encampment complete with white tents and dilapidated trucks, a couple of camels loaded up with a merchant's goods, the flat roofed dwellings which made up the houses of the small Ismailian villages and fishermen sailing by in long narrow boats. Tugs and ferry boats criss-crossed the narrow isthmus and ships' horns from cargo boats in the passing bays sounded in greeting as the *R.M.S Arcadia* sailed slowly by.

"Something to tell our children" Patrick said dreamily, his thoughts drifting to the future, when he and Mel would have settled down and begun to raise a family – a little girl with long dark hair and a sturdy boy with big, blue eyes.

"Our children?" Mel gazed at him curiously, whilst fleetingly asking herself if that was what she wanted, to settle down with this bashful young man. Thoughts of travel and a career as a lecturer in European history came also; it was what she had always wanted to do.

"Don't you want them too?" Patrick looked lost as he realised that maybe her vision of the future was not the same as his.

"One day" she acknowledged slowly. "But Patrick we've hardly got to know each other, don't you think you might be racing ahead?"

"I love you Mel," he babbled, hoping he could persuade her with his feelings. "I have from the first day I saw you by the souvenir shop. We're meant together. I'll get a job, we'll travel if you want, the children can wait until you're ready for them. I want to have what my parents had, until some selfish bastard who wanted world domination destroyed their world." He quickly got down on one knee, much to the embarrassment of Mel and the surprise of the other passengers, who like themselves were watching the ship's progress along the canal. "Marry me Mel."

"Get up, you idiot, you're making a show of us." Mel hissed, looking at him in annoyance because in her eyes, he was humiliating himself. "We'll talk about it."

*So what was he supposed to do?* He asked himself, when after what he had thought was a romantic proposal, Mel suggested that they go for a drink and discuss their future without an audience. Was it wrong of him to have made his proposal in front of other people, though wasn't that what a man who was in love with his girlfriend usually did? Didn't they go down on bended knee to pop the question? He was sure that was what one of the lead actors in a recent film that he had seen had done. He supposed he'd blown it now, as he trailed miserably behind her shapely figure, dressed as she was once again in her puffed sleeved blouse and short, dirndl skirt, this time barefooted. He'd made a fool of himself by asking her to marry him when she had dreams of becoming a lecturer and he was a farm worker, "a bog trotter" as those boys had called him, not even good enough to wipe her boots.

"Patrick" she said gently, taking her hand in his, after he had ordered two glass of iced tea from the waiter and was sitting at her side, unable to meet her eyes. "Patrick, it's not that I wouldn't want to marry in the future, but I've only just finished college and I was hoping to see a bit of the world, get my studies over, get a job, be independent."

"I thought we loved each other, I thought that what I was supposed to do. I don't know how to act, how to behave myself, I've never had a girl in my life before."

Mel nodded. "I know that, but now is not the time for you and I."

"Well, there's nothing more to say then" he said bitterly, getting up to go, already beginning to feel his ready tears about to surface. "I wish you luck with your future Mel, but you'll never find anyone to love you more than me."

"Patrick…"

He walked away to sit in his cabin reflecting on the people that he'd loved and had been taken away. To be fair, he couldn't say that of Kathleen, although he knew that there might be a parting of the ways when they got to Tilbury because of Harold, but she had always shown her love for him, no matter what he did.

# Chapter Twenty One

"Mel not joining us for dinner tonight?" asked Harold, as the three of them met up for a pre-dinner drink, whilst waiting for the maitre d' to announce the restaurant open.

"Lover's tiff," said Kathleen astutely, after noticing that Patrick's eyes looked a little red and and he was wearing a "hang dog" look. "Still you're young yet, Patrick, plenty more fish in the sea and you don't want to go tying yourself down just yet."

"It wasn't a tiff; I stupidly went down on one knee and asked her to marry me. It's not funny." He glared at the couple, who couldn't help but laugh at the seriousness on his face.

"You did what?" Kathleen chuckled. "You and Mel must have been watching that film they were showing, *Seven Brides For Seven Brothers*. Did she turn you down, is that why you look as if you've lost a pound note and found a sixpence?"

Patrick nodded. "I really thought she felt as I did."

"Well, she told me only the other day that she was having a gap year, seeing a bit of the world and returning home to study at university. You can't expect her to give up her dreams just because she met someone she liked on holiday." Kathleen felt relieved at the turn of events.

"I suppose not."

"Come on Patrick, cheer up, we'll be docking at Port Said in the morning and Harold has said he'll treat us to something from the bumboats, seeing as its just been Christmas."

Port Said, "the valiant city", was situated at the west side of the

Suez Canal, a little further up the Mediterranean coast. It was founded by President Sa'id of Egypt when, as Ferdinand de Lesseps, the architect, gave the first symbolic swing of the pickaxe at the beginning of the construction of the Suez Canal, Port Said and its twin city, Port Fuad on the eastern side of the canal which could be reached by little ferries, was deemed to become a vital part of the area's economy. The ship was to anchor there for a few brief hours, intending to top up with fuel for the final leg of its journey then take on more provisions and a hold full of cotton to sell in London. Most passengers were anxious to be on their way, as the weather was hot and humid and the only relief was to sit in the air conditioned lounges. They preferred to bargain with the dusky faced traders who swung their goods on poles from their little boats that abounded around the vessel, calling out "cheap, very cheap," in high pitched, pidgin English.

Of Mel there had been no sign, neither sitting with her friends in the restaurant that previous evening, nor later when they watched a show in the entertainment lounge. Patrick assumed that she had taken her meals in her cabin and hadn't wanted to be seen around. He missed her – missed the way she held his hand, laughed at his attempts at making jokes, her sweet tasting lips when she had offered to kiss him and the cute little outfits in which she liked to dress. His world had been brighter since she had walked into his life.

Harold, told of the situation by Kathleen, who was relieved that the young lady hadn't got her claws in him, sought him out to commiserate.

"You know, Patrick, marriage is a commitment for life and I can vouch for that. My wife and I were wed for thirty years before the cancer took her, God bless her. You need to really know that person before you ask them to marry you. You've known Mel for what, a couple of weeks and you were ready to propose to her?"

"But I love her, Harold. She's the first girl who has ever made me feel this way, well, the *only* girl that has made me feel this way. I've never had a girlfriend before. To be honest Harold, that is what

I thought you had to do if you love someone, go down on one knee and ask them to marry you."

Harold patted the young man's knee in sympathy. The lad hadn't got a dad to guide him, to tell him about the birds and bees and how to woo a young lady.

"Tell you what, Patrick, how about you and me having a couple of jars together? I'll tell you about my conquests before I settled down with Joan."

She watched him through the window of the library door. Patrick was hunched over a book at one of the tables and Mel, her heart going out in sympathy as she looked at his lonely figure, wondered at her readiness to let him go. He was a nice bloke, a kind bloke, better than any of the boys she had met back home in the Barossa, better than this gang that had been her and Sue's companions whilst being on board. The problem was that he was too nice. He wasn't tough like her brothers, strong minded or self willed. He was an innocent, rather immature, he behaved in an awkward fashion and was difficult to get to know. He wasn't the type of man she would want if she were to ever marry, if the truth was told. And yet – No. It was a career, not a marriage, that she looked forward to – a brilliant career as a lecturer, or even a professor one day of European history. A husband and children would come later, of that she was sure.

Kathleen, aware of Patrick's descent into despondency, tried to cheer him up with promises of what they would do when the ship docked at Tilbury.

"I'll come with you to Ireland. We'll see if the name of Mayo in my ancestor's letter is one and the same" she said, staring at him fondly. "We'll catch the train to Liverpool and travel by boat to Dublin. Harold said it docks in a place called Dunleary. You'll remember where you lived before your parents went to Liverpool, won't you? Yes – then we'll go there, have a look around, then decide if you want to stop there or travel on with me."

"It isn't fair that I continue to be your burden, Kathleen, which I have been for the past ten years. Don't think that I'm not grateful for all you've done, but you should be following your own dreams of the future, your independence from your brother Joseph. I'm a big boy now, I can manage on my own." He gasped as she pulled him tightly to her, giving him a motherly hug.

"Never say that, Patrick" she cried, her voice muffled against his chest, as he was at least a foot taller than her. "You've been the reason for my existence for all these years."

She suddenly pushed him from her and sat back on the settee where they were sitting together in one of the lounge rooms. Her eyes were full of tears and she groped into the black leather handbag that Harold had bought her from one of the Aden bumboats, frantically looking for a handkerchief. "Have you any idea what it was like for me as a woman, not having a chick nor child that I could call my own? You coming into my life gave me purpose and helped me to feel that I was needed. I wouldn't be at all happy if I lost you from my life after all this time."

"But what of Harold?"

"Yes, Harold and I have tentatively discussed a future together. He is undecided whether he wants to go back to Melbourne or stay with his elderly parents and help out on their farm. Either way and most of all, he has agreed that your happiness should be my chief concern."

It was a few days later, when on entering the beginning of the Bay of Biscay, the ship began to feel the effects of a storm that had been brewing in the unpredictable Atlantic. It started with scudding rain and an unfamiliar lurching of the decks. The passengers, unused to more than a heavy swell in the oceans that they'd been travelling, felt alarm and more than a little seasick. With no sun to warm their limbs and a chilly whistling wind that heralded that they were definitely now in the northern hemisphere, many passengers crowded into the public salons or sat in the safety of their cabins, surveying the waves through their portholes as they lashed over the ship. Sick bags began to appear at strategic points along the bannisters, corridors began to stink and fights broke out amongst fractious families, who hadn't bargained for any of this.

It was just after dark, when those people who had sea legs, or hadn't visited the doctor for pills and had managed to finish their dinner, felt as if the ship had plunged to the bottom of the ocean, sighed, pulled itself up, then hit the depths once more. It was a stomach churning experience and Patrick was thrown to the ground as the ship keeled over, whilst he waited in the salon for Kathleen and Harold to appear for an after dinner drink. He couldn't help but think that this was the end for him. There would be no return to the land of his birth, no listening to the chirrup of the birds in the trees outside his window, just a watery grave for him and the other passengers. He heard screams, thuds, the sound of breaking glass as he lay there winded, feeling other bodies close beside him and listening to their cries of alarm, because the lights had gone out. As the vessel buckled under the weight of the mighty waves, he felt panic, then grief that he might never have a glimpse of Mel nor Kathleen again.

Then above all the mayhem came the sound of the loud speaker and the authoritative voice of the captain from his precarious position on the Bridge. He asked for "lock down", all passengers must make their way calmly to their cabins and stay there until the vessel was under his control again. There was a rush as those not thrown from their perches on the bar stools or armchairs, began to find their way to the exits, helped by sympathetic members of the crew with light from their torches. Patrick got to his feet unsteadily and began to follow suit.

"Which deck?" A crewman shouted over the roar of the wind, then grabbed Patrick by the shoulder, whilst trying to marshal the crowd that had gathered by the doors in consternation, not sure which way to turn.

"C Deck." Patrick spoke quickly, looking over the railings uneasily at the huge, white tipped waves that might engulf them at anytime.

191

"C Deck, wait over there. When I've enough of you, I'll guide you down to the corridor."

"Patrick" Her hand gripped his and they were pushed along together, the crewman deciding to tell his group to follow him to the carpeted landing below. The ship lurched, causing them to be hurled into the bulkhead, there were screams from the females and stalwart gasps of consternation from the men.

"Patrick? I came looking for you. I was scared that the ship might go down and I had never had the chance to tell you –" Mel shouted above the melee, but he didn't hear her words, lost as they were in the din of confusion as people began to head down the next set of stairs.

"Mel!" He grabbed her hand as they made it to the corridor, fumbling in his waistcoat pocket for his cabin key. There was no time to think of the niceties of convention; he dragged her through his cabin door and set her on his bunk.

"Patrick–" Then her mouth covered his with joyful kisses and explanations were no more.

It was with noticeable relief from all on board, when the ship nosed its way into Tilbury Docks and the last twenty four hours could be put down in history as a passing nightmare. Amazingly, the *Arcadia* was only four hours late, even though the captain had hove to once out of danger, to give all his passengers a chance to sleep and those who had suffered from broken bones or scalded by boiling water, as two stewards had, chance to be seen to by the doctor.

Not that there had been a lot of sleeping going on in Patrick's cabin. A lot of talking certainly, interposed with much physical contact and lots of giggling, and to give them their due, the couple were respectful of Patrick's wish to wait until they were married, before the ultimate intimacy. It had been difficult for two young people to deny themselves the pleasure of each other's bodies, confined as they were for hours on a narrow bunk suitable for only one person, but their decision felt justified when Kathleen, worried that Patrick had come to harm and had made her way during a lull to check on him, brought them back to reality. Whilst Mel hid herself under a blanket trying not to laugh, as Patrick assured his 'aunt' at the cabin door that he was well and not worried about the storm in the slightest, the seriousness of their situation could not go ignored. In a few hours time when the ship had moored at its destination, decisions must be made.

♣

# Chapter Twenty Two

It had come as a bit of a shock when Kathleen, hearing the knock on her cabin door the next morning, found that not only was Patrick grinning from ear to ear before her but Mel, the girl who had caused so much anguish to the poor fellow, was standing right behind him. Looking a bit sheepish admittedly and rather windblown as if she hadn't had access to a brush since waking, she stood without speaking whilst Patrick explained her presence there.

It appeared that Sue, the girl with whom Mel had been sharing a cabin with, had pleaded with her during the terrible storm the night before, to allow her boyfriend to share their quarters to keep them safe from harm. He was not a man that Mel had much liking for, as arrangements had already been mooted, thanks to him, for Mel to continue alone on her European journey, whilst Sue and her crewman beau, who was going to ask for his discharge papers at the end of the voyage, were planning to look for work together in London. Here Patrick wavered in his explanation, causing Kathleen to have the horrible suspicion that it hadn't been three people who had shared the young ladies' accommodation, it had been only two.

"So we wondered –" Patrick stuttered a little, not used to telling lies to Kathleen. "Well, Mel and I met up this morning when the captain said we were allowed to move about the ship freely. Mel was sitting in the salon and I passed her by when I went up deck. We wondered if perhaps she could join us, Kathleen, now that she's on her own, that is? She'd be happy to travel to Ireland with us and if we were to get a bit of a move on, we could all be there to celebrate the new year."

It was the hour of disembarkation, something that the passengers and crew had prayed for, as many had thought that their time had come and they wouldn't reach the safety of the docks at Tilbury. It was also decision time. Kathleen and Harold had talked about the situation often, once they had realised that the feelings between them were reciprocated. Suddenly Kathleen, she who had thought that her days as a spinster would be played out as the Aldridge pioneer of travel and Harold on his part, knowing that Australia held too many painful memories of watching his wife affected by the horror of cancer, were faced with a dilemma. It would feel like abandonment of the chick that had fulfilled her yearnings of motherhood if Kathleen was to choose Harold. Patrick was penniless, of no fixed abode and she couldn't see herself cutting off the apron strings and allowing him to go to Ireland alone. Harold could picture a future. It was one where he and Kathleen moved to his parents' farm, married, settled down and perhaps even started another family. She'd be an asset, someone who would work as hard as he did to make the place prosperous. His cousin could buy him out from the construction firm that they ran together and there'd be a bit of money in the bank. But what of Patrick?

It seemed to Kathleen that now it was Mel that was pulling Patrick's strings. He was a gentle soul, rather naïve, unused to the wiles of women and she wondered if perhaps this sudden wish to be together was on Mel's part, a calculated ruse. How long would she stay when she realised that Patrick hadn't got a penny to his name and that the very clothes that he stood up in had been bought and paid for by her, his benefactor? And did she want to part from Harold, journey to Ireland for the sake of a promise that she had made to Patrick, when now there was this Mel in the young man's life? As Harold had said to Kathleen after she had cried in frustration upon his shoulder, when he had come to check that her luggage was ready for the porter, parting from the very person who had made her life worth living for the past ten years was a tough decision, but there was nothing much that she could do. He was twenty two, a young man who imagined himself to be in love with the young woman and objecting may well cause a rift forever between the two of them.

As Kathleen waited with Harold in the warmth of the salon, all dressed up in their heavy overcoats, Harold wearing a trilby and Kathleen a felt-brimmed hat that would keep her recently styled Marcel wave in place, whilst they listened for their call to disembark, Patrick and Mel stood on deck looking out across the busy dock land, with its ocean terminal, grain stores and a dry dock for ship repairs, towards the iconic River Thames with all its ancient maritime history. It was an awesome scene, especially for Mel, whose nearest city of note had been Adelaide, with its history no older than a hundred years. Patrick, for whom places had no appeal unless it was a town or village in his homeland, was anxiously scanning the cloudy skies for the threat of snow. If he was to be in Ireland with the intention of celebrating New Year there, he didn't want a downfall of snow to disrupt his plans, nor his methods of transport to be delayed in any way.

Mel shivered as they stood there in a temperature of five degrees, both used to the summer temperature that they had left behind six weeks before. She wasn't as warmly dressed as Patrick was in his thick three quarter length coat. She had just a blue, single breasted jacket which she wore with black, tailored trousers and a pair of black ankle boots. She tucked herself under his arm where he drew her trembling body to his to keep her warm.

"I've been thinking Patrick," she began, not wanting to upset his plans in any way because of her presence, but wanting to clear up a few misunderstandings that might occur over the next few days. "We haven't really talked about it but if you and I are going to travel on together, where does that leave Kathleen and Harold? I know that Harold wants to travel back to his farm in Lincolnshire.

He told me so when he and I first met and I thought that Kathleen would want to accompany him, not trail along with us, when she has the chance to hook up with him."

Patrick nodded. It was something that had passed through his mind too. Was it fair to expect Kathleen to continue her substitute motherhood, when she had a life of her own that she was entitled to?

"Is it money, Patrick?" *There she'd come right out with it.* She knew of his background, the orphanage, the petty Uncle Joseph who had never given him a penny piece for his labour on the farm. "If it's all down to money and having Kathleen along means that money won't be a problem, well I've got plenty. I only have to send my dad a wire and he'll send me more if needs be."

Patrick stiffened and took his arm away from Mel's shoulder.

"So that's it" he said rather sharply. "You think that the only reason Kathleen's in my life is because of her money. I am not a parasite. I worked long and hard on the Aldridge Farm and it wasn't my fault that Kathleen's brother was stingy. I was given bed and board and love from a good woman, who by a twist of fate was never given the chance to have children. No, it's not down to money, I just don't want Kathleen thinking I'm abandoning her, just because I have given my love to you."

His face softened after he had said those words, on seeing her surprise at his reaction. It wasn't right to take his frustration about the situation out on her. "You know how I feel about you, Mel, don't you?" He said quickly.

"I do, Patrick and I didn't mean to have come out with it like that. I'm sorry. It's just –"

"When Joseph asked me to leave the farm, it was Kathleen who decided that she wanted to come with me. She knew that I would never have made it back to Ireland on my own. As you know, I'm not very confident. I suppose in her eyes, she was finishing the job, taking me back to the place where I was uprooted as a lad. To me she's worth her weight in gold."

"Then I'll finish the job on her behalf, Patrick." Mel reached up and kissed his cold cheek, the temperature having plummeted, whilst they waited to disembark. "Let's go and see what she has to say about our plans."

There was that heartrending moment, when saying goodbye would last in the longest of memories. Saddened by their parting, there was a sorrowful silence as the taxi made the twenty five mile trip to Euston Station, where Patrick and Mel would catch the train to Liverpool and Harold and Kathleen would book into a small hotel on Earls Court Road. Not even the thought of being shown around the sights of London, could cheer Kathleen.

She fussed, whilst they stood in the queue to buy the tickets, two for the train journey to Liverpool which Kathleen insisted that she pay for and two platform tickets so that she and Harold could wave the couple off. Had Patrick remembered the name of the village where he was born? Did he remember if there were any relatives living close by? He was to write to her, the minute he had access to a pen and paper. Harold's address was an easy one; the Cooper Farm at Nethercote. Lincolnshire. As Kathleen held him close, murmuring in his ear that she would always love him and would always have a home for him, she slipped an envelope into the pocket of his coat.

It was to be a seven hour journey from London to Liverpool, changing at Crewe and travelling aboard a steam train that pulled along five carriages with corridors. Once aboard, it was difficult to find a compartment that they didn't have to share; it was so full of people returning from a visit with loved ones at Christmas, or travelling to stay with family for the New Year. Feeling strange, disorientated after spending six weeks on sea legs, they stowed their luggage on the overhead rack and as the train steamed north towards their destination, the swaying of their carriage began to mimic the rhythm of the ship. It wasn't long before they slept.

It was as they were pulling into a major station, when a woman caused a blast of chilly air to wake the sleeping couple, having lowered the window to see if a member of her family was waiting for her on the platform. Mel's watch, having been set to Greenwich Mean Time, showed that it was still some hours to their destination. Dusk was on its way, as the compartment lights were beginning to brighten up. She yawned, then got up to search in her vanity bag for a wrap of sandwiches that she had bought from a kiosk at Euston. It was hard not to hear the sound of rumbling in Patrick's tummy and she was feeling quite hungry herself. The compartment, recently emptied of its passengers, except for an old woman who was reading a magazine on the seat opposite was silent, but for the clink of the engine as it waited in the station. A screech from Mel brought Patrick swiftly to his feet.

"It's gone! Oh Patrick, my vanity case! It's got my money, my passport, all the things I need for–"

Her words hung in the air, as Patrick shoved his arms into his overcoat. He was out of the carriage like a gun salute, searching for the stupid woman who must have mistakenly picked it up. *Though where to look?* There were a couple of dozen passengers milling on the platform, some walking along to the exit and some others were waiting to board the train.

His heart was in his mouth. He could feel it beating, threatening to overwhelm him as he searched high and low for the woman, whom he remembered had red hair. Then, just as the guard had checked his fob watch, blown his whistle and waved his flag in the direction of the engine driver, the woman appeared, full of apologies for her lapse of concentration. She had been looking for her son who was to drive her to Solihull, as she was staying with him and his family for the New Year.

Without a word of thanks as he felt so angry, Patrick turned to see the train pulling out of the station, with Mel frantically waving from out of the window, asking if she should pull the communication cord. As he ran, feeling the weight of the case pulling on his arm, as Mel had stowed her makeup and toiletries inside it as well as all her valuables, the squeal of the wheels as the driver slammed on the brake and the whoosh of steam that escaped from the funnel, was music to his ears. The guard, shaken by events, after seeing the young man running and the young lady waving wildly from the carriage window, raced to the end of the platform and along the track until he had reached the stationary engine, where after mounting the steps he found the driver to be very shaken up indeed.

"I could have killed her" the man said in a wobbly voice, sitting on the bucket seat with his head in between his hands. "Came right out of nowhere, like an apparition if I believed in such a thing. A little girl with long, brown hair, wearing a long white, dress with black boots on."

# Chapter Twenty Three

It was early evening when feeling tense and exhausted, they emerged from Lime Street Station, where street lights shone weakly through a misty fog. After their fright at nearly losing Mel's vanity case, and grateful to whoever had pulled the emergency cord so that Patrick could climb aboard again, they had spent the journey in a bit of a dither, whilst checking that their luggage was never out of sight.

Patrick, upon talking to a soldier that had joined the train at Birmingham, who had a three day pass to visit family in Liverpool, learnt that the ferry that would take them to the port of Dunleary, a short train ride from Dublin, left from the dock nearest to the landing stage at the Pier Head. He seemed to think that an Irish mate of his always caught the ship at 9pm, which got him to Ireland in the early hours of the next day.

"I'll walk yer there, if yer like," said the soldier, quite keen to be seen in the company of this handsome couple, especially the Aussie girl, who if she hadn't been courting, he wouldn't mind a crack at. "I could see me mates in the Baltic Pub, that's just up the road from where you're goin'."

"I'm sure we'll find it" said Mel, answering for both of them, as she had seen him leering at any pretty girl who had passed them by on the station platform. "If the ship doesn't sail until then, we've chance to get a bite to eat, Patrick."

"There's the Kardomah, or Lewis's has a restaurant, though it's probably shut by now. Oh and there's a chippy just down the road from here, over across the road. I'd come with yer, but I fancy a pint not a coffee."

The soldier gave a mock salute, then ducked into a public house that was standing on a nearby corner.

"Do you remember any of this, Patrick?" Mel asked as they set off down the road towards the city. "Perhaps the funny accents? I could hardly understand that soldier or the woman who sat across from us. Look at those streets full of houses, they look so narrow and mean. I much prefer our stone built houses, with our wooden verandahs and slated roofs."

"Terraces, yes I remember they were called terrace houses. We lived in one in Bootle. That's where I lost my parents because of the bomb. Then they moved me to a place in Walton. That's when they let me out of the children's ward and put me into Dorricott House, which was an orphanage."

He shuddered, more from remembering the terrible time that he'd had in the children's home, when his accent was mocked so badly that he never bothered to speak in case he was jeered at, than because of the bitter wind that was whooshing up from the Mersey and starting to attack his bones. "It's a city though. You'll see a difference when we get across to Ireland, you'll never want to leave the place once you've seen the lovely loughs and glens. I'll show you the Round Tower, the village of Killala and the town of Ballina. We'll walk along the headland, look across Killala Bay and sit on the banks of the River Moy."

"Whew, Patrick," said Mel, changing over her case to carry it in her left hand in an effort to get closer to him, as her body was also beginning to shiver. " I'm feeling dizzy with all this talk of the sights that you'll be showing me. Let's go and get a meal at that cafe."

It had been while Mel was visiting the ladies room, after eating their meal of fish and chips in a cafe with red gingham tablecloths, that Patrick searched in his pocket for the envelope that Kathleen had hidden there. He whistled in surprise when he saw the white pound notes and a couple of fivers nestling within it. As it didn't do to bring attention to himself by sitting there counting lots of money, he put them back in the envelope again. There was a rush of love for the woman who had taken him to her heart so easily, tinged with a tingling of excitement, when he realised that she must have put at least twenty pounds in there. It seemed a fortune, which would pay for their dinner, the boat and may even last him until he got a job, if he was careful!

They window shopped, as they strolled down the street towards the River Mersey. Stores in readiness for the coming New Year sales were lit up brightly, advertising all the things that they hadn't sold at Christmas at knock down prices. Mel quivered in her jacket, as she stared at a fox fur coat in the window of Littlewoods and boots that looked warm and cosy, which she knew she couldn't afford. Oh, she had money and could always wire her father and ask for more if she wanted to, but what if she needed funds in an emergency? She might not like this place that Patrick was intent on taking her to and she might decide she didn't want to stay. Not that she had said any of this to Patrick, who was looking with studious interest at the wedding rings that were on display in a jeweller's window. He was under the impression she was his forever and was it fair to hurt him, when she hadn't made her mind up either way?

They'd made it. On the 29th day of December, in the early hours when dawn was still some hours away, Patrick Mayo walked down the gangplank of the Dublin ferryboat. It was hard to stop the tears of joy weeping from his eyes, as he and Mel stood hand in hand on the upper deck, looking out across Dublin Bay to the shapes of Dalkey Island and the Muglins. He was back in his beloved homeland. Even the air that he was breathing seemed fresher here and he loved the lilt of the Irish voices. They'd take the train along the coast to Dublin, where they'd inquire about how to get to Ballina, the town that Patrick remembered fondly from his youth.

*This was the boy who would take her home, back to the green fields of her hamlet, the sparkling river that ran down the side of the hill and to the little church which overlooked the crashing waves of the sea. She would meet her beloved sister either in her native Killala or in the spirit world of the dead.*

It was eight o'clock before the train chugged into the little station, with many miles of countryside travelled on the way. Cattle grazed on lush, green pasture. Forests, dark and eerie, lay at the foot of the many hills. Whitewashed farms and small holdings, still using their peat beds for fuel, villages and towns, rivers and loughs abounded throughout their journey and Mel, warmly dressed now after making a quick visit to purchase a thicker coat from Switzers in Dublin, thought it was the prettiest place she had ever seen.

Having changed trains for a branch line from Manulla Junction, as the main line continued on to Westport, a town on the coast past the city of Castlebar, it was a tired and grubby couple who arrived in Ballina that evening, hungry and badly in need of a change of clothing. It had been a long and arduous day. Patrick, who had remembered that his childhood friend Billy, had an Aunty Bernadette who had a hotel at the bottom of the High Street, carried their cases wearily, whilst Mel, looking with interest in the windows of the little shops, trailed along behind. There was a chemist, a haberdashery, a dressmakers and tailors, their premises darkened as the trading day was over, but earmarked for a visit by a curious Mel.

"Is it Patrick? Patrick Mayo?" The woman who was standing behind the reception desk in the foyer of the grey stone building named The Heaney Hotel said, as she came bustling around to greet him with a broad smile.

"We thought you'd gone to Liverpool. Freddie, Freddie." She shouted to someone in the back room, who by looking through the door which was ajar, they could see was a man who was sitting at the table drinking from a glass of beer. The man rushed out in alarm, no doubt thinking that his wife was having trouble with these strangers who had just blown in through the door.

"What is it Bernie?" He asked, pulling his braces up around his shoulders and acting a little menacingly.

"Would yer ever look to see who's come visitin'. It's Patrick,

Patrick Mayo, come all the way from England and this is 'is –" She stared at Mel's gloveless hand and continued, "His girlfriend."

"Oh Patrick. Jesus, Mary and Joseph, where's Jack? Where's Aileen? We wondered. The last time I saw Jack we was having a beer in Flanagans, then a few days later I heard you'd all gone ter Liverpool, something about a run in with Father Cronin –Aye that was a bad business."

"They're dead, Mr. Heaney – a bomb got us a few weeks later. Dad was working on the demolition. As you'll know, Liverpool got a terrible pounding. We were just sitting down to our tea when the siren went. The house got a direct hit and –" Patrick's tears, which were never far away when he spoke about his parents, began to fill his eyes and Mel patted his arm in sympathy.

"God love yer." The woman he had known as Aunty B, took him in his arms and gave him a hug. "And you've come back to see us love – Well our Billy's up above in Dublin with Jessie. Do you remember she was in your class at school? They got married last September and me sister, our Mairaid, is over the moon as she's going to be a grandma in the summer. Oh". She suddenly looked at Mel, who had been standing looking on in silence

"I'm Patrick's girlfriend – it's a long story." This was in response to Aunty B raising her eyebrows at Mel's accent. "I'm dying to use your lavatory, could you show me the way?"

"Of course, of course, we're so excited at seein' Patrick after all this time; him and Billy were such good friends when they were little. We've a single room and a double room available and there's a bathroom just down the corridor from there. Patrick, give yer bags to Freddie and he'll show yer where and I'll take Mel along to the convenience."

It was late the next morning when Patrick and Mel walked hand in hand together down Tebley Street. It was a fine, crisp day and Mel, all wrapped up in her new coat and a woolly hat and mittens borrowed from Aunty B, felt warm and cosy and grateful that after a good night's sleep, the floor wasn't coming up to meet her as it had yesterday. Patrick, eager now to visit the place where he was born and grateful that he had achieved his dream, with plenty of time to spare as it was the last day of December, felt elated as they strode past the familiar buildings of his childhood.

They walked over one of the two stone bridges which spanned the sparkling river and its salmon weirs, then on along the street which would bring him to the same winding footpath which had been the route he took on his journey to and from his school. He spoke with pride, as he pointed out the little place that had been his seat of learning, the monumental church, its graves holding the remains of his ancestors and the ruins of a castle on a hill. He spoke of his friends and their mischievous ways when they were children in their Sunday school, about how it was always Brendan Hanley's fault, the one who forever got the cane.

He'd felt angry though the night before, when even though he was dead on his feet, he'd picked up on Freddie's words, when he had said that something had been "a bad business". Leaving Mel to settle in her room, he had sat with the man into the small hours and learnt the reason for his parents flight to Liverpool. It appeared that Jack Mayo had felt he'd had a calling. From a child, when he'd first looked up and saw his Saviour dying on the cross in the Catholic church along the coast, to growing up and being a leading member of the choir, Jack's only wish was to be accepted as a priest and train at a seminary. Visions of bringing the sinful to purity lasted throughout, even when he became a novice priest in one of Dublin's parishes. Until one day when he was visiting a family in the area, he fell in love with the pretty Aileen Burns, who was working in the city as a shop assistant.

His family, amazed at his decision when he brought his beloved back to Killala to meet them, could only give their blessing on their union and so did the local priest. Life was fine, Jack, earned a living rearing rare breed cattle, alongside Danny, a tenant farmer and family friend, who lived across the way. Until a few years later, when the old priest was replaced by Father Cronin, a zealot and upholder of the power of the Roman Catholic Church, who reprimanded Jack for failing in his vows. According to him, a mortal sin had been committed because if Jack had continued with the priesthood, then the land that had belonged to his parents, should have gone to the church when they passed away.

They'd made it. They had walked along the coastal path from Ballina and had reached the hamlet by the early afternoon. It had been a tiring journey, not helped by their need to rest after so many miles had been travelled from Australia and if it hadn't been for Patrick's determination to see his birthplace before 1957 had come to a close, Mel would have advised a few more days with their feet up before they ventured out so far. Though it was worth the blisters and the soreness of her soles, in shoes that were designed for pavements, not the wild and rocky muddy tracks that often wound its way through small dense copses, when she saw the joy in Patrick's face, as they came across the small hamlet that he'd called home. The old stone farm, which was four square with a barn incorporated and a cobbled yard where a gaggle of geese honked and pigs grunted in their sty; the row of stone built cottages; the materials brought across from Foxford over a century before and the footpath which Patrick had said led to the place where his ancestors had lived their lives in turf roofed cabins. All of this had gone now, it had all been demolished when an absentee English aristocrat had wanted grazing on his pastures, instead of the lowly potato plant which had grown on his land before.

They sat for a moment on the wall that ran along the perimeter of the farmyard, looking across with pleasure at the fine row of cottages with their grey, slate roofs and walls of weathered stone, sturdy and attractive, with white, lace curtains at the lattice windows. The end one, which an earlier owner had knocked through to the dwelling next door, had a pretty rose bower in the middle of the picket fence.

"That's where I lived" Patrick said, sounding choked as he gazed over, not able to believe that here he was, outside the place where he had been his happiest.

"And considering how old these buildings must be, someone has kept them in good repair" said Mel, thinking that the cute little cottages must be older than some of the settlements of Australia.

"That's down to me" said the voice of a man, who had been quietly listening to the newcomers, as he had been standing just inside the farmyard gate. "Me dada decided to turn them into weekend lets a couple of years ago, said it wasn't right to let good property like this go to rack and ruin. Don't usually get people up 'ere in the winter though, if yer were wantin' to rent one of 'em."

Patrick turned. He knew that voice, it had been part of his childhood from when his parents had helped out on the farm.

"Danny Douglas. It's me, Patrick Mayo. You know me. I used to live across the grass in the old Dockerty place?" He smiled with delight, as the man, in his late fifties, grabbed him roughly in a bear hug and let out a cry of anguish as he did.

"Patrick! Jesus, Mary and Joseph, is it yerself that's come back here agin? Where've yer bin? Where's Jack and Aileen? Jack said yer'd stay away a couple of years until the dust 'ad settled with that tub thumper, Cronin. 'E said 'e'd write, get in touch and tell us what was to 'appen to 'is land and property. We never 'eard, so me dada decided to do up the cottages, keep 'em nice, do the gardens and keep the rent from the lets for yer daddy in the bank." He stepped away, then pushed his cap back above his forehead, letting out a sigh, as he realised what must have happened with only Patrick returning after all those years. "E's dead. Jack and Aileen are dead aren't they? God Bless 'em. I said as much to Dada when Jack didn't come back to face up to old Cronin. I told 'im it was a dangerous world out there before 'e went, but would 'e listen."

Danny wiped his eyes with the back of his hand and shook his head mournfully.

"So all this land and property belongs to you then, Patrick. Passed down through the generations from Maggie and her brother Bernie Mayo, or so the story goes."

He brightened when he looked at Mel, who'd been listening quietly at Patrick's side, whilst she gazed around at the beautiful scenery. "So this'll be yer wife then, Patrick. Well, come on in Alanna and I'll brew yer a pot of tea. Yer can meet me dada. He'll be very glad ter meet yer, so he will."

*This was the boy who had brought her home, back to the green fields of her hamlet, the sparkling river that ran down the side of the hill and the little church that overlooked the crashing waves of the sea. It had taken Molly a century, but now at last she could meet her beloved sister, either in her native Killala or in the spirit world of the dead.*